PRAISE FOR THE NOVELS OF DAVE WHITE

"Everybody wins when a classic form, such as the private-eye novel, meets up with a class act, such as Dave White. In his remarkable debut novel, *When One Man Dies*, White manages the neat trick of respecting the genre's traditions while daring to nudge it toward something new and unexpected. And Jackson Donne is a wonderful character, someone with whom readers will happily share many beers in the Olde Towne Tavern for years to come. Lots of promise here—in Donne and White. I'm rooting for both of them."
—Laura Lippman, Edgar Award-winning author of *What The Dead Know*

"Every now and then you find a debut novel that carries the clear promise of big things to come. WHEN ONE MAN DIES is one of those. Fast and funny, with plenty of classic action but a setting and character that are entirely new, Dave White is creating a winner with Jackson Donne. Alwaysgood to get in on the ground floor."
—Michael Koryta, *L.A. Times* Book Prize-winning author of *The Prophet*

"Will grab most readers from its opening sentences. Fans of hard-hitting, uncompromising private investigators will hope that Donne ditches his college dreams and continues to pound the pavement."
—*Publishers Weekly* (starred review) on WHEN ONE MAN DIES

"A terrific novel, a unique and artful blend of the PI and the Police Procedural in a plot as nicely tangled and sexually violent as a cat fight, a story as deceptively simple as your first love and as fatal as your last car wreck. It's a great read."
—James Crumley, Dashiell Hammett Award-winning author of *The Last Good Kiss* on WHEN ONE MAN DIES

"When I read my first Dave White story, I knew that he was going to be huge someday--like, Robert Parker huge. *When One Man Dies* is the first bold step in fulfilling that promise. It's the great American private eye novel reborn for the 21st century, with a fast-moving, spare style that punches you in the gut at the same time it squeezes your heart."
--Duane Swierczynski, author of *Canary* and *Hell And Gone*

"Stunning...fulfills the promise of his debut...the author does such a fine job of depicting the inner conflicts of his fallible but ultimately heroic protagonist."
— *Publishers Weekly* on THE EVIL THAT MEN DO

"Intricate plotting and nonstop action make this a nail-biting read from start to finish. White, winner of the Derringer Award for When One Man Dies, is a writer to watch."
— *Library Journal* on THE EVIL THAT MEN DO

"White makes good use of the urban and suburban geography, accurately depicting the terrain. But that's not what makes his sophomore effort so readable and engaging. Rather, it's White's realistic depiction of family dynamics--readers will be struck by the sheer humanity on display in this novel, from Donne's strained relationship with his sister and brother-in-law, to the tragedy of the PI's mother's valiant but futile struggle with Alzheimer's disease, and finally, to the sacrifices that are sometimes required to keep one's family intact and safe."
— *Mystery Scene* on THE EVIL THAT MEN DO

"Dave White's second novel, *The Evil That Men Do*, absolutely confirms and fulfills the promise of his highly regarded debut Jackson Donne novel, *When One Man Dies*; so, simply stated, readers looking for top-notch hard-boiled noir fiction featuring an intriguing protagonist and complex characterizations need look no further than Dave White's deftly plotted novels."
— Bookloons

DAVE WHITE

NOT EVEN PAST

A JACKSON DONNE NOVEL

Dave W

Copyright © 2015 by Dave White

Cover and jacket design by Adrijus Guscia

Interior designed and formatted by E.M. Tippetts Book Designs

ISBN 978-1-940610-36-8
eISBN 978-1-940610-03-0

First trade paperback edition February 2015 by Polis Books, LLC
60 West 23rd Street
New York, NY 10010

POLIS BOOKS

ALSO BY
DAVE WHITE

The Jackson Donne series
When One Man Dies
The Evil That Men Do

Witness To Death

For
Erin and Ben

"The past is not dead. It's not even past."
—William Faulkner

PART I
JERSEY COMEBACK

CHAPTER
ONE

When Jackson Donne saw the eight-year-old picture of himself, he thought the email was the weirdest form of spam he'd ever gotten.

It was taken on graduation day at the police academy, and Donne was in his dress blues, smiling in front of an American flag. His hat was tilted down, leaving two fingers of room between the brim and his nose, exactly as they'd been taught. Jeanne had taken it. They had only been dating three months, and he remembered how happy she was that he'd completed training. Now, they would have some extra time to spend together. Donne was smiling more about that than he was from actually graduating from the academy.

He hadn't seen the picture in years. It had been boxed up somewhere with the rest of Jeanne's things. Had her parents taken that stuff after she died? He didn't remember. Donne scrolled down some more and saw the email's text. The muscles in his shoulders tightened as if someone had grabbed him. Written in bold italics was **_Click and watch. Her life depends on it._** Next to that was a link, but not to a website Donne recognized.

Don't click on it, he thought. Probably some virus, something that would eat up all the files on his computer. He couldn't afford that, not now, with exams looming. Of course, the only reason he logged on in the first place was to procrastinate.

But this email tickled his brain. The picture. Who had found and sent him that picture? He looked at the email address again, a string of numbers and a domain that just read "di. com." Nothing familiar jumped out at him.

Donne quickly forwarded the email from his school account to his personal one. Then he closed it, without deleting it. Scrolled through the rest of his email. Nothing from his professors. No study guides, no cheat sheets, no rubrics. No help at all. His time at college had been tedious, full of syllabi, message boards, readings, and essays. But this was his life now.

No gunfire. No one dies.

Life was what it should be. Boring. Work on what you have to, have pizza and a beer on Friday night. Watch some movies. Tweet.

And now that he was so close to the end, closing out his degree, he wanted it to be even easier. Kate said he had senioritis. He didn't disagree.

Which was why this email bothered him. Donne clicked on it again and looked at the time stamp. It'd been sent at six this morning. Now, according to his iPhone, it was 10 AM. Four hours that email had sat there waiting for him. The Microsoft Outlook email system Rutgers used didn't jibe with his phone, otherwise he might have gotten it earlier.

But no, that picture had sat there while Donne had gotten up and gone for coffee and a bagel. Surfed through some New Jersey websites looking at the news and procrastinated overall instead of studying.

The mouse arrow hovered over the link, turning from arrow to finger. His own finger hovered over the button.

A bead of sweat formed at his hairline.

He clicked the link. And his gut gurgled when he got the pinwheel cursor. His computer had frozen, and for an instant he worried about every one of his files disappearing into some abyss of zeros and ones. About spending the next twelve hours waiting in line at the Genius Bar at the Menlo Park Mall.

The pinwheel stopped and his browser opened up. Donne stared at the screen. A black square, then a play button in the middle. He clicked on the triangle and waited. *It must be buffering*, he thought, because nothing else was happening.

There was a loud *swoosh* from his speakers and the screen went bright white, like sun reflecting off snow. Donne flinched and squinted as the camera adjusted to the light. The picture came into focus. A nearly empty room. Gray walls, gray floor. The camera was positioned behind two spotlights. Donne could see the tripods and big round head fixed on top of them. Beyond that was a chair. In the chair was a woman.

Donne leaned closer to the screen. He couldn't tell who it was.

The camera zoomed in slowly. The spotlights were out of view. The woman wore blue sweatpants and a white tank top. She was slumped over. Her wrists were tied to the arms of the chair. Her brown hair had fallen in front of her face.

The camera pulled in tight on the torso of the woman. She was shaking and her arms appeared bruised. The bruises had occurred some time ago, however, because they had yellowed on the outside. The woman lifted her head and the hair fell away from her face. Her mouth was covered in duct tape. Her nose was runny. And her eyes looked directly into the camera.

Donne's throat closed.

Jeanne Baker stared back at him, eyes wide at the camera, a tear trickling down the left side of her face. He could hear muffled screaming through the duct tape.

He said her name. He said it twice.

The screen went blank.

"No!" Donne shouted and grabbed the monitor. He shook it, as if that was going to help.

He clicked on the mouse, hoping the triangle play button would reappear. It didn't. Donne didn't know long he sat there clicking. It felt like only seconds. He didn't stop until he heard the door open behind him.

He turned and saw Kate, two boxes in her hands.

"Hey," she said. "I thought you might want to take a break from studying and help me with the invitations."

CHAPTER
TWO

"What's wrong?" Kate put the box of invitations on the coffee table.

Donne blinked. "I didn't expect to see you this morning."

She smiled. It was the same smile she gave him the first time he opened a car door for her. The time he brought her roses at work. Each time, she'd smile the smile she was giving now and call him "the gentleman." And then remind him it was the twenty-first century.

"Well." She tilted her head. "I'm here. Let's get stuffing."

Kate waited for him just for a moment, as if she expected him to take the initiative. He didn't move. It felt like he was stuck to his computer chair, as if the seat had iced over and caught his body with it. When he didn't move, she pulled the first envelope.

"Got to do my mother first, right? She'd probably be offended otherwise." She took an invitation, glanced over it, and then slid it into the pink envelope.

If this had been a normal moment, Donne would have laughed and asked why her mother even needed an invite. She was paying for most of the damn thing. They would have laughed, and Kate would have reminded him about tradition.

Not today.

"Kate, I—" He turned and looked at his computer. The web browser was still open to the blank video. He clicked it closed. "I have to study. I haven't even started yet."

She licked the glue of the envelope and sealed it. Put it on the coffee table next to the box. Donne leaned back in his chair and watched her stand up and walk toward him. Slowly, like the first night they made love. The smile changed now. No longer confused. Confident.

She put her hands on the arms of his chair and leaned in close. Her hair smelled like apple shampoo.

"You said you were going to get up early and work."

"When did I say that?"

"When don't you say that?"

She leaned in closer and her lips parted slightly. "You work too hard."

"If I don't, I won't be finished with this."

"I'm sure you'll do fine."

Before their lips could meet, Donne flashed on to Jeanne. Tied up in that chair. Her eyes wide. Screaming behind duct tape.

He tilted his head out of the way of Kate and stood up. She stepped back and brushed hair in front of her face, as if she was trying to hide it.

"What is wrong with you?" Her voice was the edge of glass.

"I told you, I have to study."

She shook her head. "That's not it."

He stood up, feeling ice form in his chest. Someone must have turned the thermostat down when Donne wasn't looking.

Jeanne—no, Kate—had her arms folded in front of her. Donne stepped in close to her, put his hands on her elbows. Squeezed gently.

"I'm—I'm sorry," he said. "I'm stressed. There's a lot to be done. Finals. The wedding. We have a lot to do. You surprised me."

"But you ..." Kate shook her head. "You've been doing this a lot lately."

Donne closed his eyes and took in a long breath. He kissed

her on the cheek. "I don't mean to."

He wanted to explain, tell her about Jeanne. Tell her about the video. Tell her about the blood on his hands. All the blood. He should have done that a year ago. But it never felt like the right time. It still didn't.

"Then why do you do it?"

"Did you take today off?" he asked.

"I have a meeting later this afternoon. Last-minute preparation for court. Took the morning off, thought we could stuff some envelopes and then get lunch."

That sounded good. It sounded like exactly what he needed. But the walls felt like they were closing in on him. His mouth was dry and his throat was tight. He needed to go do something, anything, to try to find out what that video was about.

"I really need to study. Get this over with. What time is your meeting over?"

Kate pursed her lips. "I'm done at four."

"In that case, I'll be done at four," he said. "I'll pick you up and we can go to Silvio's and get a real meal. Then I'm good for some beer and all the envelope stuffing you want to do."

The glint returned to her eyes. She didn't smile. Didn't unfold her arms.

"Okay."

Donne dropped his hands to his sides. "I really need to study. Why don't you stay here? I'll go down to the library and get some work done. Hard to procrastinate there."

"If you end up at the Olde Towne—"

Donne laughed. "That's the last place I'll be."

"I was just going to say 'call me.'"

They didn't say anything for a moment. The silence hung in the air like gnats on a summer night. They stared at each other, Donne waiting for Kate to move first. Either toward the couch or the door.

She didn't.

He gave in. After kissing her on the cheek again, he went toward the door. Pulled it open and stepped out into the hall. The door swung shut behind him. The hall smelled of wet pizza boxes. He took two steps but stopped when Kate opened his door again.

"Jackson," she said.

He turned and waited. The ice in his chest got colder.

"You forgot your books."

The knot in his stomach eased, and he went back to gather his things. There wasn't much. Two textbooks, a binder, and a pen. He shoved them into his bag, zipped it closed, and headed back toward the door.

"I love you," he heard Kate say.

He pulled the door shut and kept going.

CHAPTER
THREE

Donne sat in the Olde Towne Tavern staring at his phone. Seemed to be what everyone else was doing as well. The days of pub arguments that went unsettled were long gone. Pub arguments turned into quick Google searches and Wikipedia answers.

That wasn't Donne's concern at the moment. No, he'd clicked on the link in the email and opened up Safari on his iPhone trying to get another glimpse of Jeanne. Or whoever it was in the video.

Couldn't be Jeanne. She was dead. Car crash. Dead.

Each time Donne tried clicking on the link, the browser would open and just show a blank white page. Nothing would load. The activity bar at the top of the screen didn't appear, so he knew nothing else would load on the page. He shook the phone, as if that would help. When it didn't, he slapped the phone on to the bar. And then cursed himself for almost breaking it. He couldn't afford another one.

Artie appeared across the bar, eyed the phone, then eyed Donne.

"Cutting class?" he asked.

Donne shook his head. "Jameson. And a Kane Head High."

Artie exhaled and leaned over for the glasses.

"Sorry for making you do your job," Donne said.

Artie poured the shot. "I was wondering when this Jackson would show up again. Been a while."

Donne took the shot in a quick gulp. Felt the slow burn up his throat. His chest and stomach warmed. He welcomed the feeling.

"Exams are coming up," he said.

Artie put the IPA on a coaster. "*That's* why this place is empty." He made a show of looking around. "Well, that, and the fact that it's not even noon yet."

"I should be studying." Sweat slid down the side of the pint glass.

"Instead you're doing shots."

"One shot."

Artie shrugged. "Don't want to talk about it?"

Donne picked up the beer and drank. The taste of whiskey washed from his mouth, replaced by bitter hops. The nerve endings that been jangling for the past hour settled into a rhythmic throb.

Artie turned and went to the other end of the bar. Donne pressed the home button on his phone and stared at the picture Kate on his lock screen. He took another sip of beer. Kate looked over her shoulder, a wisp of hair cutting across her brow. The corner of her lip was curled up in a smile. Behind her was the sunset over Garret Mountain.

Jeanne, meanwhile, was tied to a chair.

Thirty seconds of footage, something that could have been faked by anyone.

He looked at his lock screen again. He grabbed his beer and froze.

"You shouldn't drink that," Kate had said the night they first met, last year.

Donne was sitting in nearly the exact same spot he was right now and had just finished his first winter exams. Artie was hosting a benefit for State Senator Henry Stern, who'd worked with Jeanne years earlier.

"Why not?" he asked.

Kate was wearing tight jeans and a turtleneck sweater. Her

hair was pulled back in a loosely tied bun. As far as he could tell, she was alone.

"Because if you drink that now, you'll be drinking by yourself. But if you wait and buy me one, you'll have someone to talk to. And that's less weird."

It was the kind of line that usually made Donne cringe, but she'd said it with such a wide, goofy smile.

He signaled Artie, and she ordered a vodka tonic.

"Really?" she asked. "You couldn't even try to say something funny?"

"No matter what it was, it would have bombed."

She tilted her head to the left and some of her hair fell out of the bun. "That's the point."

"You know the senator?" he asked, nodding toward the back where Stern was holding court.

She shrugged. "Old family friend. You?"

"A lifetime ago."

"So we're both here for the free food and booze, then?" She touched his arm.

And that was the start. Now, a year and a half later, he was engaged and actually supposed to be filling envelopes. They were getting married in two months. Middle of July.

He put his phone down and drank some more beer. Kate deserved to know. He picked the phone back up.

She picked up on the second ring.

"Hey," she said. Her voice was soft and she spoke slowly. "You okay?"

"I'm going to be back soon. We'll talk." He stared at his half drank-beer. He could leave it. "And I'll help fill some envelopes too."

Kate exhaled. "Don't you need to study?"

"I will. I am."

"All right, get back here. You've got some licking to do."

Donne started to speak. Stopped.

"Envelopes," she said. "What were you thinking? Envelopes, Jackson."

He laughed. "Anything I could have said would have

bombed."

"That's the point. See you soon. I love you."

This time she hung up before he could respond. He looked at the beer again. Times had changed. He didn't need it anymore. He couldn't believe he even came here. Like muscle memory.

He waved to Artie and got up. Just as he was putting his phone in his pocket, it vibrated a text message. Kate needed something from the store, maybe?

He looked at it. The recipient was marked unknown. But the message read:

She needs you. What are you waiting for?

CHAPTER
FOUR

Two—no—three years ago, Donne would have known what to do next. But his investigative skills had faded, and technology had passed him by. He didn't have much access to anyone who could track IP addresses and wasn't a skilled hacker himself. If the person who'd sent him the email had put any sort of security on the website at all, Donne wouldn't be able to track him down. Hell, Donne wouldn't have been able during his PI days either.

At the same time, his phone company contacts had dried up, either moving elsewhere or retiring. Investigating certainly wasn't like riding a bike. Instincts sag, and intellectual focus is put elsewhere.

He couldn't go to the cops. Talking to them meant talking to Bill Martin. He wasn't ready for that.

Donne stepped out of the tavern into the noon sunlight. It reflected off the glass of the store across the street directly into his eyes. He blinked and wiped at his watery eyes. The temperature had crested somewhere into the high seventies, as businesses let out for lunch and some students who hadn't gone home after finishing exams loitered.

What he should be doing.

Instead, he opened his text message and tried firing off a quick text to the blocked number. *Who are you?* It didn't go through.

Donne took a deep breath and leaned against the wall of the Olde Towne Tavern. He needed to go talk to Kate and tell her what was going on, but he wasn't ready to do that yet. At the very least, he had to try to get a step closer to figuring out what was going on.

His mind flashed on the video again. Jeanne's eyes wide open. She was screaming through duct tape.

Closing his eyes, Donne thought back to his brother-in-law, another kidnapping victim. So many people were involved then: local police, state police, the FBI. Who took the lead? The FBI—they always took the lead, pushing cops off the trail, using their massive budget to track people down.

That's who Donne needed now.

FBI headquarters was a thirty-five-minute drive up the Turnpike, with no traffic. Easier than calling. If he called, he'd bring two agents down to his home and just worry Kate.

He walked back to his apartment. His car was parked across the street. Kate's was parked right behind his. She'd noticed he was gone, and if he didn't call he'd worry her. She picked up on the second ring.

"Where are you?" No hello, no smile in her voice.

"I'm outside, but I have to take a ride."

"Where?"

Donne looked up at his apartment window and saw the curtains part. He waved and saw Kate wave back.

"Newark campus's library." Not a total lie. Well, maybe a total lie, except for the location.

"Why?"

"An article for Siva's class. I need it for the exam."

"You can't get it on campus? Or on the Internet? Like normal people?"

"It's in one of those journals you can't find online. I missed class the week he handed it out."

Kate sighed. "You need to make some friends."

"I need someone to cheat off."

She paused, squinting. Then she grinned.

"Be safe," Kate said. "Be quick."

The drive was quick. The roads were mostly clear, and he hit green lights on the way there. He found a parking lot just two blocks from the FBI building. This wasn't like walking into a police station. People didn't just call the FBI about a kidnapping. There was procedure. Call the police, and eventually the FBI would be brought in. He knew the drill. He hadn't been out of the game that long.

Claremont Tower rested along the Passaic River at Newark Dock, on the outskirts of the city. Donne imagined few people actually knew what was inside the tall, unmarked building. It looked like any other office building but without corporate logos. Donne crossed McCarter Highway and walked down a side street to the front of the building. He could smell dead fish and gasoline rising off the river and wondered if that made agents ornery on a daily basis. They did have a reputation to uphold, anyway.

Donne pulled open the glass door and a security guard waiting by a metal detector stared at him. The lobby looked like the TSA line at the airport.

"Can I help you?" the guard asked.

"I need to see an agent."

The guard picked up his iPad and touched the screen a few times. "Which one?"

Donne exhaled and said, "The one you report a kidnapping to."

The guard looked up. "Excuse me? Did you call the police?"

"I'm a former private investigator. I know the routine. It's easier to go right to the source."

The security guard put down the iPad and unbuttoned his suit jacket. Donne kept his hands at his sides.

"How long has this person been missing?"

"I'm not sure," Donne said. "For the last six years, I thought she was dead."

SPECIAL AGENT Fullbright's office was overdecorated. The guy wanted you to know he was from New Jersey. There were framed autographed pictures of Fullbright with Martin Brodeur, Yogi Berra, and Jon Bon Jovi. Next to those were vinyl copies of Springsteen's *Born to Run* and *Darkness on the Edge of Town*, also framed and autographed. Sports pennants for the Devils, Seton Hall, and the New York Giants hung from the ceiling. His desk, though, was clear. No memorabilia. No photos. Just files and a desktop computer.

Fullbright, sleeves pushed up, tie loosened, stood behind his desk. Donne sat across from him, feeling completely underdressed in his jeans and Pearl Jam T-shirt.

"Do you have the email?" Fullbright asked when Donne was finished telling him the story.

"I do." He pulled out his phone and handed it to Fullbright, with the text message open. "And the text message."

Fullbright looked at the text. "Can't do anything with this. Where's the email?"

"I need to access it on your computer."

"Like hell. Just pop it up on here." Fullbright shook the phone.

"It's Outlook. Doesn't really work well on the phone."

Fullbright shrugged. "Apple sucks anyway. Listen, Mr. Donne, you don't have much to go on here."

Donne's nostrils flared. He knew where this was going.

"Let me show you the email."

Fullbright nodded. "Our tech guys will take a look if your forward it to me. Just don't send me a virus."

"This isn't funny."

Fullbright put his hands in his pockets. "Jeanne Baker, by your account, has been dead for six years. There is a record of that. The medical examiner signed the death certificate. We have it on record here."

"I saw the video. I saw Jeanne."

The special agent nodded. "Someone is messing around with you, Mr. Donne. Someone with a sick sense of humor."

"If—"

"Forward me the email, Mr. Donne. I promise you I will look into it." Fullbright went into his desk, came out with a business card. Slid it across toward Donne. "Has my email on it too."

Donne took it and stood up. He left without thanking Fullbright. Why thank a guy you'll never hear from again?

Forty-two minutes later, Donne was parked in front of his apartment again. He looked up at his building. Kate wasn't looking out.

There was one contact Donne hadn't lost track of. He got out of the car and walked south on George Street. Traffic eased the closer he got to the theaters. It was the midpoint of New Brunswick. Here, the fancy restaurants and college pubs faded. Houses with faded siding and broken windows started to appear. Only residents and campus buses traveled this part of town. The city was expanding, and expanding in this direction, but the gentrification was slowed by the economic collapse. The university and Johnson & Johnson had been unable—or unwilling—to jump-start it again.

Eyes were on him because he didn't fit in. Even if they couldn't see his face, they could see his skin color. He was either buying or busting.

It took only five minutes before Donne heard his name being called. He whirled to his left to see Jesus Sanchez limping up Dumont Street.

"What the hell are you doing here, man?" Jesus asked as he crossed the street to Donne.

Jesus had ascended the ladder. After some cops had knocked off his boss, Jesus took over and now wasn't a street dealer anymore. That was three years ago. Sanchez apparently had an eye for business, or the cops had an affinity for him. He probably gave his boss up to the cops.

Jesus shook Donne's hand. He didn't say anything, just waited for Donne to explain.

The story of the email and Jeanne came easily out of Jackson, like a waterfall. He spat the words out, and when he was done he was out of breath.

"Holy shit," Jesus said. He wiped at his nose. "Why are you

here?"

"Where else would I go?"

Jesus shoved his hands in the pockets of his jeans and turned away from Donne. He headed up Dumont toward Douglass College. He stopped after a few steps.

"Go home, Jackson. I don't know shit."

For an instant, Donne believed him. He ground the heel of his shoe into the sidewalk and started to turn. But something tickled at the back of his neck. Maybe just a spark of his old instincts trying to fire up again. He froze.

"You're lying," Donne said.

Jesus tilted his head. "What you say?"

"You heard me."

Now Jesus's head started to shake. Back and forth slowly.

"Don't do this, Jackson."

"Do what?"

Jesus turned back toward Donne, but he was looking further down the road. He waved. Donne turned his head. As he did, his gut tightened. A black car rolled toward them. Tinted windows, shiny rims.

"I like you this way, Jackson," Jesus said. "The new you. You're happy, and this new girl, she seems good for you."

"How—"

Again Jesus shook his head. "The old you rushed into things. Didn't think. Fuck. You should be dead."

Donne didn't say a word. The car rolled up and stopped at the curve.

"I didn't like the old me either. Scared. Talkative. Not no more. I buried him." Jesus pulled the passenger door of the car open. "You should do the same. Old you comes back, it ain't gonna be for long."

"It's Jeanne," Donne said. "They have her. And they said I have to help her."

"You don't even know who *they* are. And you're better off that way. Go home. Study."

"She might die."

Jesus got into the car and shut the door. He rolled the

window down.

"And how is that different from what you thought yesterday?"

He rolled the window up as the car pulled away from the curb.

CHAPTER
FIVE

Three minutes.

The parking meter had been expired for three minutes. The driver, who had exited the car thirty-three minutes ago, was nowhere in sight. Bill Martin tapped twice on the steering wheel, exhaled, and allowed himself a smile.

Time to go to work.

He grabbed the summons and got out of his car. After straightening his tie, he crossed the street and stopped at the Volvo—one that belonged to a Mr. Shaun Smith. Smith—Martin loved the alliteration—couldn't be more than a sophomore and was probably getting used to parking on campus. And by getting used to it, Martin meant not doing it. The university had one of the largest private bussing systems in the country. Don't try to goose the meter.

People like Bill Martin were watching. And he was going to do his job.

After writing down the license plate number, Martin started to fill in the rest of the summons. The scratch of pen against paper made his smile grow even wider. None of this newfangled computer crap. Pen and paper—the right way to do things.

"Hey! Hey, wait!"

Martin looked up from the pad. Shaun Smith was running away from College Avenue toward him. Two pieces of change flew from his hand and clattered against the sidewalk. The kid stopped for a second, looked at the sidewalk, and then gave up—rushing again toward Martin.

Martin let his arms fall to his side, still gripping the pen and pad.

"Officer, please!" Smith skidded to a halt in front of Martin. "I'm just—wait a second. Are you even a cop?"

"I'm writing you a ticket, aren't I?" Martin asked.

"Where's your uniform?"

Martin shrugged his shoulders. He pulled his sports jacket open and flashed the badge on his belt.

"I've been around a long time. Wearing a suit on the job is a perk for me."

Smith opened his mouth, closed it. Then said, "You can't give me a ticket."

Here we go.

"Why not, son?"

Smith ran his hand through his shaggy blond hair. "Because I was just coming back to feed the meter."

"But you're three minutes late."

The kid looked behind him, then back at Martin. "I dropped my quarter back there, but I have the cash."

"Cash for the next half hour."

Smith nodded. "Come on, I have an exam. I'm going to be late."

"But you didn't pay for these last three minutes."

Smith shoved his hands in his pockets, feeling around for another coin. Behind them, a campus bus rumbled by. Martin figured it was headed to Busch Campus. That one seemed to be on schedule.

He went back to writing.

"Come on, man, don't be a dick."

Martin shook his head. "I'm not. I'm doing my job."

Smith exhaled. "Is this fun for you? Torturing college students?"

Martin tore the piece of paper away and handed it over to Smith. The kid took it and read it over. He shook his head.

"This is a blast," Martin said.

He turned around and went back to his car. As he crossed the street, he heard Smith call him an asshole.

"Don't forget to feed the meter in another thirty minutes," Martin called out.

Another stream of curses followed. Martin couldn't hold the smile back any more. Great start to the week.

Just a year after his promotion, after the shakes started, they demoted him to this job. They wanted him to retire.

And miss out on all the fun?

Hell, no.

Time to go back to the office to drop off all the tickets he'd written.

CHAPTER
SIX

Donne headed back toward home. Off to the north, some thunderclouds hung over Piscataway, threatening a midday storm. It felt like it was too early in the year to be expecting a heat-breaking thunderstorm, but it was already early May. Time passed quickly when you weren't paying attention.

Jeanne had already been gone six years, cut down in a car accident with a drunk driver. She was coming home from work, only a few weeks after Donne had left the force and started his own private investigator business. Someone came too hard around a curve and slammed into her. She was dead before the ambulance got on scene. The driver of the car had run off, leaving the car and several liquor bottles behind.

Now, as he passed the theater district, he tried to remember the days that followed. They were fuzzy, blurry — no, that was wrong. They were nonexistent. The weeks following Jeanne's death were a black hole of alcohol and drugs, exactly what he'd promised his fiancée he'd give up for her once they decided to get married.

A sober man may have gone on a quest, tracked down the drunk driver. But he just let it go. He let Jeanne's parents handle everything. Never asked if they found the guy. Never asked if they'd checked the plates to the car and caught anyone.

And then, just three years ago, her parents told him they never wanted to see him again.

Now, somehow, Jeanne was back in his life and Donne had nowhere to turn. His phone vibrated again, and his fingers tingled as he reached for it. He expected another warning from the blocked number, but all it was only Kate asking where he was. A few clicks of the keyboard later, and she knew he was on his way. But Donne had to make one more stop. Only one place left to turn.

If that car accident was faked and Jeanne was in danger, there was only one other person who could help him. It was not a place Donne wanted to go, not a place he ever wanted to walk into again.

THE NEW Brunswick police station was a big, modern brick building off the beaten path of downtown New Brunswick. Kirkpatrick Street was buried behind a parking deck and was considered a small side road. Donne hadn't walked down that side road in many years.

When he pulled the glass door open and stepped across the threshold, it felt as if a boa constrictor had wrapped itself around his neck. Air caught in the back of his throat.

He walked up to the reception desk, and the cop on duty looked up and did a double take. Maybe there was a picture of Donne in the break room and all the new recruits had to curse it out.

"Can I help you?" The cop sounded like he'd swallowed a thornbush.

"You know who I'm here to see," Donne tried.

"Because I'm psychic?"

Donne closed his eyes. A tough guy act wasn't going to work in the building where it was perfected.

"My old friend, I know he's still here."

"Well, I'm not about to announce you, so go find him yourself."

Clearly this guy knew Donne wouldn't be able to walk two feet without being stared down by six or seven other armed men. He just crooked his neck and nodded Donne toward the back. Didn't even check his ID.

Sometimes being hated makes things a lot easier.

Donne walked past the desk and into a series of cubicles. The police department always reminded Donne of a small-town business.

Cubicles, coffee, and water coolers.

The clicking of computer keys and mumbled chatter.

He expected all that to stop as he made his way through the office, but it didn't. He heard a few people mutter sounds of surprise, but the world didn't end. The boa constrictor left, but a rat had nested in his stomach.

He and Kate liked to joke about this when they went out for dinner. In New Brunswick, it was easy to walk to a restaurant, especially in the spring and summer. Kate knew about Donne's history with the police, and knew if they had a few drinks and there was a beat cop around, he'd be out to bust Donne for disorderly. So she would whisper "beer goggles" to him as they walked back to his apartment. It meant "Keep your eyes open" when the cops were around.

She'd be screaming "beer goggles" right now.

He came to the corner he'd rounded three or four hundred times when he worked here. The office was at the end of the hallway. As he strode, the doors to other offices closed. In the age of texting, word travels fast. He felt like he was in a bad, old comedy and had walked in to the wrong bar. The only thing missing was the scratch of a record stopping.

Donne reached the doorway and hesitated, his hand hovering over the knob. He used to have a key to this office, spent hours drinking coffee, reading files and sniffing cocaine. It was in this office that Donne had finally decided to go snitch, to give them all up.

It's also where he tried to protect his partner.

The same partner who wanted nothing more than to see Donne completely ruined. And, three years ago, had almost succeeded.

Donne turned the doorknob.

Bill Martin looked up from his desk, blinked, and dropped the mug of coffee that was in his hand.

It rattled on the desk, and the last sip of coffee dripped out on to the carpeted floor. The liquid seeped in, joining a multitude of other coffee stains.

"What the hell are you doing here?" Martin asked.

"We need to talk."

Martin blew air out of his mouth. Then said, "Like hell."

"It's important."

"Like hell it is." Martin turned toward his computer.

"I think Jeanne is still alive," Donne said. The words seemed to float from his mouth. He wanted to reach out and grab them. Stuff them into his pocket. Forget this ever happened.

Martin paused, hands above his keyboard. The blue screen reflected on his cheeks, making them look pale. Donne waited. Martin put his hand on his lap and swiveled his chair back in the direction of Donne.

"Who do you think you are?" he said. "Get the hell out of my office. Now!"

CHAPTER
SEVEN

Donne didn't leave, though every nerve ending in him fired and tried to force him to run.

"I think Jeanne's alive," he said again.

Martin's hand shook as it hovered over the desk.

Years ago, his old partner dropped a bomb on Donne, one that shook him to the core. Donne would have been lying to himself if he didn't hope this news did the same to Martin.

"What are you talking about?" Martin said. He put his trembling hand flat on the desk to stop it and pushed himself up into a standing position. He looked like Perry White in just about every comic book drawing ever. Two hands on the desk, leaning over it, about to scream.

Donne quickly ran through the email and text message story. Martin's mouth was parted, but he didn't speak.

When Donne was finished, Martin said, "Gotta be a fake."

"But I—"

Martin shook his head. "Let me see the email."

Donne started to take out his phone.

"No, idiot. Come around to my computer and login. I can't see anything on those screens."

Donne did as he was told. He stepped around the desk, leaned over the keyboard, and got to his email. He opened it, then opened the email. He was about to click on the link when

Martin nudged him aside. They stared at Donne in dress blues.

"I remember that picture," he said. "That was when you were smart, kid."

The last word came out sharp, like Martin bit the end of it off.

He grabbed the mouse away from Donne and clicked on the link. The blank website opened up with the video box in the middle. They waited. Nothing happened.

"It must have been a one-time-only deal," Donne said.

"Are you just here to ruin my day?" Martin clicked the mouse a few times.

"You think I want to be here?"

"Then go home."

Donne didn't move.

Martin stood up turned away from him. He opened a file cabinet and started to flip through files.

"Think about it, Bill. I had to walk through a gauntlet to get here. Would I really come here just to pull a dumb joke?"

Martin didn't speak, but stopped looking through his papers.

"Jesus already told me to stay away from this. I have no idea what he knows, but this is real, Bill. And I have nowhere else to turn."

"Jesus is doing pretty well for himself these days," Martin said. "Thought you were out of the PI business. I believe I took your license."

Donne clenched his fists. "I keep in touch with old friends."

"You don't keep in touch with me." Martin's shrugged his shoulders.

"Enough." Donne looked out the window and watched a car pull out of its parking spot in the deck across the way.

"Let's say I do believe you," Martin said. "What's the next step for you and me?"

"I don't know."

"We're not working together. What do they call it in the comic books? A team-up."

Donne smiled despite himself. Martin loved to read comics.

He also liked the Hollies.

"No," Donne said. "We're not working together."

"Then, I ask again, why come here?"

Because I didn't know what else to do. Donne wanted to shout it at him.

"I'm out of the game, you said it yourself. Investigating is not something I do any more. I don't have any contacts—"

"You just said you keep in touch with old friends." It sounded like Martin was speaking through clenched teeth. He turned back around to face Donne.

Getting somewhere.

Donne plowed on. "I don't have any contacts. I can't make any headway on this. But you—you slept with Jeanne." He had to spit the words out. "You loved her. If Jeanne's alive—"

"'If'? You came all the way down here for 'if'?" Martin shook his head. He picked the mug off the floor and kicked at the liquid, rubbing it deeper into the rug.

Donne exhaled. "Find her. Please find her."

"The text message and that email said you were the only one who could help."

"We're going in circles here, Bill."

Martin took a step toward him, and Donne tensed. Martin leaned in closer, until they were nearly nose-to-nose. Donne could smell old coffee on his breath.

"I want to punch you in the face." The words oozed from Martin. "I want to see nothing more than you lying on my carpet creating another stain. You know how many men out there lost their jobs, are in jail, because of you?"

Without flinching, Donne said, "Do what you have to do, Bill."

Martin pursed his lips and rolled his right shoulder. For an instant, Donne actually expected a right cross to connect with his jaw.

"I want to hear you beg."

Donne's shoulders slumped.

"Beg me to find her, Jackson. Do it."

Donne took a deep breath. He hoped his smelled as bad as

Martin's. "Help me, Bill. Help me find her. I need you to find her. Make her safe."

Martin held his position as another long puff of coffee breath exploded in Donne's nostrils.

"Forward me the email." He rattled off his email address. "And then go the hell home."

"Thanks, Bill."

"I never want to see you again."

Martin turned and slammed the filing cabinet shut.

"When you find her, call me."

Martin laughed. "Who are we kidding, Jackson? You're not going to leave this alone."

Donne didn't say anything.

"You're going to be out there looking too." Martin paused. "You are the only one who actually believes what you're saying."

"I'm not—"

Martin waved a hand at him. "Save it."

Donne turned and left. Seconds later, he heard the door slam behind him.

CHAPTER
EIGHT

The drive to the shore took just over an hour.

Bill Martin took a left turn on to a street named after some sort of tropical flower and cruised down it. Lavallette, like most Jersey Shore towns, was still cleaning up from Hurricane Sandy. There were empty lots where one-floor houses used to be. Garbage bags lined the curbs waiting for pickup. Damaged boats sat in driveways, waiting for repair.

Martin hoped his destination hadn't been harmed. He hadn't come this way in more than six years, not since Jeanne died. Couldn't allow himself to. Jeanne had made her choice, choosing to go back to Donne rather than be with him. There was no reason to go to the funeral or contact her parents other than to send condolences. But now, with the news Donne had brought, seeing Jeanne's parents was the first logical destination.

They deserved to know.

The road curved around away from the lagoon that cut through everyone's backyards. In this area of the shore, people didn't have lawns. They littered their front and backyards with stones. If the lagoon every crested, as it did with Sandy, the stones were supposed to be better somehow. Martin never cared to ask how.

He saw Jeanne's parents' home up ahead. It appeared to be in good shape. Being off the lagoon must have provided some form of security. He checked the clock on his dashboard. It was just before three, but he assumed they were home. The Bakers were long retired—both teachers—and collecting their pensions.

Good for them.

Martin parked across the street, turned the car off, and put both hands on the steering wheel. He hated that his hands had shook in front of Donne. And now the shakes were worse. He'd tried everything, giving up coffee and smoking. Eating better. More exercise.

His heart pounded hard and his breath was ragged. He closed his eyes and tensed his upper body, willing it to slow down. Once it did, he got out of the car before the tremors could start again. He crossed the street, crunched his way over the front yard rocks, and stepped onto the stoop. The doorbell played Big Ben's theme.

Someone moved behind the door, and Martin's heart rate picked up again. He put his hands behind his back and clenched them into fists. As the door opened, Martin focused on his breathing.

Leonard Baker stood in front of him, and the years hadn't been kind. His once salt-and-pepper hair was completely gray. The crow's feet that had been at the corner of his eyes now stretched out across his face.

"Bill Martin," he said, his voice strong and full of bass.

"Hi, Leonard. Can I come in?"

"Is something wrong?"

Martin dug his nails into his palms. "We should talk."

"Come in." Leonard pushed open the door.

"Is your wife here?"

Leonard shook his head. "She's out. Be back soon."

Martin followed Leonard into the living room. The floors were tiled, with a throw rug resting under the coffee table. There were no pictures in the room, just displays of the shore, sea shells, bottles full of sand, and a craft sign that said ON THE BEACH, IT'S ALWAYS HAPPY HOUR.

Martin sat on the couch. Leonard took the loveseat across

from him.

"How did you guys do during the storm?" Martin asked.

Leonard shrugged. "We're still here."

"No damage?"

"What's going on, Bill?"

Martin leaned back on the couch. Coming here wasn't a good idea. No matter what he said, he was going to hurt Leonard. He didn't expect such an older man. He expected to deal with the strong man Leonard had once been. The one who accepted him when he and Jeanne started dating. And who, six years ago, told Donne to stay out of the Baker family's life once and for all. No, Martin wasn't really thinking when he hit the Parkway.

Martin said, "Jackson Donne came to see me."

Leonard Baker's cheeks fired up red, but he didn't respond.

"He told me Jeanne's still alive."

Baker looked toward his front door. "That's ridiculous." The bass left his voice.

"He said he received an email with a link in it. When he clicked on the link—"

"Did he show you the email?"

Martin stopped for a moment. He studied Leonard and tried to pick up his body language. Leonard wasn't looking at him, and his body went stiff in the chair. He kept staring at the front door.

"He said when he clicked on the link, Jeanne was on it. Bound and gagged."

"Why are you telling me this?"

"You're her dad."

Leonard tilted his head left, then—as if it was attached to a piece of elastic—snapped it straight back up again. "She's dead. And Jackson is a drunk, drugged-up moron." Leonard's eye flicked upward. "He doesn't know what he's talking about. How can you listen to him?"

"He wasn't drunk when I talked to him."

"Do you believe him?"

Martin glanced toward where Leonard gazed. The clock. Ten after three. "Do you believe me?"

Leonard turned back toward Martin. The red in his cheeks had faded. "I believe Jackson Donne came to you and told you lies. I believe he is trying to hurt you, and now you're here to hurt us."

Martin said, "That's not it. There was something to this. It felt legitimate."

"You have to go."

Martin flinched. "We need to talk more about this. If Jackson isn't lying—"

"He is."

Martin shook his head. "If he isn't lying, we need to find Jeanne before someone hurts her."

"You can't hurt a dead person."

"I don't know if—"

Leonard stood up so fast, it was as if he leapt. "You have to leave. You have to go now. Get out of the house. Thank you for coming, Bill. Get out."

Martin didn't move. Leonard started to walk to the door. "Come on now."

Martin stood up. "I wish you'd let me talk."

Before he could take another step, Leonard froze in front of him. Martin heard the front door swing open. He looked toward it expecting to see Mrs. Baker. He did. She stood there, looking just as old as her husband. She covered her mouth with her hand.

By her side was a young boy, no older than five.

"Grandpa!" the boy said, and ran toward Leonard.

CHAPTER
NINE

Part of Bill Martin had always hoped she'd been lying. The day before she died, when she told him she was going back to Jackson Donne, Jeanne lied about being pregnant. It made things less painful, less horrible. He pushed it down, just like he pushed everything about Jeanne down. Hiding it away in the dark recesses of his memories.

But now, with the boy in front of him, one whose age lined up with what Jeanne said, it was impossible to deny.

The room tilted left and Martin dropped back on to the couch. He shook his head to clear his vision and looked up at the boy who was hugging Leonard Baker. Brown hair styled into a crewcut, a slight tan to his complexion. Spider-Man T-shirt and khaki shorts. A Thor bookbag. Smiling. Laughing.

Sarah Baker was staring at Martin, and he could feel it on his skin. He rubbed his face and stood up again. The floor seemed to have regained its equilibrium, so he had little trouble standing.

"Sarah," he said, as a way of greeting her.

Sarah turned toward Leonard and opened her mouth.

Leonard nodded. "I'm taking care of it. Why don't you and William get a snack?"

"I think I'm going to have cookies," William said. He ran out of sight. Martin remembered the kitchen being in the direction

William ran.

"Wash your hands," Sarah called and stalked off after him.

"You still need to leave," Leonard said when she was gone.

Martin's hands were trembling hard, and squeezing them into fists didn't stop it. He thought about jamming them in his pockets, but didn't want to look like a three-year-old. They remained at his sides, shaking.

"You have to tell me what's going on."

"I can't. I made a promise." Leonard turned toward the front door again. He pulled it open. "Leave us alone."

"William is hers. I know he is. Before she—" He paused, not sure how to say it. "Died. Before she died, she told me she was pregnant."

"Why are you chasing this?"

Martin curled and then stretched his toes inside his shoes. He needed to be doing something.

"Jackson Donne came to me and said she was in trouble."

"Please go." Leonard's cheeks weren't red anymore. They were the opposite. Pale, as if all the blood had drained from his body and pooled in his feet.

"How do you have a child in this house if she's dead?"

"It's the neighbor's kid." The words were ice chips.

"He called you Grandpa."

Leonard closed his eyes. Opened his mouth, closed it. Opened his eyes again. They were glistening.

"Please go. You can't—."

"She's alive."

"Go, Bill." His voice cracked.

"I can help."

Leonard shook his head. "No. No, you can't."

Martin waited a beat, then walked toward the front door, but turned left toward the kitchen. The hallway used to be barren of memories. Now, the Bakers had lined it with framed pictures. Martin's eye registered them as he passed. William on a slide at a park. William eating cake. A picture of Jeanne graduating high school.

William and Sarah sat at the kitchen table eating sugar

cookies. Sarah was flipping through a magazine, but not really reading it. Her eyes were on William. He was looking at a comic book.

They both looked up at Martin in the doorway. Martin felt Leonard's hand on his shoulder. It was a gentle grasp, with a quick squeeze. Like he was saying *please*.

"I'm so sorry, Sarah," Martin said.

Sarah looked back at William.

"Hi, William," Martin said.

"Hi."

"What are you reading?"

"Spider-Man."

Martin nodded. "He's the best."

William held up the book so Martin could see Spidey flipping through a hail of bullets. A thug had been firing a machine gun at him.

"Can I ask you something?"

William nodded.

"Where's your mom?"

Sarah made a noise. Her hand flashed up and covered her mouth as if trying to push the sound back in.

"She's working," William said.

"Where does she work?"

William looked at Sarah, then up at Leonard. If he read something on their faces, he didn't show it. He just went back to looking at the comic book.

"Far away," he whispered.

"Do you ever see her?"

William shook his head. "Not for a while."

Martin nodded. "Don't worry. Spider-Man always gets the bad guy."

"I know," William said. "And sometimes he has help."

Martin paused. "You mean like Doctor Octopus?"

"No. Doctor Octopus is a bad guy. They don't work together. Doc Ock would hurt Spider-Man. I mean the Avengers."

A thought crossed Martin's mind. He reached out and shook Will's hand. "It was nice to meet you."

William nodded.

Martin turned, trying to ignore the tears in Sarah's eyes. Leonard stared at him as he walked by. He felt like he was passing through needles. It took until he got to the front door until it hit him.

He'd been alone for so long, years. Martin didn't go out with people. Didn't talk to anyone.

No one ever had long conversations with him. And when someone did need his attention, it was either by calling him "Bill" or "Martin."

No one had used his full first name in years. Maybe Jeanne was the last one. She liked the formality of it. It wasn't a boy's name. It wasn't a baseball player's name.

The realization froze him cold at the doorway.

He hadn't been called William in six years.

Bill Martin turned on his heel and faced Leonard.

"Jesus Christ," Martin said. "He's named after me."

CHAPTER
TEN

Kate Ellison stared at her fiancé. He sat across from her, not making eye contact, jamming invitations into envelopes. She'd already asked him once to be gentle. He did for about three invitations, and then the jamming started again.

"Do you want a beer?" She really didn't want to nag or ask what was wrong. He'd get to it. Jackson always got to it.

Eventually.

Jackson shook his head. He jammed another invitation and it bent at the corner, like a dog-eared page in a book. A tremor went through her, a short bolt of electricity.

"Stop it," she said, hoping the words came out evenly.

Jackson froze, except his eyes, which finally met hers. He held them for an instant, then his shoulders slumped and he looked down. After placing the envelope on the table, he sat back on the couch.

"What the hell, Jackson?" Even just went out the window.

"Kate, I—"

"No, seriously. You've been acting weird all day."

She searched her memory for another time he'd acted like this, sullen and quiet. A petulant child. All she wanted was a moment to compare this to, something to latch on to and help her understand. This wasn't like him at all.

Nothing came back to her.

Their fights were always full of screaming, but open and honest. They always knew where the other stood. The first night Jackson promised to come over but didn't—their first fight, actually—she knew he was right for her. There were no games. His phone had died, and without the clock on it, he lost track of time bullshitting with Artie. She argued he could have checked another cell phone, or—for pete's sake—looked at a clock. The Olde Towne Tavern was littered with them.

Their points were clear, even if they shouted them at each other. She always understood what he meant Hopefully, Jackson understood her too.

But now, he was obtuse.

"It's nothing," he said. "It's … it's just exams."

"Oh, come on. I've been with you for at least three exam sessions. You've never been like this."

Jackson looked at the table, strewn with envelopes, stamps, and address labels.

"Jeanne Baker? Remember?"

The name didn't come up often, but it did come up. Kate knew who Jeanne was. The hair on her arms stood.

"I think she's alive." He slumped deeper into the couch.

The muscles between her shoulder blades stiffened.

"That's not possible," she said. "You told me—you …"

Donne blinked. He put the envelope he'd been stuffing on to the cushion next to him.

"You were gone all day," she said. "You went to Newark, you were … You promised lunch."

Kate got up, and the muscles in her back grew tighter, turning into sailor's knots. She went into the kitchen and surveyed Jackson's fridge. When she'd first met him it was a mess of leftover Chinese food or pizza and Molson. At least she'd gotten him to upgrade his beer choices. Better beer, but less of it. He thought the prices of a six pack were ridiculous.

She grabbed two Troegs Hopbacks, popped the caps and poured each into its own pint glass. That was the other thing she'd taught him: Use a glass to drink your beer. It tastes better. Might actually enjoy it.

And he did.

Small things. He started to drink less and take his time when he did. They would watch movies together, and he'd only drink three beers. Friday night alternated. Either they'd do takeout, Jackson's choice. Or they'd go out, Kate's choice.

Compromise.

She brought the glass to him and put it on the end table — away from the envelopes. After she sat, she took down half the pint in one gulp. Jackson didn't touch his glass.

The first time he told her about his dead fiancée, she held him close. He told Kate how Jeanne called to see what they needed at the supermarket while he was on a case. Something about her own father needing help. Suicide watch, maybe? She couldn't quite remember. After he finished talking, Kate and Jackson sat there for a long time. They didn't make love. They didn't go to sleep. They just sat, until he gave her a small kiss on the cheek.

Today, he told her about the email. About going to the FBI and how they didn't believe him. How he went to the bar and drank, when she asked him to call her if he did that. After he finished talking, he rested his elbows on his thighs and let his head hang between his knees.

"We should do something," she said.

"No."

"Come on, someone can help you. We can get to the bottom of this."

Donne shook his head. "I don't want to involve you." He paused. "But I didn't want to lie to you either."

"Senator Stern. He knew Jeanne. Remember? The night we met. I'll get my father to put us in touch with him."

"No."

The buzzer to his apartment rang, and Kate jumped in her seat. The electricity that had been buzzing through her veins sent another jolt. She looked at Jackson, who bounced up out of his seat, as if the buzzer was as starter gun. He rushed to the intercom.

"Hello?" he said.

"Come on, I'm downstairs."

"Bill?"

Who the hell was Bill?

"Yes, asshole. Turns out, I think you're right. We have work to do."

"Who is that?" Kate asked.

Jackson looked her, his face flushed. She couldn't read his expression. His lips were pressed tightly together, and his nostrils flared a bit when he inhaled.

"I have to go."

"Go where? Is this about Jeanne?"

"I—" he said. "I have to go. I don't know where."

After putting his hand on the doorknob, he turned back toward her. She felt the muscles in her back relax for the moment she thought he was going to stay.

"I'll call you," he said. "I promise."

Jackson pulled the door open and left. It closed with a soft click behind him.

Kate looked at the piles on the table in front of her and finished her beer. Once she was sure Donne was gone, she picked up her phone and called her father.

Myron Ellison picked up on the third ring.

"You better not be calling in sick tomorrow. Opening statements are next week," he said in a nasal whine.

"No, Dad," she said. She took a second to try to catch her breath. Working for your father was a pain in the butt. When he hired her, it was supposed to be an easy job while she studied for the bar. Now it took up all her time.

There must have been something in her voice she didn't realize, because the bounce went out of Dad's. "Tell me," he said in a hushed tone.

She did. About the way Jackson was acting. The intercom conversation. The email. He took it all in, asking for clarification here, a bit more description there. She obliged, trying to not to rush. It was like a client interview, each detail pored over until she had it right.

Clients hated the process. And now Kate knew why. It was

tedious, down to the color of the intercom. At one point she asked her dad if he wanted to know how many scratches were on it.

"Not this second," he said.

Fifteen minutes later she was done, and exhausted. She waited while Dad hummed. He was thinking. He always hummed Neil Young while he thought. Depressing.

"Can you blame him?" Dad finally asked.

Kate waited.

"Let's just say you had a guy you really loved ten years ago."

"I was an undergrad."

"So's he." Dad chuckled. "Just listen. You're going to get married to this guy, but you know, he dies."

"Dad," she said.

"Then all of a sudden he's back. He might be alive. What are you going to do?"

"I get it." She could feel the burn of the beer at the back of her throat.

"Good, then you're not allowed to be mad at him."

"That's not why I'm calling you. I can be mad at whoever I want, whenever I want."

"Great," he said. She heard papers shuffling.

"I need to find him."

There was a moment of silence. Kate stared at the door, willing it to open, willing Jackson to come in and explain everything. Instead, she heard Mrs. Mullins from upstairs shuffle past with her shih tzu.

"You think he's coming back tonight?" Dad asked.

"No."

"I'm sorry. You want to come stay here?"

Kate clutched the phone tighter, but didn't respond.

"You have to let him deal with this, Kate."

"I want him to talk to me. How can I find him?"

"You don't want to go down this road."

Myron's voice was scratchy and soft now — the whine gone. It reminded her of bedtime when she was little. He used to read her a book, basically whispering it until she nodded off. She wanted him to whisper her to sleep again. Do what dads do and make everything okay again.

"Please, Dad. What can I do?"

More paper shuffling. "I'll get back to you. Stay put."

"I'm nervous, Dad."

"It'll be okay."

Kate put the phone down. The stabbing pain in her skull said otherwise.

CHAPTER
ELEVEN

Martin drove for miles without speaking. They cruised south on Route 18, out of New Brunswick, through East Brunswick, and into Old Bridge. He pulled off the highway and tracked through backroads Donne didn't recognize. Soon they pulled into Union Beach, a town that had been hammered by Superstorm Sandy.

"Where are we going?" Donne finally asked, unable to wait out the silence anymore.

Martin didn't speak, and his eye remained fixed on the road. Donne wasn't sure why he'd even gotten into the car in the first place. Martin said they had work to do, and that seemed like enough for Donne at the time.

"Come on, Bill, tell me what's going on."

Martin stopped at a traffic light and reached down into his cup holder for his coffee cup. Took a long sip. The light changed green. Donne's ears burned.

Three blocks later they parked in front of a one-story cape. It was the typical Jersey Shore house, right down to the rocks on the front lawn. Donne got out of the car and immediately smelled the salt from the sea. It brought back memories of Jeanne and his first vacation to Cape May. They only stayed three nights — it was all they could afford. But they hit every hot spot at night, and burned their skin to a crisp during the day.

"Come on," Martin said. He walked up the front walk to the door and knocked.

"I think I'm owed an explanation," Donne said.

Martin looked at the sky. "You think I'm going to drag your ass down here and keep quiet the whole time?"

"You didn't say much on the ride."

Martin said, "I'd rather focus on the road than listen to you prattle on."

The door was answered by a woman in shorts and a T-shirt. It wasn't Jeanne. This woman was older, and her shorts didn't fit right, as if they'd shrunk in the wash. She was blond, her hair cut short.

"Hey, Bill."

"Hi." He motioned for Donne to come up with the walk.

Bill went into the house. As he passed the woman, his hand grazed her hip. Donne followed. The hallway smelled like old pipe tobacco and caramel.

"This is Eileen," Martin said. "Eileen, Jackson Donne."

Eileen blinked, then looked at Martin. Donne's skin prickled. Not his favorite feeling.

"Here's what you're going to do," Eileen said. "You're going to log into your email and show me what Bill here was talking about. I'll take a look and tell you where it was sent from."

"Just like that?" Donne asked.

"Shut up and do what she says." Martin shook his head. Eileen gave him half a smile. "You're a two-year old."

They followed Eileen into a room full of computers. Hard drives hummed, wires were taped to the wall or strewn across the carpet. Donne counted three modems and five monitors.

"Who are you?" Donne asked.

Eileen looked at Martin and said, "You're right—he is two. Mr. Donne, have you read about the people in the government who've been tracking your Internet and phone records? I used to do that professionally. Now I do it privately."

"You mean illegally."

Eileen shrugged. "I still feel like a patriot."

She gestured for Donne to sit down at the computer. He

did. She told him to bring up his email. He did. Then she rolled Donne and his chair out of the way. She leaned over the computer and clicked around with the mouse. Occasionally she'd type on the keyboard. Donne tried to follow the flashes on the screen, but they flickered away too fast.

"I got a text too," Donne said. He reached for his phone.

"I see that. I assume you don't mean the one from Kate."

Martin laughed. Donne glanced toward Martin. He wasn't smiling. Donne rubbed at his wrist. The prickly feeling moved from his arms to the back of his neck.

"There's a bodega in Perth Amboy," Eileen said.

Donne turned back to her and saw Google Maps open on his screen.

"The email was sent from there." Eileen shook her head. "Maybe not. This email is connected to that place."

Donne didn't even try to venture a thought as to what that meant.

"What about the website and the video? Can you tell where that was filmed?" Martin put his hand on her shoulder.

"Not yet. Working on it." Eileen clicked a few more keys. " I can see the code of it, when your computer connected to their camera. It was shot this morning."

"Jesus," Bill said.

Donne's mouth ran dry. "Why would the video come from a bodega?"

Eileen sighed. "Here's what I can tell you. The email was encrypted and pretty well. If I wasn't so good at what I do … Listen, they sent it from a computer, and they're professionals. They really didn't want you to know where it was sent from. I'm still not 100 percent sure."

"Then why did the text say I was needed?"

Eileen blinked. "Bill's the detective."

Another gust of sea air came through the window, and Donne flashed to Jeanne in Cape May. She was in a bra and panties, lying on the bed of their hotel room. She beckoned him.

Someone was beckoning him again.

"Maybe a couple of years ago, the kid would have figured

it out," Martin said.

Donne said, "It doesn't matter. What's the address of the bodega?"

Eileen started writing on a Post-it note.

CHAPTER
TWELVE

Perth Amboy was once a bustling shipping and resort town. History, however, hadn't been kind to Perth Amboy. The streets started to crumble, and tourists left for the more scenic Jersey Shore.

Today, it was much like the area of New Brunswick beyond the theaters. Untouched, unloved, and falling apart. People sat on stoops, drinking from bottles in paper bags. Martin accelerated at every yellow light to beat the change.

Gentrification hadn't hit downtown Perth Amboy yet. The government wanted to focus on the ports and bay area. And the media was focused on an ongoing battle toward privatizing the schools. Downtown was littered with bargain stores, bodegas, and caged windows.

Martin parked the car. Donne's neck seized as if he'd slept on it funny. Adrenaline pumping through his veins, he whirled around and looked across the street.

No one around. His old cop instincts were firing.

He rolled his shoulders and glanced at Martin who'd just stepped on to the sidewalk. Martin didn't seem to notice.

"What's the deal with you and Eileen?" Donne asked.

Martin turned and glared at him.

"I saw you touch her back. She laughed at your jokes."

Martin shrugged. "A friend."

"That's all?"

"Come on," Martin said.

"You would think a 'friend' would have made you relax a little."

The bodega was on the corner, the first floor of a three-story apartment building. The awning was yellow, and the name of the store, Convenience, was written in both English and Spanish. They advertised coffee, newspapers, lottery tickets, and cigarettes.

Donne didn't follow Martin. Instead, he glanced up the street and saw two men in suits walking their way. They stuck out like chocolate chips on a pizza.

"Bill," Donne said. "We have visitors."

"Oh. Nice."

Martin stepped up next to Donne and watched the guys walk. They looked like linebackers, and the seams of their suit were struggling to hold on.

When they were two feet away, they stopped. One guy went for folded arms, the other went for hands in pockets. Other than skin color, the guys looked alike. Close cropped hair, sunglasses, and muscles. Military, Donne guessed.

"Jackson Donne?" the black guy asked.

"Uh-huh." Donne's witty banter had gone the way of the rest of his investigative skills.

"Mind coming with us?

"Yeah. Kinda."

"I'm afraid we insist." He nodded down the block. "Now, if you'll follow us."

"Boy," Martin said. "You two are flat-out Shakespearean in your conversational skills."

The two pro wrestlers glanced at each other, as if Martin was an alien.

"Sir?" the white guy said. "Can you get back in your car, please?"

"Yeah ..." Martin flashed his badge. "I don't think that's going to happen. Do you men have some identification we can see?"

The black guy leaned in close to the badge. "We're in Perth Amboy. You don't have jurisdiction here."

Martin sighed. "You think I can't make a quick phone call and get ten Perth Amboy comes here tout suite?"

As the man stood back up, Donne could hear the fabric of his suit stretch. The white guy cracked his knuckles.

The bodega must have put on a fresh pot of coffee, because the odor suddenly permeated the air. Behind the two men, a bird landed and pecked at the ground. Donne felt his heart ticking off the milliseconds in his chest.

"So what do we want to do here, boys? Mr. Donne goes, I go with him. We're … pals."

The two men looked at each other and seemed to make a wordless decision. He watched the black guy's muscles relax, and the air seemed between them seemed to change. The two men smiled like customer service employees at a Walmart.

"We will be in touch, Mr. Donne. There's some business we'd like to deal with. But it's best handle it between us."

Donne wanted to ask about Jeanne. He wanted to go with them. But the sweat in his palms and the pounding of his heart stopped him.

The men left, heading back the way they came. Once they were out of earshot, Bill Martin clapped.

"This is the most fun I've had in years," he said. His voice was flat.

Donne checked his phone and didn't see any texts from Kate. His stomach fluttered and twisted and he thought about texting her. Just to say he was okay. But he didn't want her to worry. A text would more than likely cause more problems and not ease his nerves.

"They're in a car about a block and a half down," Martin said. "They're not going to go anywhere until we do."

"Jeanne could be dead by now," Donne said. "Maybe I should have gone with them."

"Yeah, then you'd be dead too." Martin paused. "You know, you're right. Why don't you head down the block and take a ride."

Donne said, "You called me your pal."

"I didn't have a better word, and calling you 'asshole' would have given them a better sense of who I was." He looked at his watch. "Or at least given them more information than they had before."

Martin turned and walked into the bodega.

CHAPTER
THIRTEEN

*B*ill Martin just bought me a coffee.

It was burnt and overly sweetened, but it was bought by Martin and given to Donne without asking. Donne expected tectonic plates to shift beneath his feet and the entire block to get swallowed up into the earth. Martin downed his coffee in one long gulp, as if the heat didn't exist.

He drank it so fast, Donne almost didn't notice the tremor in his hand, the way the cup swayed just a hair just before the lip hit his mouth.

Martin tossed the cup into the trash next to the counter and pulled out his badge. The cashier leaned in to take a better look, but it disappeared into Martin's jacket.

"I need to take a look around," Martin said the words like it was a fait accompli.

"I haven't been robbed. That was two blocks over." The clerk, a short, round man with a thick Spanish accent laughed. "Cops don't know nothing."

Martin exhaled what must have been the sarin gas equivalent of burnt coffee right into the cashier's face. He recoiled.

"Not about a robbery."

The cashier wiped his mouth. "You want to buy something?"

"How about health inspection?"

Donne picked up a package of Tastykake coffee cakes and

looked at the expiration date. A year old.

"My stuff is fresh!" the cashier shouted. "I run a good business."

"Then we'll be out of your way in ten minutes," Martin said. He nodded at Donne, and they walked around to the back of the store.

Martin made a show of looking at the coolers. He opened one and pulled out a bottle of Gatorade. He twisted off the cap, smelled it, and gagged. The old routine started to come back to Donne. How many times had they done this when looking for drug runners hiding out in the back?

"You have to pay for that!" the cashier yelled.

Martin took a gulp, then spat it onto the floor. Donne turned away from him. This time they weren't claiming drugs as evidence and snorting or selling half the coke themselves after their shift was over.

"I'm not going to pay for my own poison," Martin said. Donne could have said the words, right down to the cadence, along with him.

"Fuck you!" the cashier spat.

"You're not my type." It was as if Abbott and Costello were doing "Who's on First?" at a funeral.

Martin tilted his head toward the door that lead to the backroom. Donne's gut lurched. He wasn't armed, and he had no idea what was back there. Martin dropped his hand to his waist. His fingers grazed the gun at his hip.

Donne went first. Martin always told him the point man never got shot at in Vietnam. No, the Viet Cong were smart. They didn't shoot at the first guy that came through; they waited for the rest of the platoon.

Donne was pretty sure Martin never served.

Pushing the door open, he stepped over the threshold. No one shot at him. The only sound was the whir of the engine running the central air-conditioner. To his right were metal shelves, filled with old boxes, waiting to be tossed in the bailer. To his left were pallets filled with potato chips and K-cup coffee packs. And a desk with a computer on it.

Martin noticed the desk first and went to it. Now the tremor showed in both hands. Donne couldn't remember if Martin had always displayed this tic.

Moving the mouse, Martin clicked through several different screens. Each window got a few seconds of his time before he moved to another one. Occasionally, he'd mumble something that Donne couldn't decipher. His tone of voice, however, was sharp and cutting.

"Do you want help?" Donne folded his arms. He hid his fists behind his elbows.

"No."

Donne looked at the small backroom again for something that stood out. Nope, the bailer, the rotten food, and disorganization were the room's best features.

"You sure? It seems like you're having trouble."

Martin clicked a few more times.

"Forget it," he said. He pushed the mouse hard and it fell off the desk, suspended in air by its wire.

Donne didn't wait for an invitation. He stepped in between the desk and Martin and picked up the mouse. Pressed it down on the mouse pad and started scrolling. Martin had opened Internet Explorer and was stuck on the Yahoo! homepage.

Donne closed that and looked at the programs on the desktop. Nothing out the ordinary. Microsoft Word, an Excel spreadsheet with inventory numbers on it, web browsers, and Skype. He was stunned this place kept an inventory. Donne clicked on Start, then froze.

Skype.

"We're looking for an iPad," Martin said.

"Yeah, I know."

"That's a computer," Martin said.

"Have some more coffee." Donne squinted and willed his eyes to stay focused. "Don't you hate computers?"

"That's why I didn't realize it wasn't an iPad at first."

Donne clicked on the Skype icon. The hourglass appeared on screen for a moment, then then the Skype window appeared. The username and password were saved to the computer, so

Donne didn't have to login.

He counted to ten while waiting for the contacts to load up.

The usual screen full of usernames showed up. Most didn't have avatars, and were just images of phone handsets. Donne scanned usernames and didn't recognize any. He scrolled the down the screen and pictures started to show up.

That's why his gut pitched and for an instant, Donne thought he was going to throw up. One of the icons, one with an avatar was very familiar to him. He recognized it.

It was someone he hadn't seen in years.

It was Jeanne's father.

CHAPTER
FOURTEEN

Donne closed Skype and exhaled.

"Jackson?" Bill Martin's voice was far away.

He felt his nerves endings firing—like he'd drank too much Coca-Cola. Muscles tensed.

"Donne? You okay?"

"Yeah," Donne said.

He dropped his arms to his side and closed his eyes. His ears were burning. He opened his eyes again.

Then he burst through the door back into the front of the bodega. He spun on his heel into a rack of potato chips knocking them over and headed down the aisle toward the cash register. The cashier's eyes went wide as he stared at what must have looked like a madman rushing at him.

Blood pounded in his ears. He slammed into the counter of the register and reached across, grabbing the cashier by the front of his polo shirt. Donne pulled him close and punched the him in the face. The cashier's head snapped back and blood burst from his nose.

Donne pulled him in again and unleashed another blow to his jaw. The cashier slipped from Donne's grasp and smashed into the cigarettes and condoms behind him. They clattered to the floor along with him.

Just before he could hop on to the counter, someone grabbed

Donne by the shoulder and held him in place. He pulled against it, the fabric of his T-shirt rubbing and stretching against his neck.

"Where is she?" The words thundered from Donne's mouth.

The cashier looked up at him eyes wide. He had covered his nose with both hands. His mouth was moving but no sound came out.

"Why do you know her father?" Donne could feel his vocal chords straining. "Where is she? How is she alive?"

The cashier shook his head. Blood was dripped between his fingers. His mouth moved even faster.

Donne pulled free and leapt onto the counter. He was about to jump down into the pit with the cashier when his he was hugged around his waist. His body fell backward and he was lowered to the ground. He tried to get his feet under him, but couldn't and landed on his ass. Hard.

"*Jackson!*" Martin's voice came into the focus. "Jackson! Stop it. Calm the down."

"I will sue! I will sue all of you. The police. The state. Whoever the fuck! You punched me."

Donne shook his head as the cashier rambled. He tried to let the world come back to him. His breath was ragged and felt like it was getting caught in the back of his throat. Trying to scramble back to his feet wasn't an option. Pain shot down his legs from his tailbone.

"Kid. Jackson," Martin said again. "Breathe, kid."

Donne looked up at him and the room spun. He felt like he'd had too much to drink, and his stomach lurched left. Focusing on the plain front of the counter, he forced the contents of his stomach to stay on the inside.

"He knows where Jeanne is," Donne said.

"Okay."

The cashier was still screaming. He'd changed his tune from suing everybody to just getting in contact with his lawyer. He also wanted paper towels.

"Get up," Martin said.

Donne got to his knees and started to push up.

"Not you. *You*." Martin pointed at the cashier.

"Fuck you," the cashier shouted.

"Yeah, okay. Listen, get up. Let's talk."

The cashier stood. Donne could see him peeking over the edge of the counter. The blood was dripping faster now. Martin tossed him a roll of paper towels from one of the shelves.

"Fix your face."

The cashier unwrapped the towels and tore them from the roll. He wadded them up and pressed them against his nose.

"Going to be fucking rich."

Martin nodded. "You haven't had a customer in here in the last twenty minutes, at least. Why is that?"

The room stopped spinning for Donne. He started to get up again. Martin put a hand on his shoulder.

The cashier spat on to the floor. The wad of reddish phlegm splattered just inches from Donne.

"My friend here," Martin said. His voice was like a schoolteacher who wanted everyone's attention. Quiet and calm. "He thinks you know where a friend of ours is."

"I don't know anything."

Martin nodded. "I'm sure. But tell us. Whose computer is back there?"

"It's mine."

"Anyone else use it?"

"Just me." He spit again. It missed Donne but got closer. Donne felt his pulse race again.

"Yeah. I'm sure. Anyone *besides* you."

"It look like anyone else is here?"

Martin sighed. "Not today. But ever?"

"Go fuck yourself.

"Nice." Martin put his hand back on Donne and pushed him back to the floor. "Does the name Jeanne Baker ring a bell?"

"My nose is broken. I need a doctor."

"Yeah, and your lawyer. I know. Jeanne Baker?"

"I don't know who that is."

Martin let go of Donne and leaned against the counter. He looked left, then right. The cashier didn't seem to want to move out of his way, but did when Martin stuck his shoulder into the guy's sternum.

"You have a silent alarm, over there. But the switch is still in the off position."

"You're not robbing me."

"My friend beat the hell out of you."

"I—um ..."

"How about Leonard Baker?"

The cashier froze, just for a second. A slight hesitation before reaching for the silent alarm.

"Stop," Martin said. He pulled out his wallet. Pulled a couple of bills and dropped them on the counter. "Clean yourself up."

Donne looked at him. Martin put a hand under Donne's arm and pulled. He got up. Martin tilted his head toward the door.

"Have a good day, sir," Martin said.

They walked out into the daylight. As they walked to the car, Donne scanned for the two guys in suits. He didn't see anyone. A kid ollied on a skateboard a block away. That was the only action on the street.

"He hesitated," Donne said.

"I know." Martin pressed the button on his keys and unlocked the car doors. "You probably shouldn't have punched him."

"He knows something."

Martin nodded. Pulled open the driver's side door. He got into the car. Donne walked around and got in on the passenger side.

Bill Martin didn't start the car.

"Let's take our time here," he said. "See if anything interesting happens."

He leaned back into his seat.

"You got him good," Martin said. Then he laughed harder than Donne had heard him laugh in ten years.

CHAPTER
FIFTEEN

Martin drummed the steering wheel in time with the Hollies' "Carrie Anne." They'd already tracked through "Bus Stop" and "Long Cool Woman." Donne was ready to shoot himself. It was easier to focus on hating the music than the bruises that were starting to form on his knuckles.

When he opened and closed his hand, a dull pain radiated up into his wrist. Been a long time since he punched somebody, and his mind had been so clouded, he didn't even take the time to do it right. He'd be lucky if he didn't fracture anything.

The tapping slowed as Martin's mix CD—yes, a CD—transition into "The Air That I Breathe." Donne wondered what Martin would do if he just reached over and hit the AM button and flipped to sports talk.

"Chances are he didn't call the cops," Martin said. "They'd have been here by now."

Donne looked out the passenger window, but couldn't see the bodega. The kid with the skateboard had disappeared nearly ten minutes ago. The street was empty, save a couple of birds who landed, pecked away at something on the sidewalk, then took off into the air. He twisted his neck and looked down toward the bodega. Nothing going on there either.

"What are we waiting for?" Donne asked.

Martin blew out air out of his nose sharply. "What have you been doing the past two years?"

"Studying." He wished he hadn't said the word. The impending morning exam flashed in front of him, and he realized he was going to miss it. He pulled out his phone. No messages.

"We're waiting for something to happen. Come on, kid. You've done this before."

"Don't call me kid." Donne looked out the window.

"You would be dead," Martin said. "They would have killed you."

"You're psychic now?"

"I remember that look. You always thought the risky option was the best." Martin pulled out a pack of gum and offered it to Donne, who turned it down. Martin shrugged, then popped a piece in his mouth. He almost missed because of that tremor in his hand.

"We'd have more information."

"Remember Levison Street?"

Donne closed his eyes and tried to pull up the memory. It wouldn't come. He'd hoped it was just because too much time had passed, not because he'd been on that much coke and booze at the time.

"No," he admitted.

"Three guys upstairs. At least we thought they were in that old apartment, counting their money, making their meth. We were waiting for them to come out when the bathroom window blew out, big flames, black smoke. Loud as hell."

The memory didn't come. Donne's stomach twisted into a sailor's knot.

"We thought—they had to be dead. Wait for the fire department to come, put it out. We'd go up and drag out a couple of crispy corpses. But not you. No, you thought it was a distraction, remember?"

Jesus.

Martin blew a bubble, popped it. "You thought they were gonna wait a few minutes, and then sneak out the back, while we were distracted by the sirens and flames. Wait a second."

Martin turned his head and Donne followed, craning his neck. A dark Cadillac pulled up to the corner near the bodega. The black guy hopped out of the passenger seat and headed into the store. Donne should have gone with them. He opened and closed his right hand again and winced.

"This should be interesting," Martin said. He put one hand on the key in the ignition.

The motor fired up.

"You don't remember running into the fire by yourself?"

"Shut up, Bill. Let's see what happens."

"You caught them. By yourself. Spent the night in the hospital with smoke inhalation. Soot all over your face. But you got them."

The owner of the bodega came out, covering his face with a red cloth. The black guy followed, but stopped to close and lock the door. Martin started the car.

"How fucked up were you back then? No wonder Jeanne left."

Donne took a deep breath. "She came back," he said.

"Yeah," Martin said. "She did, right?"

The words seemed to be laced with something. Donne didn't feel like playing this game. The knot in his stomach tightened.

Martin waited until the Cadillac was halfway down the block before pulling out into the street. If these guys were military, they'd make the tail quickly. Maybe they didn't care.

But Donne couldn't let those last words from Martin go. "What are you talking about? What happened with Jeanne?"

"You've always been paranoid too."

"Stop screwing with me."

"I have to concentrate. Let's see where these guys are going."

They were winding down toward the docks. Donne could smell the bay through the cracked windows. Bill Martin hated air-conditioning. Donne felt lightheaded and energized at the same time, as if he'd drank two cups of coffee and taken a sedative simultaneously.

The Cadillac acted like they didn't know they were being

followed. Martin said a few car lengths back, but it never felt like they were going to lose them. If these guys wanted Donne to go with them, having him follow them was an easy way to accomplish it.

Three minutes later, Martin stopped the car. The Cadillac kept cruising up to on old shipping warehouse. Behind it was the water. One way in, one way out.

"Looks like we're both about to learn something new, kid."

Martin turned off the car and got out. Before Donne could do the same, Martin was ten feet away and heading toward the warehouse.

CHAPTER
SIXTEEN

Kate deleted the text message without hitting Send.

Outside the sun was starting to set, reflecting off the glass of the building across the street. The sun always made the apartment warmer in the late afternoon. She got up and turned on Donne's air-conditioner and then found an unopened bottle of pinot in the fridge. She took it out, removed the cork, and poured herself a glass.

After taking half the glass in one sip, she topped herself off again. The cool liquid spread thread her body, and she felt her muscles ease. Playing the scene in her head again, she tried to place the voice on the other end of the intercom. Nothing registered.

Another sip of wine. She tried not to think about going into the office tomorrow; fighting through a hangover to catch up on the case she was working on.

Her phone rang. It was a number she didn't recognize. She answered.

"Kate? Your father asked me to call." It was a voice from a million TV commercials over the past year. Senator Henry Stern.

"I'm in trouble, senator."

"Your father filled me in. Jeanne Baker's been dead for years, Kate." He took a breath. "This can't be real."

"So you haven't heard anything? You two were close when you were at Rutgers."

"She's dead."

"Jackson doesn't seem to think so."

"Why do you need me?"

The question rolled through her mind. "I didn't know where else to turn. Jackson's run off with someone."

"Jeanne?"

She exhaled. "No. A man. They were on to something. They must have been looking for her."

"Who, then?"

She finished the second glass of pinot. The alcohol was rushing through her veins now, a good buzz going on. Sitting back, Kate closed her eyes and ran through her memories as if they were a Rolodex, trying to figure out who was in the picture. It had to be someone Jackson knew, maybe someone he'd introduced to to at a party?

Jackson had said a name before he rushed out. Bill. Kate got up and went and poured the rest of the bottle of wine into her glass. Then she went into Jackson's office, cell phone at her ear. The room was a cluttered mess: old textbooks strewn across the floor, paperbacks dumped on the table, and four old shoe boxes pushed off in the corner.

"She said his name was Bill."

"Doesn't ring a bell."

It was the shoeboxes she was looking for. Jackson kept them out in the open, but never went through them. She asked him about them once, and he just shrugged. Old pictures, he said. Time to throw them out. When she asked if she could look through them, he just shrugged and asked if they could do it another night.

They were of his old life. Mementos of his dead fiancée that he never talked about. Times he tried not to remember.

Hell, he always said he *couldn't* remember a lot of them.

She didn't bother him about it again. But now she wanted to find a picture of him in his old uniform. See if there were pictures of this Bill person. Maybe if she could see what he looked like, it would jar an old memory loose.

"Is there anything else, Kate?"

"If you hear anything, please help."

"I'll look into it." He paused. Then, "Listen, Kate. Do you love him?"

"Of course."

"I've been divorced. Twice."

She knew. Everyone knew. Anyone who ran against him brought that up.

"And here's what I've learned." His voice was soft, like a kind uncle. "Find him. Don't let him go. Call him. Text him. Facebook him. Talk to him. Hold on to him as well as you can."

Her eyes burned. "Goodbye," she said.

She pulled the first box and started scanning through the pictures. It felt funny looking at developed film. She'd become so adjusted to seeing pictures on Facebook or a phone. The real thing felt odd; smooth, but sticky at the same time.

The first few pictures were of Jackson at a bar, eyes slightly closed, crooked smile, toasting the camera or pretending to throw a dart. They were silly, drunken nights of his early twenties.

Kate flipped through them quickly, not allowing herself the smile she would have if he'd been sitting next to her. Arm around her, pulling her close. She would smell his aftershave and tell him how cute he was in those pictures, and then give him a kiss on the cheek.

The next picture was what stopped her short. Jackson was still in the bar. It must have been the Old Towne Tavern—where else could it have been? Must have been early in the night too. His eyes were clear and the smile was wide. He had his arm around another woman. The woman from the website.

Kate's heart was slamming against her rib cage, and the buzz had gone from her system. She picked up the wineglass and took another slug. Then she flipped the picture over. It was dated nearly eight years ago. Beneath that it said "Jackson and Jeanne" with a smiley face drawn next to it.

She wondered if Jackson would do the same with a picture

of the two of them. Her phone suddenly vibrated, and she snatched it up. It was a message from her father.

Does Jackson have an iPhone?

CHAPTER
SEVENTEEN

Martin slammed his fist on the front door of the warehouse. It was metal and clanged against its hinges. The music of the banging made Donne's ears ring. He jammed his hands in his pockets and looked out toward the water. He tried to focus on the sloshing of it against the docks, rather than the churning in his stomach or Martin's slamming.

The image of the two military men busting out of the door, guns blazing, tearing the two of them to shreds wouldn't escape Donne's mind. As Martin knocked, Donne felt naked without his own gun.

Martin stopped banging and said, "Someone's coming."

Taking a step back, Martin rested his hands on his hips. Donne couldn't tell standing behind him, but he assumed Martin's hands were as close to his weapon as possible. The lock in the door turned and Donne tensed. He was ready to run, dive, jump, duck, or whatever the hell else he had to do to save his own skin.

The door swung open.

"Hello, gentlemen." It was the white guy this time. He'd taken his jacket off. Donne wondered if his shirt could take such strain against those biceps. "Can I help you?"

"Yeah," Martin said. "I never caught your name."

The white guy stuck out his hand. "I'm Calvin. My partner over there is Nick."

Martin nodded, but didn't return the invitation for a handshake. "Nice to meet you, Cal."

"Calvin," he said, then cleared his throat. "What do you need?"

"You said you wanted Donne to come with you. Then I showed up and you changed your mind. I was wondering why."

Calvin tilted his head. "You're not needed."

Martin looked around the docks. "Isn't most of this area owned by the mob? *La Cosa Nostra.* The mafia? Goombahs? What's left of them, anyway."

Calvin shrugged. "There is no mob around this area anymore. Not since President's Day."

"I must have missed that news."

"You must not read a newspaper."

Donne felt out of place, a spot on a pair of white pants. This wasn't what he needed anymore. Again he thought about Kate. He thought about the exam he should have been studying for. The future he was throwing away.

Calvin frowned, shook his head.

"Listen," Donne said, taking a step forward. He was reasonably sure if he was going to be shot, it would have happened already. "I'm here. What do you want from me?"

Calvin shook his head again and stepped back from the doorframe. He put his hand on the door and was about to slam it.

"Mind if we take a quick look around?" Martin said. "Five minutes."

Calvin said, "You beat up our friend."

"That was him." Martin pointed his thumb and fist at Donne. "He can stay outside if you want."

His hand still on the door, Calvin hesitated.

Martin folded his arms in front of him. "Listen, remember that ruckus I was going to make back on the street? A ton of cops, sirens going, showing up? That'll be nothing compared to what I bring here."

"I don't understand. Why do you want to look around?" Calvin folded his arms too. Still, his shirt didn't tear.

Martin shrugged. "Gut feeling?"

"You don't have a warrant."

"I'll find a reason. Come on, it'll make both yours and my day easier."

"Easier. We should sue for what you did to Juan."

Martin thumbed over his shoulder at Donne again. The tremor was gone.

Calvin took his hand off the door and Martin stepped in. Donne followed.

They were in a small office, like one in a gas station. There were a few shelves with paperwork on them. A metal desk. On one side of the desk sat Nick. The other side was Juan, who still applied pressure to his nose. Donne wanted to apologize, but didn't.

"What the hell?" Nick said.

Calvin held up a hand.

"Just taking a quick peek around. No worries." Martin looked at the door to his left. One that probably led into the big hangar. Donne wondered if this warehouse was built specifically for ship repair. Years ago, this area had to be bustling with shipping, but now the shipments went elsewhere. New York City or Baltimore, usually. Sometimes Newark.

Next to the door was a hole that was cut into the wall. Through the hole ran a wire, thick and black. It was taped to the floor and went across the room to a giant electrical outlet. The outlet was the cleanest thing in the place.

"Okay, thanks," Martin said.

Nick said, "What the fuck?"

"Thank you for coming," Calvin said, not missing a beat.

"Anytime." He pointed at Nick. "Watch your fucking language." Paused. "Get it? I said fuck and he said—ah, nevermind." Martin waved it off. "Let's go, Jackson."

ONCE THE door to the warehouse closed and locked, Donne said,

"That's it?"

"Not now," Martin said, striding ahead.

"You went in, took a glance around, and leave? That's a search."

"Shut up. We'll talk about it in the car."

Donne had to pick up the pace in order to keep up. Pretty soon, they'd be jogging. "And what's going on with your hands? I see that slight shake. Are you okay?"

Martin glanced at Donne. He said, "I'm fine."

They got to the car. Martin got in first. Donne rubbed his face and thought about how to the ask *What the hell was that about?* more politely. He pulled open the door, got in, and then slammed the door shut.

Before he could even open his mouth, Martin cut him off. "Did you see that wire?"

"What about it?"

"You never worked a commercial shoot when you were with us?"

Donne shook his head. "Get to the point."

"You should have. Good money, double time. Easy money too. Plus Craft Services."

"*Get* to it."

"That wire on the ground. I've seen those before. They're camera wires. Like I've seen on those commercial sets."

Donne processed what he was saying. "Like in the video."

"From your email. Yeah."

The car went cold and still. Donne felt a rat nibbling on his shoulders. He rolled them to ease the pain, but to no avail.

"Jesus," he said. "She's in there." Donne undid his seatbelt. "Let's go get her."

Martin shook his head as he started the car. "Tonight."

CHAPTER
EIGHTEEN

"I need a gun," Donne said.

Martin peered over his steaming cup of coffee and blew on it. "You didn't bring a gun?"

"I don't have one."

Donne stirred sugar into his cup. The Starbucks was nearly empty, a few people on line asking for Venti this or Grande that. Off in the corner, someone typed furiously on a laptop. Starbucks wasn't too popular in Perth Amboy, especially not at night, Donne guessed. He was surprised they even found one.

He opened and closed his right hand. It was swollen from his punches and ached at the knuckles with each movement.

"We should talk to Leonard Baker," he said.

"A private investigator who doesn't own a gun?" Martin's voice remained at a whisper, but it was now as tense as a Wallenda family tightrope. "I seem to remember you shooting up a National Park about two years ago."

Donne took a sip. The roof of his mouth burned. "Leonard's avatar was on Skype. We should talk to him. We'll be more prepared."

"You're not speaking English to me." Martin drank coffee. "What did you do with your guns?"

"Got rid of them."

Martin shook his head. "I knew I should have kept better

tabs on you. I hope some drug dealer didn't end up with them."

It was too easy to fall back into their old patter. Years of working together would do that, but this wasn't what Donne wanted. Too much history, too much tension. Martin had destroyed Donne when he told Donne about his relationship about Jeanne. The cloud hung over him for too long. The life he believed he was living wasn't reality, and now his past was twisting even more. The taste of coffee went bitter in his mouth.

"Did you go to the wake?" Donne asked.

"There wasn't a wake," Martin said.

Donne put his cup down so hard that some coffee splashed through the hole in the lid. He put his palms flat on the table as if to steady himself.

"I was there," Donne said. He remembered the coffin, he remembered how clean Jeanne looked, but how plastic as well.

Martin tilted his head. "Couldn't have been. There wasn't one."

The guy at the next table tapping on his computer pressed Play on a Springsteen song. One of the baristas looked at him and pointed toward her ears. He plugged in headphones. Now they were left with John Mayer on the store's speakers.

"That …" Donne trailed off. He remembered the Bakers sobering him up. Didn't they? The time period was so foggy in his mind. He couldn't have just imagined things. Not possible.

Martin drank. Then said, "Jeanne was cremated. What was left of her. The car burned badly, and she was inside. I was in touch with Leonard the whole time. They didn't want a wake. Didn't want an autopsy. Just wanted to start the moving on process." He had more coffee. Then shrugged. "It made sense at the time, I guess. I didn't ask too many questions."

"No one did," Donne said. The muscles in his lower back tightened. The chair was uncomfortable.

Martin shook his head. "Two cops. Neither of us thought to ask questions."

"I need a gun," Donne said.

"When was the last time you went to a range?"

Donne rubbed his face. "Sometime before I got rid of my

guns."

"I don't want to get shot." Martin tilted his head back to get the rest of his coffee. "If I knew I was working with an amateur ..."

"And I'm not walking in there unarmed." Donne's cup was still three-quarters full.

Martin looked out the window and tapped his fingers on the table.

"Are you ready for this?"

Donne leaned back trying to stretch out his muscles. "I'm not going to get you killed, Bill."

"Not what I meant." Martin scratched his chin. "I have an extra gun in my trunk. Fuck that. You need one. Are you ready for what we're going to find?"

After taking a deep breath, Donne said, "I can't believe she's alive. How can I be ready for what we're going to find?"

"What if she's alive?"

"How?"

The Springsteen guy slammed his laptop shut and left the coffee shop. It was just the two of them now. They'd had these conversations before, ten years ago. They'd talked about where they'd hide the "extra" drugs they'd found on a raid. Or how Donne was going to propose to Jeanne. And they'd spent one final time in a coffee shop, where the mood was just like tonight. Donne was about to throw the entire NARC division under the bus. And Martin tried to stop him.

Martin tightened his jaw and flared his nostrils. He looked toward the ceiling fan. Then back at Donne.

"I'm happy," Martin said. "This afternoon I was doing my job, and I was happy."

"What happens if we do find her?" Donne asked. "If you're so convinced she's alive, and we're going to save her. What happens then?"

Martin stood up. "Let's just go get her."

"I thought you said I was the one who wanted to run into the fire."

"Let me go get your gun."

Donne didn't get up. "Let's think about this."

Martin's hand tremor was back. "They know we're close. How much time do you think we have?"

"What if she's not there?"

Martin pushed his chair in so hard, it clattered against the table.

The barista looked up, waited to see if he was going to keep yelling, then went back to cleaning the coffeemaker.

"Let's go. Now."

Martin left the Starbucks. Donne sat for a second. He could just stay here. Call Kate, have her pick him up, and be done with it.

No.

He got up and followed Martin out the door, and into the fire.

CHAPTER
NINETEEN

Kate grabbed Donne's laptop and opened it. The home screen was password protected, but she knew the login: KateJan14. The day they made things "official."

That January evening, they sat on the edge of his bed, her bra strap hanging off her shoulder, hair out of sorts, and the last remaining buzz of beer running through her veins. Her heart pumped hard, and she could feel a few beads of sweat drying at the nape of her neck. Jackson sat next to her shirtless, his hand on her thigh. He was breathing heavily.

The scene reminded her of being a senior in high school. Creeping up to the edge of sex, but backing off at the last moment. Getting that rush, but feeling no release.

It was their fifth night in a row hanging out together. Always started out the same, a couple of beers while watching TV or a movie, then ending up in the bedroom, edging close to the line.

Kate exhaled and willed her heart rate to lower, and reminded herself she was an adult.

"This is fun," Jackson said.

She smiled and nodded. Her heart beat faster instead.

"I like you," he said.

She ran her hand through her hair, curling a strand over her ear. She bit her lip. *You are not in high school,* she commanded herself.

"I like you too."

Oh, God. Shut up, Kate.

Jackson laughed. "Your cheeks are turning red."

Her hand went from her ear to her left cheek, finger tips grazing her warm skin.

"Shut up."

"I want to keep doing this," he said. "I want to keep hanging out."

"Have I said I wanted to stop?"

Jackson shook his head. "What do you think about making things official?"

She said, "You mean like boyfriend and girlfriend?"

Jackson leaned in and kissed her on the lips. A short peck, not like the kisses earlier. He lingered just long enough.

"We could do a trial run, if you want." Jackson backed up. "See how it goes."

It was her turn to lean in. She kissed him long and hard. When she pulled away his cheeks were red.

"I don't need a trial run," she said.

Now, she played with her engagement ring while she searched his computer. The Find My iPhone app wasn't along the bar on the bottom of the screen. She stopped twirling the ring and reached for the touchpad. She scrolled through the finder and the app popped up. She clicked on it and it opened.

The laptop prompted Kate for a password. She tried "KateJan14" again. Rejected.

She typed it one more time, watching for typos, and was rejected again. The password the computer asked for was the same as his iTunes account, according to the window on the screen. He'd had iTunes long before he met her.

Kate blew a strand of hair out of her face, placed the laptop next to her on the couch and got up. Pacing would help clear her mind. Trying to guess what Jackson liked before they met was a needle in the haystack. She leaned back over the computer and typed in "Molson."

Rejected again.

Would an iTunes account lock you out?

The last vestiges of wine sloshed in her stomach. Maybe if she ate something, it would settle her stomach. She wasn't hungry, though. Not even a craving for chocolate. Rubbing her hands together, Kate circled the couch. A number of password combinations ran through her head, but none of them seemed right. They all keyed on names and events that had occurred after they met. Jackson wasn't the kind of guy who spent time switching his passwords around to fool hackers.

Pictures of Jeanne were still spread across the coffee table. Jackson with her in a park. At a Christmas party. In an office. They were all smiles. They were all touchy-feeling, arms around each other. Kate sat back down, picked up the stack and started to flip through them again. A chill ran through her.

Tossing the pictures back on the coffee table, she watched them scatter and flip on to their backs. On the back of one was scrawled "I love you—10/15."

And then it clicked.

Kate grabbed the laptop and typed in "JeanneOct15." The pinwheel whirled for a moment, and then a red pin appeared on the computer screen map. It said "Jackson's iPhone." The address was in Perth Amboy. An option popped up on the screen to send the phone a text.

Kate's heart started to pound again, just like that night when they started their trial run. She clicked the mouse and sent the text.

Then she grabbed her purse and ran out the door.

CHAPTER
TWENTY

Martin passed the gun over to Donne. Donne took it and hefted it once, twice. It was a police issue—a glock like he'd used in the past. It felt comfortable in his hand. More comfortable than he expected.

They sat about three-quarters of a mile away from the warehouse, waiting for the last legs of the sun to fade away. In front of them, it was mostly dark, only two streetlights illuminating the dark asphalt ahead of them.

Despite the car's air-conditioning, Donne was sweating. Life could change in an instant, and he wouldn't be surprised if tonight was one of those instances. No cars passed them either way. In fact, there hadn't been any movement around them for at least twenty minutes. And, then, it was only seagull landing, picking something off the ground, then flying away.

Martin shook his head. "Dammit. I thought at least one of them would have left for the night."

"That makes sense." Donne hefted the gun again. He tried to remember the last time he fired one. Was it just two years ago, along the Passaic River? Before his mother died? Didn't feel that long.

"Say what you want to say."

Donne sighed. "If Jeanne is in there, do you really think they'd leave her alone? I mean, it seems they want her alive.

They want me for God knows what. Someone has to feed her, give her water. Let her use the bathroom."

"I thought at least one of them would have taken Juan home."

"Might they did already. And came back."

"Or maybe they're still gone." Martin tapped his hands on the steering wheel.

"There's two of us, and two of them." Donne bit his cheek. "No problem."

Martin nodded. "Right. And when was the last time you shot a gun? You gave yours away."

"I'll be fine. Let's just be quick and get Jeanne out of there."

Martin turned the car off and opened the door. "Spread out. You see one of them, shoot 'em." He paused. "Don't shoot me. Let's go."

IN WHAT was probably not the smartest move of the millennium, Donne kept his eyes on the ground as they walked. He didn't want to trip over a twig or a cracked piece of pavement. He was moving slow, feeling the *thud thud thud* of his heart ahead of his foot's pace.

Martin was about ten yards ahead of him, in a jog. The warehouse sprawled beyond that, illuminated by a pale light in the office window. Martin's plan, as he laid it out to Donne, was simple. Get them outside. Take them out. Get Jeanne. Figure everything else out later.

When they reached the parking lot of the warehouse, Martin swung out to the left. The door to the office opened out that way and would give him a moment to aim before they appeared. Donne agreed to stay to the right, because it'd be a clearer shot. He wasn't sure this plan was going to work, and he'd voiced that to Martin.

Martin ignored him. "When the bullets start flying, instinct goes the hell out of the window. You know that."

Donne found a patch of tall grass to kneel in. He took a breath, trying to settle himself. He cell phone dinged that he had a text. Martin's head snapped up and looked in Donne's direction. He fumbled for his phone, but gave up. There was movement inside the office.

Martin picked up a rock the size of a softball and hurled it

It slammed off the metal door with a clang, and landed right in front of it. Donne counted the seconds in his head. He got to fourteen before the door moved. It opened quickly, at first, but stalled when it hit the rock. He could see Nick push on the door. To the right of the door, he could see a shadow pressed against the window. Calvin, cloaked in darkness because of the light behind him.

On one knee, Martin leveled his gun. Donne did the same and squeezed off a shot. The gun recoiled and Donne's wrists snapped upwards. The bullet whizzed over everyone's head.

Nick pushed the door fully open, turned and leveled his gun in Donne's general direction. Donne aimed as Nick cleared the frame of the door. He took another breath to steady.

There were two pops before Donne could fire and Nick dropped to the ground. Martin was the quick draw.

There was a muffled curse from inside the warehouse, and then the glass exploded outward as Calvin fired his own gun from the window. Donne hit the dirt flat. He heard bullets whizzing off to left, and then a few thuds as they buried themselves in the ground.

Donne could see Martin, down on one knee, edging himself toward the warehouse wall. Calvin didn't have a good vantage point from the window and wouldn't be able to hit anything without getting lucky.

Maybe if he laid some cover fire down, a few random shots toward the warehouse, it would flush Calvin outside. He aimed the gun and squeezed the trigger. Two more shot flew into the night.

There was another volley of bullets from the window. Martin was standing now, pressed flat against the warehouse wall. Calvin must have know where Martin was because of the way Nick had fallen.

The gunfire stopped, and for a moment, all Donne could hear was the water licking the docks. The odor of sulfur and gunpowder filled the air.

The door swung open even farther, and Calvin filled the frame. He toed Nick and said his name, but there wasn't a reaction. Donne could see Martin tensing. Calvin took another step, his gun in front of him. He snapped his body to the left, jumping out of the door frame, but it was too late. Martin snapped off two shots and Calvin's body whirled away from him. Calvin's gun went off once, and then he dropped to the ground.

Martin stepped up to the bodies and kicked one gun away.

Donne was up and running toward him. "They dead?"

Looking up at him, Martin said, "Get that door open in there. I'll be right behind you."

Donne was going to argue further, but he needed to know if Jeanne was inside. He went through the doorway, trying not to step in the dark red puddle that was forming. He looked at the door, and saw it was padlocked. He went to the desk, and realized that at some point they had to have taken Juan home. The office was empty.

He pulled doors open and found nothing. But he still had the glock. He approached the door, aimed and fired. The padlock shattered, and Donne fell to the ground when he heard the whine of the ricochet. After he got up, he jammed the gun into his belt.

A gunshot went off outside and Donne froze.

"Bill?" he asked.

"Get inside. I'm just making sure here."

Donne pulled the door open and stepped into darkness. Behind him there was another gunshot, but he didn't care. He reached out for the wall and felt for a switch.

"Jeanne?" he called out.

There was a soft, muffled moan. His heart jitterbugged.

His hand found a switch and he flicked it. He heard the loud clunk that he heard when he opened the website.

Jesus Christ.

The spotlight went on and illuminated Jeanne. She was duct taped to a chair by her wrists and her face was slumped over on to her shoulder. He hair was in front of her face. Donne's heart was pounding. His forehead was wet.

He ran.

Jeanne's head lifted and looked in her direction. Her eyes went wide, and she was trying to say something, but was gagged. Donne fell to his knees in front of her. He remembered the day he proposed to her, outside the Olde Town Tavern. He tried to go down to only one knee, but the beer decided otherwise. This time, it was nerves. Then she'd laughed. Now he could see tears in her eyes.

He pulled the gag off her mouth.

"Jackson," she said. "You found me."

"I—I—" He didn't have the words. Too much was trying to get out of his brain. Things he'd wanted to say for years. Questions. His eyes burned, and his temple throbbed.

"We have to get you out of here."

"I'm so tired," she said. "So thirsty."

He pulled at the duct tape, but it didn't give. She groaned as he did it, and he apologized. Over and over again. He was so sorry. The lead ball in his stomach was expanding, pressing against his ribs.

The keys in his pocket. They sharpest thing he had. Donne retrieved them and began to saw at the tape.

"What happened?" she asked. "I heard shots."

"I want to know what happened to you," he said. He kept sawing, and then her left arm was free. She put it on his shoulder. He tried to remember the last time she'd touched him, but couldn't.

The second piece of duct tape was easier. It was her right arm, and it seemed that she'd been working on it already. He pictured her, slowing tugging against it when she was alone. Trying to free herself.

"Don't worry," he said. "It's going to be okay."

"I'm so tired," she said.

The tape came loose and Jeanne fell forward. As he caught her, his keys clattered to the ground.

He felt air on his neck. Jeanne's breath. He started to shake.

He remembered mornings, rolling over into her. Smelling the shampoo in her hair, and the faint scent of Puddles, her dog. The dog she gave away when they got engaged. Now she smelled like dirt and glue.

"Oh my god." The voice wasn't Donne's and it wasn't Jeanne.

Her head lifted off Donne's shoulder. *No,* he thought. *Just give me one more minute.*

"Bill?" she said.

Donne tried to hold tight, but felt her pushing against him. Pushing him away. She stood up, but stumbled. Donne tried to catch her.

"Bill? You're here?"

"I'm here," he said.

The lead ball in Donne's stomach exploded and pain radiated through his entire body. He got to his feet in time to see her fall into Bill's arms.

She said his name. Again.

Bill held her tight with his left hand. His gun was still in his right. Donne dropped his head and started to walk toward them. The corners of his eyes stung and his cheeks felt wet.

He thought of Kate. He should call Kate.

"Thank you, Jackson," Martin said. "But I don't need your help anymore."

Bill Martin lifted his free arm, and time stopped for Jackson Donne. He didn't have time to say anything.

Martin pulled the trigger three times.

PART II
RESTORE THE SHORE

CHAPTER
TWENTY-ONE

Donne's eyes snapped open and he gasped for breath. He was on his back, but he wasn't sure for how long. His nerves, muscles, and brain were screaming for him to get up and run. A warm, thick liquid was making his clothes sticky. His body felt heavy and he was having trouble getting to his feet. Every time he tried to push himself up, he fell back down.

Intellectually, he knew he'd been shot. He was getting cold. He knew he was covered in blood. And it was hard to breathe.

The funny thing was it didn't hurt.

Donne rolled over on to his stomach and started to crawl. The warm liquid now spread to his pants and palms of his hands. He looked at them and saw they were covered in red.

This is how I'm going to die, he thought. *Covered in blood in a warehouse in Perth Amboy.*

He pushed himself forward and tried to figure out if Bill Martin and Jeanne were still there. His only urge was to crawl, find a way to escape, but part of him expected to be shot again. One last bullet to the brain to make everything go dark.

Air was getting caught in the back of his throat, and he spit to try and clear his mouth. He wondered where he'd been shot and why it didn't hurt. When he was a cop, Martin and he interviewed a gangbanger who'd been dealing dope to college kids. The guy told them he'd been shot three or four times, but it didn't hurt. The heat from the bullet numbs the wound.

"People don't scream because of the pain," the guy said. "They scream because they're scared to die."

And Donne realized he wasn't screaming. Maybe he should. Yell for help. Yell for his mother. Yell for someone.

He pulled himself forward some more, away from the chair Jeanne had been bound to, and toward the office. He couldn't see Martin and Jeanne. They must have left.

Did he black out? Had he been dead for a few minutes? Why did they leave without finishing the job?

Donne got some air down into his lungs. It helped. He pushed forward, imagining a trail of blood behind him, like that Sean Connery scene in *The Untouchables*. He was a slug. A shot and dying slug, leaving a trail.

He tried to talk, but nothing had come out. He wondered if he'd been shot in the throat, and that's why he couldn't speak.

Listen, he told himself. *Try to hear something that can help you. A truck, a ship in the distance. Maybe a ringing phone.*

His phone. He could dial 911. Even if they couldn't hear him, they could track the call, couldn't that?

Or was that only landlines?

He could hear the lapping water again. The wind blew through the open hangar of the warehouse, and metal creaked. No one drove by, that he could tell. It seemed like his hearing was malfunctioning, though. The wind would fade in and out, and the lapping water seemed to transition to static.

Inching backward along the floor, Donne moved his arms from in front of him down to his right pocket. He slipped his hand inside and found his iPhone. He wrapped his fingers around hit and started to pull. That's when the pain came. It was hot and burned and shot throughout his body, radiating out ward like sonar.

He opened his mouth to scream, but only a gasp of air came out.

He inhaled again and pulled on his phone. It slipped from his pocket, but once his hand was free, his fingers went slack.

The phone clattered out of his hands. Donne tried to twist his head to look for it, but he couldn't. His motor functions were impaired. His limbs weren't working, and even if he found his phone, he wasn't sure he'd be able to dial.

Better to focus on crawling.

Donne pulled himself forward again, his nails digging into the grooved floor. He pulled himself ahead, each inch feeling like a country mile. The door swung open and closed in the wind before him. At this point, there was no plan. All he wanted was to get out into the open. Try to get to where someone could see him.

Where someone could find him.

Stay alive long enough to be found and get to a hospital. He opened his mouth again and tried to force the words out.

"Help," hissed from his lips. "Me."

It worked. But now he was out of breath. The strength had gone out of him. He couldn't pull himself any longer. His arms went slack and his head slammed into the floor. He was able to turn it sideways, as if he was sleeping on his stomach.

The static faded and he could hear the water again. Somewhere a bird crowed. He worked his mouth again, fought air into his lungs.

The image of Jeanne formed before his eyes. But it twisted and morphed into Kate. She reached for him. Donne tried to lift his arm to reach for her. Like a professional wrestler mugging for the crowd, he got his arm up, but it slammed back into the ground.

"Help me," he said. A full sentence this time.

"Oh my God, Jackson! Oh my God!"

Brakes screeched. Car doors opened and closed.

Donne shut his eyes and waited to die. Kate faded away from him. Pain bubbled in his chest and his side. He wanted to scream, but couldn't muster the strength.

Footsteps clattered against the metal floor. More than one person.

"Mr. Donne?" he heard. The voice was familiar. "Don't worry. He'll be fine. It's good you called."

He tried to open his eyes, but it felt like anvils had been tied to the lids. He couldn't call for anyone.

"No, no, no. You can't die." *Was Kate really here?*

"Your friend made quite a mess outside." The man was crouching over him.

Donne turned his head and forced his eyes open. He looked up, but could only see a body covered in shadow.

The shadow reached out his hand.

"You can't die yet, Jackson." Kate's voice was shrill and whimpering.

The world went black.

CHAPTER
TWENTY-TWO

Bill Martin wanted to ask a million questions, but he felt like Jeanne should start. Jeanne, however, didn't say a word. She reclined the passenger seat and had her forearm resting over her eyes.

The Parkway going south was empty, which was a good thing, because Martin was having a hell of a time concentrating. His hands wanted to shake, they begged him to shake, but he gripped the steering wheel hard to stop them. His knuckles turned white instead.

Twice he opened his mouth, then shut it again. Instead of talking, he stared ahead at the glowing lights of a sedan or two in the distance.

"Where are we?" Jeanne snapped her head up off the rest.

Before Martin could answer, Jeanne said, "No. No, no, no. We can't go here, Bill."

"We have to figure things out," he said. "All of us."

Martin turned down the Bakers' street. The garbage had been removed from the curbs. Not too many cars were parked on the street.It felt like a ghost town.

And here he was with a living ghost.

"You will get them killed, Bill. They will die."

"What are you talking about? What is going on?"

"Turn the car around."

He rolled forward, scanning the house fronts, looking for her parents' place. It seemed further up the road this time, as opposed to this afternoon.

"Turn the car around, Bill."

"No one followed us here. I made sure of it."

"Who do you think you're dealing with?"

Martin pulled the car over. They weren't in front of her parents' place. Not yet. But he couldn't have this conversation and drive at the same time.

"I don't know who we're dealing with, Jeanne. As far as I knew this morning you were still dead. And—" He wanted to bring up William's name. It'd been rattling around in his brain all day. But he wasn't ready to confront that part just yet.

"I'm sorry. You shouldn't even been here."

"Why did they track down Jackson, then?"

The look on her face said it all. At that moment, it dawned on him. She hadn't even flinched when he shot Jackson Donne. She didn't cry. She didn't scream. He couldn't keep his from hands shaking if he tried.

"I don't know."

"Who is after you?"

She reached out and touched Martin's face. It wasn't a caress and it wasn't loving, but his cheek still burned warm at her touch.

"Go home. Let me run again."

Martin shook his head. "Can't."

"It's been six years, Bill."

Martin reached over and turned down the radio. The air-conditioner was pumping, but everything else felt very still. His shoulders were loose, but his stomach was tight. He'd hoped that finding Jeanne would cause his hands to go still, but the shaking was worse than ever. Part of him thought maybe he needed a doctor to check them out.

"I have so many questions."

Jeanne shrugged. "Does it matter?"

"Where have you been?"

"I can't."

Now the tightness in his stomach travelled up to his shoulders. He slammed his hands down on the steering wheel and the horn beeped. Jeanne flinched.

"I saved *you*!" Inside his shoes, his toes curled.

"I saved myself. Six years ago."

"And tonight?"

She shrugged again. Martin wanted to slam the steering wheel again but restrained himself.

"I would have figured it out." She crossed her legs. "I'm trying to save you. I'm still trying to save my parents, and I'm trying to save William."

"You let me believe he was dead too." Martin spit it out.

Jeanne turned pale.

"Years ago, years ago you told me he was mine. And then you died."

Jeanne didn't say a word.

"You needed me to hurt. Because if I was hurt, I wouldn't dig."

"I'm going to leave now," she said.

"No."

She reached for the door handle, but Martin was quicker. He hit the autolock and put the car back into drive. Accelerated before she could get out.

"We're going to talk to your parents. We're going to see William."

"This is a mistake, Bill."

Martin shrugged. He thought about the day she walked out of his life. How he wanted to chase her.

"I've made them before," he said.

"Please. Let's find a motel at least," Jeanne said.

Martin could see her parents' home now. There was a light on in the front room, and the porch light was on as well. Someone was still awake. He accelerated a little bit, and then pulled to the right to make a U-turn. He would park in front of their house.

"Please. I can't see them tonight. Not like this."

Martin stopped the car before making the U-turn. He looked at her. The bruises on her arms were turning yellow. There was a lump on her chin, swollen and red. Her eyes had dark shades under them.

"Jesus," he said. As if seeing her for the first time, he blinked. "What did they do to you?"

"Stop asking me questions."

The car idled.

"Listen," she said. "They know we're gone, and they going to come here to find us. Where else would we go?"

"If they're going to hurt your parents, that's more reason to be here." Martin rubbed his chin with his right hand. His left stayed on the steering wheel. He couldn't trust it to be steady.

Jeanne shook her head. It was slow and hesitant. Either she wasn't sure, or the movement was causing her pain.

"You don't understand them," she said.

"Make me understand!"

As if a volcano was erupting, the words shot from Jeanne's mouth. "This is on me, Bill! Me! No one else! Take me to a hotel and go home. Get out of my life. You're going to get hurt."

Martin rolled his neck, cracking it. He blew air from his nose. "You hurt me a long time ago," he said.

"For your own good."

"How was I supposed to know that?"

The porch light of the house they were parked in front of went on. Someone had noticed them. In a neighborhood like this—still rattled after Sandy and worried about looters—that likely meant the police were on their way. Martin thought about staying and waiting for the police. He'd badge them, talk to them, make them go away. At that point, though, they'd have attracted a ton of attention, and Jeanne would have no choice but to go see her parents.

He looked at her again, letting her face come into focus. There were dark circles and the hint of tears at the corner of her eyes. Crows feet had formed at the corners of her eyes. Her laugh lines were deeper.

"When was the last time you saw William?" he asked.

She flinched at the name. "When he was three months old."

Martin pulled a U-turn, but instead of parking and going inside, he kept driving. There were several motels on Route 9. They weren't clean and they weren't high-class, but they were plain. Whoever was looking for her would have a hard time finding them there. He would even pay in cash.

"You can wait one more night." He accelerated down the road. "Let's find a place to get some sleep."

CHAPTER
TWENTY-THREE

Martin opened his eyes and stretched. There was a sharp pain at the corner where his neck and left shoulder met and his legs were cramped. Sleeping on a loveseat in a hotel room will do that to you.

Especially at his age.

He sat up and reached over to the end table for his gun. He hefted it and undid the clip. Everything was still in place. If he got a chance later in the day, he'd need to clean it. Too much was at stake now to have to deal with a rare malfunction because of an owner error.

Jeanne made a snuffling sound and rolled over on the bed. Martin waited a moment, but she didn't wake. He listened to her breathing go from momentarily ragged to easy and smooth second later. It had taken her nearly two hours to fall asleep after they checked in. She tossed and turned and cried. Martin made an attempted to go comfort her once, but she moved away from him.

Now he was content to let her sleep. They'd found a semiclean motel on Route 9 that advertised DRIVING DISTANCE TO THE SHORE and HBO ON THE TV. He also expected clean towels, but that might have been pushing it. The guy behind the desk asked for ID and Martin gave it, but he paid in cash. If whoever was looking for them was monitoring credit lines, Martin wouldn't be tracked down. At least not today. He had enough money to get them through.

By the time he had to use an ATM, he was hopeful they'd be well out of state. Of course if Jeanne's warnings came true, being out of state and staying away from credit cards wouldn't matter. They would be found.

Martin put the gun back in his holster and stood up. Still Jeanne didn't move. He wondered how much sleep she'd gotten when she was captive. An hour here or there? The body can't keep up with that.

Peeking out the front window, he saw only his car in the lot. It wasn't a weekend, so the shore crowd with smaller wallets hadn't arrived yet. The college kids with their coolers of beer, bathing suits, and just enough cash to get by would be showing up tomorrow. For now, Martin and Jeanne had the place to themselves.

Coffee, though. That was a problem. Last night, he noticed a complimentary pot in the lobby. With the parking lot empty, it wouldn't be too hard to keep an eye on things if he walked down to get a few cups.

He grabbed the key off the table and left, making sure the door quietly clicked closed behind him.

A bell jingled when Martin walked into the lobby. The same desk clerk came out of the back room and gave Martin a smile.

"You stayed the whole night."

Martin went to the coffeepot and took two Styrofoam cups from the stack. He poured cream in both, but not before checking the date on the package. Then he poured coffee. He couldn't remember how Jeanne took hers, so he put a couple of sugar packets into his pocket.

"Usually guys like you, they show up, stay a few hours, towel off, and leave."

Martin shook his head. "Just looking for a place to stay."

"That's what they all say. She was cute." The desk clerk grinned. His teeth were butter-yellow.

Martin tried to picture whatever the clerk saw. Jeanne had stayed in the car until Martin had checked in, and then she took a quick walk to the room. Guy couldn't have seen too much. Just her body. Not the bruises all over her skin.

"Where did you find her? Not around here. Too many cheap dates around here."

"Knock it off. She's a friend."

The guy nodded. "Okay."

Martin put down his coffee. He remembered Donne jumping across the counter to grab the cashier earlier. He couldn't let that happen to him. Stay cool.

The desk clerk shrugged. "Future reference. That's all."

He inhaled. Exhaled.

"Shut up," he said.

"Okay. Okay." The clerk put up both his hands, palms out.

"Thank you." Martin picked up his coffee again and left.

He walked down the corridor to their room, scanning the parking lot again. Nothing out of the ordinary. It seemed like the venture would be safe. He put down one cup to retrieve his key and unlocked the door.

When he stepped in, he found Jeanne sitting up in bed. He put the cups down and pulled the sugar from his pocket.

"You're up," he said.

She looked at him, her eyes wide. There were tears streaked down her face. Her hands were shaking much worse than his.

"Where were you?"

"I went to get coffee."

"You left me."

"I could see the room the whole time." That was a lie, but he could see the parking lot.

"You *left* me here. I was alone. What if someone came for me?"

"That wasn't going to happen."

She didn't respond. Instead, she just buried her face into the pillow and wept.

CHAPTER
TWENTY-FOUR

Martin tried to wait her out. Let her fight through the shakes and the tears and find the light. He sat on the couch and sipped coffee. She was buried in the sheets somewhere. They shook as she wept. He listened to her, thinking back to the day he got the call about her death.

He didn't cry, at least not at first. He was in his office, and the chief had called him. There was a car accident. A blaze the fire fighters had trouble putting out. Another car with empty and half full bottles of whiskey on its floor. The license plate for the burning car led them to Jeanne's name. The chief was so, so sorry. Martin stared at the phone in his hands while his extremities went cold. After some time—he didn't know how much—he hung it up and went and closed the door. She'd already left him, promised herself to Jackson Donne. He was out of her life.

And he couldn't be involved in her death.

Now he just watched her. It seemed callous, and he hated himself for that, but somehow he knew if he approached her she'd just shove him away. Matters would be worse. Occasionally, he'd say her name and ask if she needed anything. Jeanne didn't reply.

The parking lot was still empty. He'd check through the blinds occasionally, sweeping the courtyard as well for anything suspicious. Other than the traffic picking up on Route 9, everything was quiet. Checkout was scheduled for 10 AM, but he'd pay for another day if he had to. Though the thought of running into the desk clerk again made his biceps twitch.

Twenty-five minutes later, the crying started to slow down. Martin finished his last gulp of coffee. It was cold, and the cream he'd added did little to quell the bitter finish. Jeanne's cup sat on the end table where his glock had sat, untouched.

Pushing the sheets away, Jeanne looked over at him. He waited. Her cheeks were streaked with tears. Her eyes were red. Bags had also formed underneath them. Her nose looked red too, as if she'd been rubbing it.

"I can't trust you," she said.

Martin wasn't ready for that one. He sank back into the couch and waited. For the first time, he noticed the cushions smelled like mothballs. The oil and gunpowder smell was finally leaving his nostrils.

"You left me here, a sitting duck," she said.

"Honey—" He immediately regretted it.

"Don't call me that," she snapped.

"I could see the parking lot the whole time."

Jeanne shook her head. "You shot Jackson. Didn't even flinch. Just aimed and shot him."

"He would slow us down." Martin tried to come up with a believable motive on the spot. "If *they* find him, maybe it'll trip them up for a few days, and we can get away."

Her head continued to shake. "Bullshit." She slammed her hand into a pillow. "Bullshit. Bullshit. Bullshit."

"Jeanne."

"Stop it! Are you with *them?*" Her eyes were wide, and he could see where the redness ended and the white started again. "Answer me!"

"I don't even know who 'them' is."

An image straight out *The DaVinci Code* flashed in his mind. A cult of people dressed in white robes staring at a book on the table. In the book were names of people who done wrong. And where they were hiding.

"You're going to kill me."

"Stop," he said, holding himself back from calling her crazy. "Jeanne, we need to get out of here."

"Where are you going to take me? Back to 'them'? To dump me in the Atlantic Ocean? I shouldn't go with you. You *abandoned* me."

"Jeanne, you're in shock. It's been a tough couple of days for you." Understatement of the year. "We need to get you some help and get you the hell out trouble."

She punched the pillow again. He wondered how cheap the pillows were that a punch sounded like a fist hitting a brick.

Martin tried to pull something up from his memory. A moment they could lean on together to get her through this. But nothing came. He could remember dinners out and nights in bed. He remembered a few spats, but nothing major. He was always worried that, if they fought badly enough, she'd go back to Donne.

In fact, when she did leave, he wondered if he had pushed her away. Once the accident happened, those thoughts went out the window.

"We're going to go see William," he said. "And your parents. They need to know you're okay."

Jeanne didn't respond. She picked up the pillow she'd been punching and held it closer to her body.

"Once we do that," he continued, "we're going to take a ride and get you someplace safe. Where were you before all this?"

She clutched the pillow tighter and said, "Arizona."

He almost asked her if she was in Witness Protection. Decided against it.

"We can drive there. It's summer. It'll be beautiful, scenic, and safe."

Jeanne shook her head again.

"Why not?"

Her mouth moved, but words didn't come out. Martin sat forward and the couch groaned underneath him.

She squeezed her lips together and tilted her head left. Tears filled her eyes.

"You can tell me, Jeanne. I'm here to help you."

"I can't go back into hiding. As much as I want to. That's why I came back."

"Why did you leave?"

"I left because they were going to kill me. I knew too much." The words ran together like one long compound word. After she was done speaking, her breath came in large gasps. He worried she was hyperventilating.

"Who? Who's they?"

"Back then, it wasn't a they. It was a him. But he's powerful. I have to stop him."

Martin looked out the window again. The parking lot was still clear. Jeanne's words were making him too paranoid. But he needed to bring her to see William again, and to get some more answers. She was on the verge of talking, he could see it in her face.

"Who is that powerful? Who do you have to stop?"

"The senator," she said.

That narrowed it down.

"Which one?"

"The state senator," she said. Her words were slower now. She swallowed. "Senator Stern."

Henry Stern. Martin didn't vote for him.

"He wants me dead. He has for six years," she said.

"Why?"

Jeanne shook her head, and then pressed it into the palms of her hands. Her shoulders shook, and she fell in to another round of weeping. This time Martin went to her and sat on the bed. He put his arm around her shoulders and pulled her in.

Jeanne let him.

CHAPTER
TWENTY-FIVE

10 Hours Earlier

Kate held Jackson's hand.

It was limp and cold, and his fingers barely wrapped around hers. With her free hand, she rubbed his arm. His eyes were closed. An air mask covered the rest of his face. A soft beeping monitored his heart rate. Kate had no idea how strong the rate was.

"You're going to be okay, baby. Help is here."

They were in the back of a van, he on a stretcher and she strapped into a bench next to it. Across from her, a man in a white lab coat worked. She didn't know what he was doing. Some sort of medical procedure, it seemed. There was blood on his coat. He didn't acknowledge her.

Senator Henry Stern sat next to him, leaned back, right leg crossed over his left. He watched as if he were admiring a painting.

"When are we going to get to the hospital?" Kate asked.

The senator didn't answer. His right hand rested on his thigh and his index finger tapped against his pant leg.

The doctor moved his hands, and the speed of Donne's heart increased. Kate looked at him, but his face hadn't changed.

"Let go of him," the doctor said.

When Kate was in sixth grade, her grandparents were watching her one evening. Her parents were out to dinner for their anniversary, and Grandma and Grandpa had taken her to Chili's for a burger. They talked about school and laughed about her role as the parrot in *Aladdin, Jr.* She promised she would show them a good end-of-year report card when school ended in three weeks.

The drove her home in their old Chevy, a big car with leather seats and brakes that squealed. The entire ride home, her grandfather coughed. A wet cough, like phlegm had been caught in his chest. Each time Grandma asked if he was okay, he brushed her off. They pulled in the driveway, and Kate jumped out of the car and ran to the front door. As she was reaching for her house keys—her first set, her parents finally trusted her— she heard Grandma scream.

Kate whirled to see her grandfather on the ground clutching his chest. She called for him and ran. Her grandmother screamed for someone to call 911. Kate hit the asphalt on her knees, scraping them. She kept repeating "Grandpa" over and over. She held his hand. She didn't let go until the EMTs pried him from her.

It was the last time she saw him alive.

Today, she would not let go. She promised herself she wouldn't. Ignoring the doctor, she clutched Jackson's hand tighter.

The doctor asked again. Kate simply said "No."

Stern leaned forward, his chin almost touching the stretcher. The heart monitor beeped faster. Jackson's eyes shot open. His pupils were glassy. His body started to shake.

"Oh my god!" Kate screamed. "Jackson. Stay with me! Jackson!"

Stern's voice cut the noise like a needle through skin. "Do you want him to live?"

Kate looked up. "Of course. Of course I do."

"Then you'll listen to the doctor." Stern sat back.

"Where are we going? We should be at the hospital already." She kept rubbing Jackson's trembling arm.

"We're taking him somewhere safe. I promise." Stern rubbed his chin. "I'm not going to let anything happen to him.

Now listen to the doctor."

Kate stared at Stern, waiting for him to say more. He didn't. She let go of Jackson's hand. It dropped to his side, bouncing slightly off the padding of the stretcher. The doctor leaned across Donne's body and pulled a curtain across the back of the van, cutting her off from her fiancée.

This wasn't going to be like the day with her grandfather. She would see Jackson again. This couldn't be the end.

Kate buried her face in her hands and cried.

CHAPTER
TWENTY-SIX

"I was wrong," she said.

Martin was still dealing with Senator Stern, trying to fit Jeanne's words into his head. New Jersey politics were corrupt; they had been for as long as the sky was blue. But this didn't feel like that. The bruises on her body, the Internet threats. Martin was so focused on that he didn't hear what she said.

Jeanne jumped out the bed, and then leaned against it, steadying herself.

Martin was still in his seat, fingers dug into the arms of the loveseat. He was staring at his glock, trying to keep the room from spinning. When he looked up, Jeanne was at the door to their room. How long had he been staring down for? The shakes in his hands were starting up again.

"We have to go, Bill." She pulled open the door. "I want to see William."

He wished she'd stop saying his name, like he was a child.

"What changed?" He looked up. She was wiping tears from her eyes. She was taking deep breaths. She wasn't shaking.

"What changed? I started thinking, Bill. I started thinking like them. You're right. You were right. They wouldn't find us here. We could stay here until you ran out of money, and they wouldn't find us. They're not that powerful. How else could they try to track me down?"

Martin blinked. He could still see Senator Stern in his brain. His mind didn't move as fast anymore. Not after a long night and uncomfortable sleep.

"Even if they didn't want to kill my parents, they could use them. What's the only other connection I have?"

"Your parents," he said.

"They don't know about William. For six years, they thought I was dead. But now — oh my god, Bill!"

Martin pushed himself off the couch, holstered the glock, and went to the door. Jeanne was already in the parking lot, running to the car. Martin hit the alarm button on his key chain and unlocked it for her. He should be running too, but he couldn't. His legs were cramping.

This morning he should have realized it. When he went to the bathroom, his urine was dark yellow. And then he drank coffee. Caffeine? He was dehydrated.

No time.

He got in the car and backed out. Pulled into slow traffic on Route 9. If only he had a cherry top police car.

JEANNE WAS out of the car before he could even put it in park. She dashed across the pebble lawn to the front door. Martin got out of the car, hand on the butt of his gun. He scanned the street and didn't see anything different from the day before. A few cars parked outside of houses. A few new piles of garbage curbside.

By the time he got to the lawn, Jeanne was pounding on the door.

"Mom! Dad!" she yelled.

"Jeanne," Martin said. "Shut up. If someone is in there with them, you're going to get yourself killed," he said.

Her fist swung toward the door again, but Martin caught it. His left calf cramped and he grunted.

Jeanne turned toward him, her lips scrunched together. Tension at her jawline.

The door opened, and Leonard Baker stood there. Jeanne

fell forward into his arms. Her shoulders shook. Leonard's eyes caught Martin's. They were watery.

"Jeanne."

"Is your wife okay? William?" Martin's hand dropped to his side.

Leonard nodded and pulled Jeanne in tighter.

"Let's go inside," Martin said.

They complied.

In the living room, Sarah stood, her arm around William. William had an Iron Man action figure in his hand and pretended to fly it. Martin put his hands in his pockets. Jeanne ran to Sarah and William. She put her arms around Sarah and said, "Mom." William stepped out of the way.

For a minute, all Martin could think about was the scene in front of him. Not thugs coming to kill them. Not Jackson Donne. Not the cramps in both his legs. Or the shaking of his hands. Or the weight of the gun at his hip.

This was the strangest family reunion he'd ever seen.

CHAPTER
TWENTY-SEVEN

S arah Baker wanted to make lunch. Ten forty-five in the morning, and she was asking everyone what kind of sandwiches they wanted. She might have to order in, there wasn't much in the fridge. What did Leonard think?

Leonard told her to relax, they had time.

Enjoy this moment. Enjoy every moment.

Jeanne was on the couch, sitting next to William. He finally put his Iron Man toy down and realized the mood in the room was different. Martin leaned against the far wall and watched, his arms folded in front of him.

"Who are you?" William asked. The words came out soft and slowly.

Jeanne looked up at her father. He nodded.

Jeanne put her hand on his shoulder and just as softly said, "I'm your mom."

Sarah put her hand over her mouth and looked at Leonard, who stared at the couch. Martin shifted in his seat.

William looked toward his grandparents, then back at Jeanne. "Where have you been?" Still soft and slow.

"I had to run away after I had you. I was in trouble and I had to go away."

"Why didn't you take me?"

Sarah went into the kitchen and Leonard followed. Martin

didn't move. His feet felt frozen to the carpet.

Jeanne wiped at her cheek with the back of her hand. "Because you were a baby. I didn't want you to get in trouble too."

William sat back and frowned. "Are you in trouble now?"

Jeanne looked up at Martin. Before he could react, she looked back at William. The kid didn't miss the glance, though. He stared at Martin.

"I hope not," Jeanne said.

William opened his mouth, then stopped. He looked at Iron Man. "I can protect you," he said.

Jeanne couldn't hold it together anymore. She made a small noise, then wrapped him up in his arms. William didn't have any choice but to return the hug. Martin stood up and went through the kitchen. Sarah was looking through takeout menus. Leonard was pretending to read the paper.

Martin went to the backyard, looking across the lagoon. He pulled out his cell phone and called work.

"You're not in your office?" Captain Russell Stringer asked.

"I'm taking a personal day." Or two.

"Fishing?"

Martin looked down the lagoon. A few houses away, someone was unlatching their boat.

"Kind of. Let me ask you something."

"What's up?"

"You guys hear anything from Senator Stern's camp today?"

"No. Pretty sure he's busy working on the merger." Stringer paused. "Wait. What the hell did you do?"

"See you tomorrow." Martin hung up the phone and turned back toward the house. Though the kitchen window, he saw Sarah on the phone while Leonard, Jeanne, and William laughed.

Leonard noticed him and excused himself. He joined Martin in the yard.

"Thank you for bringing her here," Leonard said.

Martin said, "I'm not so sure she wanted to come."

"How is she doing?" Leonard asked.

Martin crossed his arms and looked up at the sky. "How does she seem in there?"

Leonard shrugged. "Happiest I've seen her in six years."

"How many times have you seen her in the last six years?"

Leonard shook his head.

"I don't think we can stay long," Martin said.

"I know."

The man who was working on his boat started its engine. There was a puff of dark smoke, and it sounded a lot like a lawn mower. The boat sailed toward them, and the driver gave Leonard a wave as he passed. Leonard and Martin both returned it.

"You won't lose her again, sir." Sir. Like he was a teenager. He was maybe five years younger than Leonard.

Leonard kicked at a pebble. "I hope not. Let's go back inside."

Martin followed him back into the kitchen. William and Jeanne were talking about school and the books William had to read for summer vacation. Jeanne seemed to have kept up on elementary school fiction, because she was able to give William just enough details on the stories to get him excited.

Sarah was on the phone ordering from a pizza parlor.

"Mom," William said. The kid adjusted quickly. "What happened to my dad?"

Jeanne looked up at Martin again. His knees buckled a little.

"I don't know, William. Maybe we'll find out some day."

"That would be cool," the boy said. No follow-up questions. The mob would love this kid.

Martin excused himself again. He nodded toward Leonard and went out into the living room. Leonard followed after giving William a noogie.

There was a picture window in the living room that looked out on to their street. Martin gave it a once over and still saw very little out of place. If they stayed here, they'd be endangering the kid.

His kid. It still sounded weird.

Of course, at this point, if they ran, he didn't know how far they'd get or—despite his Arizona fantasies—where they would actually go. Leonard tapped Martin on the shoulder.

"I want to know," Martin said, "how you did it."

"I don't know what you're talking about."

Leonard picked up a framed picture of his family. The three of them were on the beach, in front of the lifeguard stand. Leonard had his arm around Sarah, while Jeanne licked an ice cream cone. The picture was from the eighties and was faded, so the ocean wasn't deep blue. Leonard placed the frame next to another almost identical picture. This time it wasn't Jeanne, but William in the forefront of the picture. And instead of an ice cream cone, it was a plastic bottle of water.

"Don't screw with me, Leonard." Dispensed with the sir, this time. "I want to know how you faked Jeanne's death."

CHAPTER
TWENTY-EIGHT

8 Hours Earlier

The curtain was still drawn, and the doctor was still working. But Jackson's heart rate had slowed to a more manageable beat.

Kate sat back against the wall of the van, staring at the ceiling. She didn't speak, and exhaustion hung heavy like a rock in her chest.

Their speed slowed five minutes ago, meaning they'd gotten off the highway. Two hours from Perth Amboy could have meant anything. They could have gone north out of state, or they could be in western New Jersey or even further south. Her phone wasn't any help. She wasn't getting any reception. There was probably something to be deduced from that, but it didn't matter to Kate. What did was Jackson.

And no one was talking to her.

Not that she was pushing the issue. It had taken the better part of these last two hours just to get her emotions under control. She tried screaming at them, asking if he was going to be okay, but she didn't get any answers. At one point, Stern told her she was distracting the doctor.

The van rattled to a stop, but kept idling. It snapped Kate back to attention, electricity buzzing through her veins.

"He's stable," she heard the doctor say.

"Thank god," she said.

He wasn't talking to her.

"At least stable enough to get him out of the van. It seems he's developing a very nasty infection. Lots of antibiotics."

Stern said, "I will make sure you have what you need."

"How long until everything is set up inside?"

Kate leaned forward. They weren't at a hospital? Stern should have been bringing Jackson to the best help available. A private practice, maybe.

The doctor pulled the curtain back. Jackson lay on his back, eyes closed, air mask still covering his mouth and nose. His chest rose and fell steadily. There were two bandages on him, one at his shoulder and another at the side of his chest. A chill ran through her stomach.

She fished out her phone, but still didn't get reception.

"What are you doing?" Stern asked.

"I'm going to call my dad. Going to tell him everything's okay."

Stern shook his head. "You can't do that."

Kate looked at her phone. Still no reception.

"You're right. No bars."

More head shaking. "Not what I meant."

Stern stood up and walked around the stretcher. He reached out and put a hand on Kate's shoulder.

"In less than a month, I will have the most important day of my political career. Do you know what I'm talking about?"

"The merger," she said.

"Right." Stern took a deep breath. "I'm sorry, Kate. Your father means a lot to me, and because of that, so do you. I'm going to make sure Jackson gets well. I promise. But you can't tell anyone about this. I can't be seen at the scene of a shootout."

Kate tilted her head. "Did you call the police?"

"I will be poison. Everything I've worked for will be gone, do you understand?"

Kate didn't respond.

"You called me, Kate. You asked *me* for help. We're going to take Jackson out of this van, and we're going to bring to a place where he can get better."

"Where are we?"

Stern shrugged. "Somewhere safe."

"He's my fiancée."

Stern squeezed her shoulder. "You have to trust me. We're going to take you home, and —"

"You are not." Kate shrugged his hand off her shoulder. "You absolutely are not. I'm staying with Jackson."

"I'm afraid you'll just get in the way. I promise I'll keep you posted on his progress."

The back door to the van opened up. A man in a tank top stood in the street. Kate smelled sea water and heard the rush of waves. Stern got up and went to him. The doctor, the new man, and Stern began to roll Donne's stretcher out into the street. Their movement kept Kate pinned against the van wall.

She was able to quickly lift her phone and snap a picture of the man in the tank top. Beyond that, she was stuck.

As soon as Jackson was off the van, the back doors slammed shut. Kate leapt up and ran to them. She pushed to open them, but they were locked. There wasn't an interior switch to push to unlock them.

Kate screamed.

No one responded.

She kept pushing on the doors with no luck.

Five minutes later, she fell to the floor of the van as it peeled out and back on to the street.

CHAPTER TWENTY-NINE

They ate.

Chicken parm sandwiches and mozzarella sticks for William. Jeanne and Martin took their time eating, trying to enjoy the momentary respite. Sarah and Leonard fussed, going back and forth between bites, trying to get the guest room ready. Martin didn't want to tell them they weren't going to stay.

Not yet, anyway.

If William overheard, it might shatter him. The kid had been through enough today. Jeanne finished eating first, and William took her to see his room. Martin wondered if it was instinct, how easily they got along together.

As Martin was wiping the last bit of marinara from the corner of his lip, Leonard came in and pointed toward the back door.

"You wanted me to answer some questions," he said.

Martin nodded, and they went out to the yard. Leonard tossed a crab trap into the lagoon. The muscles in his forearms strained as he tossed. As the cage splashed into the water, a coughing fit overtook him. Martin stared out at the water until he finished.

"We never catch anything, but it's fun to try," Leonard said after he was done gasping for air.

"When I was a kid, we used to catch eels in these cages. Of all the kinds of things you could catch, we caught eels."

"Did you eat 'em?"

Martin shook his head. "Tossed 'em back."

"My mom—she was Italian—cooked them up. Everybody caught eels on these lagoons."

Martin shrugged. "At least you're catching something."

They stood in silence for a few moments. A seagull swooped down and snatched something from the surface of the water. He gave his wings a quick flap and was ten feet in the air again, heading off out of sight.

The sky was clear, and a cool breeze followed the gull down the lagoon. It wasn't a true summer day—one with humidity and unbearable heat. This reminded Martin more of late spring, just before the schools let out. Driving down the highway with the windows open instead of the air-conditioner on. He and Jeanne would get to do that again. Eileen never wanted to.

"How'd you do it?" Martin finally asked.

Leonard nodded while staring in the direction the seagull had gone. "Did you read the police report?"

Martin shook his head. "Car accident is all I know. My chief didn't want me looking into it. I didn't really want to. Not the way Jeanne had left. I was hurting enough."

It sounded more like wallowing than Martin had meant it to. Leonard let it go.

"We burnt her car to a crisp. Only let the license plate survive."

"You weren't there that night. You were out pretending to be suicidal to distract Donne."

Leonard shook his head. "It wasn't that hard to pretend. My little girl was leaving us."

"I don't get it. Who burned the car?"

After rubbing his face, Leonard said, "We lived in Middlesex County a long time. Sarah and I have a lot of friends. We knew a few firefighters who helped out that night."

"No questions asked?" Martin kicked at a pebble. "I find that tough to believe."

"I was a computer programmer. Did a lot of work for the town, once wi-fi was in style. Was owed a lot of favors."

"What about DNA?"

Leonard's eyes got watery, but the tears did not give way to his cheeks. "We had to cut some of her hair. She lost a tooth."

"There was a second car."

"Are you sure you didn't read the police report?"

"People talk. It was a drunk driving accident."

"One of the guys we used to light the fire was junking his car anyway. A couple of bottles of Jack, spill some on the front seat, you're good to go."

Martin's gut was churning, and it wasn't from the chicken parm. This was amateur hour, and he missed it. Too busy caught up in his emotions, too busy hating Jackson Donne for winning and holding on to her. He could have caught up with this and been with her. Helped her.

"It wasn't a foolproof plan," he said. "Not even close."

"It didn't have to be, we didn't think. We were grieving parents. We didn't care about the guy driving the car. We made that clear. We just wanted to remember our daughter." Leonard exhaled. "The police always have bigger issues. We gave them their out. All we had to do was fool you and Jackson. But Jackson was a drunk, so that wasn't hard. I've been lying to Jackson about a lot of things. Even about you."

"She didn't go to Arizona right away, did she?"

Leonard nodded. "We took her to Maryland. She had the baby with a midwife there. Water birth. It was disgusting and scary, but William ended up fine."

"And you agreed to take him?"

"It wasn't easy. For any of us. But she was so scared. She had to do this."

"Why did she have to do it? She mentioned the senator. Stern."

Leonard looked back at the house. Martin followed his gaze. Sarah was looking through the back door. She nodded at them.

"You'd have to ask my daughter," Leonard said.

"You know though, don't you?"

Leonard didn't answer. He started to walk back toward the house. Martin took a step forward, but movement between their house and the neighbor's caught his eye. A car had pulled out of the driveway and was rolling down the road. One of the Bakers' cars.

"What the hell?" Martin started to run and caught a glimpse of Jeanne in the driver's seat.

William was in the back.

By the time Martin got to the front yard, the car had disappeared down the road. He was getting slow.

Leonard came up behind him and put a hand on his shoulder.

"Let her go," he said.

"She's not safe."

Leonard squeezed. "She will be. Jeanne did this for six years. She's got William now. It will be okay. I promise."

Martin shook his head. His heart was pounding. "I'm not going to lose her again."

CHAPTER
THIRTY

Kate rang her father's doorbell at seven the next morning. bjkfgkjThe van had dropped her off at Jackson's apartment about three hours earlier, and she had tried to lie down for a few hours. Sleep never came. Instead, she stared at the ceiling of the bedroom. She alternated between crying and praying for Jackson to make it through the night. Once the sun started peeking through the venetian blinds, she got up and made a pot of coffee. The ache in her stomach didn't make it easy to drink, but she forced it down—fearing she'd fall asleep on the road if she didn't.

She parked in front of her father's Milltown house and trudged up the steps, her legs feeling like they were trapped in quicksand. He opened the door only seconds after she rang the bell. Once she saw him, unshaven, in a robe, reading glasses balanced on the edge of his nose, she fell into his arms and wept. Her shoulders shook against him, and tears soaked into the fabric of his robe. Dad pulled her in tight and rubbed her back.

Kate didn't know how long they stood there. She didn't care.

Finally, when no more tears would come, she pushed her self away from her father.

"Jackson?" her father asked.

She nodded.

"Come inside."

Kate's mother died four years ago of lung cancer. She had never smoked a day in her life. With each passing month, the home her father lived in unraveled, becoming more and more overrun with her dad's case files. When she started to work for him after graduating Seton Hall Law, Kate made it a point to organize his files and keep them in the basement. She remembered how, before Sandy hit, she, her dad, and Jackson lugged all the boxes out of there before it flooded. The basement never flooded, but the boxes still sat in the living room. She noticed the Gunderson case—a hit and run lawsuit—had files pulled from it.

She had forgotten about work. About her dad making her promise not to call in sick.

Now he sat on the couch and waited. Kate sat next to him, her breath coming in short gasps. She looked at her dad and tried to smile. He turned red.

Kate had rolled it all over in her head, telling her father everything—about Jackson, the gunshots, the weird van ride—and letting him pick up the pieces. It was what she'd done as a kid, and her instinct was screaming her to do the same thing.

Dad will make it right.

Instead, she said, "Tell me about Henry Stern, Dad."

Her dad sat back and looked at the ceiling. He rubbed his chin.

"How is that about Jackson?" he asked.

"I'm not talking about Jackson right now. Tell me about Stern."

"You've known him for years. Did he call you like I asked?"

Kate rubbed her palms together. "He called."

"Did he—can he help?"

The room smelled like an old book. All the files, the papers, the reports sitting in the office made it feel like a used bookstore. The pot of coffee her dad was percolating made the feeling stronger.

"I want to know about him, Dad. I don't mean the political

him."

Her father straightened his glasses then rubbed his chin. Myron Ellison could look smart even in his pajamas.

"He was a military man. That's how I met him. I was representing a case at Fort Dix and he was one of our witnesses. We become friends."

"It's all over the place that he was military. What happened next?"

"He went to Afghanistan for a year. Rumor had it he worked with the CIA trying to turn terrorists into informants. We lost touch for a while."

"And when he came back?"

"Left the army. Got married. Got divorced. Twice. He went to work at Rutgers — taught some poli sci before running for the senate seat."

Kate pulled out her phone and brought up the picture of the man who had driven the van. She handed it to her father.

"Do you know that guy?"

Her father took off his glasses and brought the phone close to his nose. Squinted. Kate's stomach burned, and she could taste coffee in the back of her mouth.

Dad gave the phone back.

"Never seen him before."

"Something bad is going on, Dad." Kate put the phone back into her purse. She pulled out a band and tied her hair back into a ponytail.

"Did Jackson find his fiancée?"

The words shook Kate. *She* was his fiancée.

"I don't know."

"Why are you so upset? Where is he?"

The words didn't come. The image of Jackson, bleeding, eyes wide, ran through her head. Jackson's face morphed into her dad's. Henry Stern had warned her to stay quiet, that he was going to take care of everything. The churning in her stomach turned into a fire.

"I'm sorry, Dad." Kate stood up. "I'm not going to be able to work the Gunderson case. I need some time off."

He stood up with her and put a hand on her forearm. "You can tell me."

Kate's eyes burned again, but she fought the tears back. "No," she said. "I'll take care of this."

She shrugged his hand away. And went toward the door.

"Kate!" he called.

She turned back toward him. Dad stood in front of the couch, shoulders slumped, arms at his sides.

"I'm worried about you," he said. "Let me help."

"This is on me," she said. "I can't put this on anyone."

"Tell me what you're talking about."

"Coming here was a mistake."

"I'm your father." His voice was soft, the same tone as when he told her Mom had died during the night.

Kate didn't respond. She opened the door and walked out into the morning.

CHAPTER
THIRTY-ONE

Someone bounced a basketball.

It thudded four times against the ground and stopped. A second later, a swish of the net. The dribbling started again. There were voices, muffled and out of breath. Another swish of the net.

Jackson Donne opened his eyes. The world blurred. He blinked it back into focus. His eyelids were dry and sticky.

He opened his mouth to speak, and his voice cracked. It felt like he'd been on a bender. His mouth was as dry as a saltine. His head throbbed behind his eyes.

He tried to sit up, but it felt like someone put an anvil on his chest. He put his hands beneath him and pushed. It felt like the skin against his chest was going to tear away. He screamed, but only a hiss of air escaped his mouth.

The ball stopped bouncing and someone said, "Hey, look who's awake."

Donne turned his head and realized he was in a church. It wasn't an active church. All the pews had been pulled out and the tile floor was bare. Where the altar should have been was a portable basketball hoop, the kind kids had in their driveways.

His chest felt like it was about to explode. His shoulder was on fire as well. No matter how many muscles he tried to tense, Donne couldn't get his body to stop shuddering. The beeping sound he heard earlier was loud now and the beeps were closer together.

A man put his hands on Donne's shoulders and eased him back into a lying position. The mattress beneath him sagged.

"Calm down, buddy. You're okay."

Donne's eyes were wide. He looked at a stained glass window, an image of Jesus passing fish out to the apostles.

"Here. Drink some water."

Someone put a straw into his mouth, and a stream of water followed it. It was cold, and his tongue absorbed it, like a starved plant. He sucked some more. The cold felt good on the back of his throat.

"Slow down."

Donne didn't take the advice and took another big sip. The water caught at the back of his throat, triggering his gag reflex. He coughed hard, and the water spilled out over his chin and on to his chest. He gasped for air and coughed some more. The hacks twisted his whole body. The pains in his shoulder and chest contracted, and again Donne felt water form in his eyes.

"Slow, deep breaths."

Donne closed his eyes and breathed in through his nose. It was a reflex from his days as a jogger. He could focus on something other than the pain. He could focus on the breathing.

His body stopped shuddering, and his aches lower their intensity. He opened his eyes again and looked up at the man helping him. He was wearing a white coat and wore plastic gloves. There was a silver plate clasped to his pocket, but Donne couldn't read it. His eyes weren't focusing correctly.

"Can you talk?" the man asked.

Donne moved his lips. At first it was just air, then he found it. "How long?" His voice was raspy and the words were broken up by phlegm.

The man shook his head. "Three days."

Donne closed his eyes again. Seventy-two hours, more or less. A lot could happen in that amount of time. Jeanne could be dead. Or she could be with Martin.

"How bad?" He wanted to spit, but the moisture from the

phlegm felt good on his tongue.

The man inserted the straw from the water bottle into Donne's mouth again and squeezed. Donne took the water slower this time.

"You've been shot twice. Once in the right shoulder and once on the right side of your chest. You lost a substantial amount of blood. We had to remove the bullet from your chest before it migrated. The one in the shoulder tore right through. There was a third shot. The men found it embedded in a wall, about head high. Whoever shot you went for the kill and missed."

Donne forced himself to breathe slowly. His mind was running too quickly, and if he let his thoughts take over, he'd have a panic attack. The air felt like it was getting caught somewhere in his throat, but he kept inhaling and exhaling. Jogging, he'd found, was like yoga. When you breathe correctly, the discomfort goes away.

"Who are you?" he said, finally. He wondered how long it was since he last spoke. It felt like only seconds, but it may have been longer. Time felt fluid.

"No matter. I'm your doctor, for now. We almost lost you two days ago."

"The beeping."

The doctor didn't say anything.

"I remember the beeping, and then everything went away."

"You didn't take to surgery well."

Donne sipped more water. The doctor's face came into focus. He was older, with salt-and-pepper hair and wrinkles on his face. He wasn't smiling, and his face was sallow.

"I'm not in a hospital," Donne said. "I'm in a church."

"You still have your powers of observation." It wasn't the doctor speaking this time.

No, it was the familiar voice he'd heard at the warehouse. Just after he'd been shot. Whoever it was stood on the other side of the bed. Donne turned his head, and more pain from his shoulder shot down his arm. It felt like an iron spike digging through his vein into his fingertips.

The man was younger than the doctor. He had brown hair

pushed to the left. He wore a suit with an American flag on his lapel. He was smiling, and his teeth reflected ambient light.

Senator Henry Stern.

"Nice to see you again, Mr. Donne. I'm glad you're not dead."

He reached out his hand as if to shake Donne's. It seemed to be a reflex. When he realized Donne could reach back, he pulled his hand away.

Donne sipped more water. The basketball started dribbling again. Donne craned his neck and saw two men in tank tops shooting hoops.

"He needs more rest, senator."

Stern smiled again, the kind of smile that wins votes. "We'll talk soon."

Donne leaned back in the bed and took the doctor's advice. He needed more rest. He closed his eyes.

As he started to doze off, he heard the someone say, "Why did you let the girl go?"

The senator's voice came back hazy. "Someone would miss her."

Then, fading, like the end of the song: "Would that be a bad thing?"

CHAPTER
THIRTY-TWO

The waves woke him up this time.

There wasn't a basketball bouncing, no cars passing, nothing but waves. The noise was constant, and almost sounded like wind through heavy brush. Donne guessed that's what the sound could have actually been, but something deep within him told him it was waves.

Opening his eyes, Donne tried to assess the situation. Wires were attached to him, and the fact that he noticed them for the first time just now was probably a sign he was getting better. He could also feel an IV in his arm. Probably trying to keep him hydrated. He wondered if it was there before, when he was drinking from the water bottle.

Next, he assessed the pain. It wasn't as sharp as earlier; the nail was no longer digging through his veins. His chest still felt like it was in a vise, but the pressure had been lessened.

Donne shifted his weight and his vision blurred. The vise tightened again, and the air went out of him. He heard someone walking toward him.

"Senator?" he asked, through gritted teeth.

"You should be so lucky." The voice was pure *Jersey Shore.*

Donne craned his neck and saw one of the guys who was playing basketball earlier. A chain rattled around his neck as he walked. Occasionally, it caught a glint of light, which illuminated the crucifix at the end of it.

"They want you to rest." He placed a hairy hand on Donne's arm.

It was then Donne realized he only had pants on. He wasn't sure why it surprised him, but it did.

"I need to walk around," Donne said.

"You're not allowed. Not yet."

Donne said, "Tomorrow morning, then."

"When the doctor says you can."

Donne bit his lip. It took more effort than he expected. "I hope my insurance covers this."

"Go back to sleep."

Donne looked over. The basketball hoop was still there. "When this is over, we'll play one-on-one."

The guy nodded at Donne's injuries.

"You're babysitting me for the senator?"

The guy shook his head, and then licked his lips. "I ain't a babysitter."

A wave of exhaustion washed over Donne. He was pretty sure this guy wanted to talk, about anything, but Donne's mind wasn't working right. He couldn't find the right questions to ask. Trying to search his memory was like trying to dig through a child's toy box to find a dropped Tic Tac. Too much work, too scatterbrained.

Donne's head lolled back on to the pillow.

"That's right," Jersey Shore said.

"Jeanne," Donne said. The name was like cream rising to the top.

Before the room went black again, he watched the guy pull out his cell phone and unlock it.

"I WANT to walk," Donne said.

It was morning. He could still hear the waves, but cars passing and the dribbling of the basketball dulled the sound. He didn't feel pain as much as stiffness this morning.

As Jersey Shore walked toward Donne, he pulled out his phone again. He tapped it a few times. Donne didn't try to get out of bed. He wasn't that stupid. He knew he'd need help. Jersey Shore would have to get the IV in the right place so Donne could push it with him.

"The doctor said you've been shot before," Jersey Shore said.

"Once," Donne said.

"Ain't that enough?"

Donne shrugged and then nearly screamed. He bit it back, then said, "I probably should have thought of that earlier, yeah."

Jersey Shore's phone went off. He checked it and then shrugged. "You can give walking a try."

Donne nodded. His neck was covered in sweat.

Jersey Shore came around and grabbed the IV and wheeled it to the opposite side of the bed. When Donne got up, he could grab it. Jersey Shore stepped back and crossed his arms.

Donne said, "You're going to have to help me off the bed."

Jersey Shore sighed and then stepped forward. He crouched near the bed and Donne put his arm across Shore's shoulders. He dropped his feet off the bed and tried to put weight on them. His calves shuddered.

"Ready?" Jersey Shore said. "One, two, three."

Donne tensed his thighs and pushed. He felt Jersey Shore lifting as well. Donne was on his feet. And out of breath. His chest heaved hard. With each exhale, the vise compressed. His chest and brow were soaked now. Donne wrapped his left hand around the IV carrier.

Every nerve, every muscle, every fiber in Donne's body screamed for him to go back to bed. He squinted against the drops of sweat in his eyes.

One step.

"You want me to put you back?" Jersey Shore asked.

Donne grunted.

Just. Take. One. Step.

"I didn't quite catch that," Jersey Shore said.

Donne wanted to lift his foot. One in front of the other. That's all it takes. Air was hard to come by. The knife was digging in his left vein. His triceps were twitching.

One step.

"Put me back," he said.

"You sure?"

"Put me back!"

Donne slumped into Jersey Shore's arms and then back into the bed. Donne leaned back into the pillow. He brought his right hand to his mouth and bit into his fist, trying to will the pain away.

"Do you need the doctor?" Jersey Shore's tan seemed to have faded.

Donne shook his head.

"Okay."

"Tomorrow," Donne said.

"I'll call him in an hour if you want."

Donne shook his head once more. "Tomorrow we try again."

CHAPTER
THIRTY-THREE

Kate couldn't get in touch with the senator. Days later, and there was no luck at his office number — his secretary said he was busy and would call back, which he didn't — and the number he'd called her from was now disconnected. She'd heard nothing about Jackson.

Her stomach sank thinking about him. Stern promised her Jackson would be okay and that he would call when it was over.

Meanwhile, the picture of the man who drove the van waited on her phone. Social media wasn't an option. If she posted the picture on Facebook or Twitter, the senator would undoubtedly find out. They had too many common friends.

And she couldn't call or text those friends either. Keeping a lid on things made it difficult to get answers.

Kate sat in her own apartment now. Staying in Jackson's only brought tears and anxiety. She'd bought a case of wine earlier that afternoon. That was probably overdoing it, but she didn't care. While lugging it back to her apartment, she passed a beat cop eating lunch in his car. She never thought her knees would go to jelly at the thought of the phrase *beer goggles*.

Now, with a glass of chardonnay at her side, she sat with her iPad in her hands. After googling "State Senator Henry Stern," Kate loaded the images tab. Six pages of images opened, and she exhaled. That would be doable. It wasn't like she ran a search for Chris Christie.

The first images were photos taken by the *Star-Ledger*. They were from Stern's first day in office. He sat at his desk, smiling. The American flag stood over his shoulder, and a medal he'd received during his time in service hung on the wall. The caption referred to Ocean County electing a decorated military hero.

Kate remembered the election. Stern basically ran unopposed. A Democrat named Michael Miragliotta ran a cursory campaign, but Stern had the governor's approval, which mean Miragliotta was poll poison. Stern won by thirty points. She went with her father to the victory party but only stayed an hour. There were too many balloons, too much confetti, and several drunk Wall Street guys home from work and wanting to get laid.

Not Kate's scene. She was still in law school.

After flipping through a page of photos of Stern in his office, Stern shaking Christie's hand, and Stern holding a baby or two, she found a few more promising photos. These pictures were of Stern out in public. In one, he held a microphone, mouth slightly open, speaking to an audience. He was at one of his town halls, undoubtedly talking about following Christie's lead with Rutgers and work their own merger in Ocean County.

A year ago, Rutgers had merged with UMDNJ, the state's medical school. It was a megapolitical and educational move that pushed Rutgers into the upper echelon of research universities. It also saved the state from covering the debt UMDNJ had dug itself into.

Now Stern wanted to do the same on a much smaller scale. The University of New Jersey and Benjamin Franklin College would merge. UNJ would gain a law school and a ton of debt as well. It wasn't the same move, but it was going to be a feather in Stern's reelection cap. Except most of the faculty and administration of BFC was against the move. They were fighting it big time. Protests, letter writing, even a billboard taken out on the Turnpike.

Kate looked at the people sitting behind Stern. Two senior citizens, and one familiar face. The guy from the picture.

Electricity buzzed across her skin. Kate scanned the caption, but there weren't any other names beyond Stern's. She clicked to another picture.

It took her another ten to find the guy in the van again. This time Stern was standing on the Jersey boardwalk, just after Superstorm Sandy. He was listening to a woman who had lost her house speak. Stern's face was politician-serious, as if he knew the camera was there. The woman, however, didn't. Tears and makeup streaked her face. Behind Stern, much clearer this time, was the man from the picture. He stood, hands clutched in front of him, wearing a dark suit, looking just as serious as Stern. Kate snapped a picture of the photo with her phone and texted it to her dad with the message *Who is the bodyguard?*

Seconds passed, then her dad wrote back *Luca Carmine. Stern likes him a lot. Good worker. Why?*

Kate's heart picked up the pace. She ignored her dad's query.

She'd forgotten the bodyguard story. Most politicians in the state had a state trooper assigned to them as protection. Stern made a show of "smaller government" and hired his own bodyguards. Three of them.

Kate opened Google again and typed in "Luca Carmine."

There wasn't much. A Facebook page, which she opened, but it was ultra-privatized. Gave her no help. There was a news article about a 5K run where a Luca and a Carmine were finishers.

And then a blog post which made her eyes light up. She swallowed some chardonnay and clicked on it.

The post was written by a former *Ledger* writer who'd taken a buyout and now ran a blog that no one read. He'd also published a few mystery novels. Kate had read one and liked it. The article was about Tony Verderese's funeral.

The former head of the New Jersey mob.

Man, Mike Miragliotta must have stood no chance in that election so many years ago. No one in the press looked into this?

It was a brief mention. One sentence. Luca Carmine was a nephew of Verderese's. He was a pallbearer.

CHAPTER
THIRTY-FOUR

"How long have you known she was alive?" Senator Stern asked.

Donne wasn't sure how long he'd been there. He was starting to wonder, however, if it was actually something to hydrate him in the IV. The way he was fading in and out, it could have been a sedative.

Fighting through the clouds, Donne said, "Not as long as you have."

"You must be so angry."

Donne thought about it. Things had moved too fast to decide that. In the morning, he got an email. By the evening, he was bleeding on the floor of a warehouse, and Jeanne was gone again. He took a deep breath. His chest didn't fight him on that too much.

Progress.

"I think I'm more pissed off I've been shot," he said.

The smell of salt hung in the air. He remembered frankincense, vaguely, but that seemed to have filtered out of the former church. The sea salt, however, was still strong. Where ever he was, they hadn't moved him too far. He may have been in a different town, but he was still at the beach. Maybe he was even just a town over, Asbury Park, Bradley Beach.

Donne tried to think of abandoned churches and abandoned

towns. A year ago, it would be impossible to find one. After Sandy, he could be anywhere.

"That's good. Go with that." Stern was sitting in a wheeled office chair.

"You're a psychologist?"

Stern smiled. "I'm a man of many talents."

A heavy door opened and closed. Donne looked to see the doctor. He shook Jersey Shore's hand, and gave them a wave. He seemed way too cheerful to being doing examinations in an abandoned church.

A wave of pain rolled off him. Donne gritted his teeth and squeezed his eyes shut. When it passed, he asked, "How long has it been, Henry?"

"About—I don't know—seven years ago?"

The doctor put on his white coat and took out a stethoscope. He pressed it to Donne's chest. It was cold. His back stiffened, and that made everything hurt again. The doctor peeled at Donne's bandages. Hair pulled with the gauze. Compared to every other pain, that twinge was almost pleasurable.

The doctor nodded. "You're getting better. No infection. The wound is healing."

"He's a lucky man," Stern said.

Donne looked around. "And it's only been a few days."

The doctor shined a light in Donne's eyes. "How *do* you feel? Groggy? Nauseous? Or fine?"

"Less groggy than last night."

The doctor nodded. "I understand you wanted to walk this morning. How far did you get?"

Donne wanted to tell him he walked across the church, picked up the basketball, and swished a three-pointer. The net was a tease. Donne had played in high school, started at shooting guard his senior year, even though he smoked weed every night. He wanted the ball in his hands right now.

"I couldn't even lift my foot."

Again the doctor nodded. "It'll come."

"No. I think the last time I saw you was the night I met Kate. The fundraiser at Olde Towne," Donne said to Stern.

Stern shrugged. "That's where you met her? Life's small coincidences."

Trying to pull those memories from the recesses of his brain made Donne feel like a spider was crawling around his gut.

Stern said, "I was poli sci. She was—"

"Education and English."

Stern smiled. "She was always so busy working. When did you ever see her?"

Donne thought about Martin and Jeanne being "pretty close," and the spider grew to tarantula size.

"She came back and left you." Stern snapped his fingers. "Just like that."

The doctor was attaching new bandages to Donne. He turned to Stern and said, "Tell Luca to keep cleaning the wounds. Try some solid foods tonight."

Donne closed his eyes. "I wish I couldn't feel that."

"Do you remember what Jeanne was working on when she 'died'?" Stern used air quotes.

"I was busy with my own small business," Donne said.

Donne kept searching his memory. As was often the case when he looked at the past, Donne wondered how stoned he was back then. It really was as bad as they said. He had memories of Jeanne's wake, but Martin said there hadn't been one.

And what else was trapped in his brain and needed to come out? Maybe he always knew about Martin and Jeanne, but couldn't bring the information to the forefront. The tarantula started to grow again. Donne felt bile burn the back of his throat.

"Tell me," Donne said. "I was pretty fucked up back then."

Stern shook his head. "No."

"You beat the crap out of her," Donne said.

Stern leaned forward. "Two of my best men are dead because of you."

"Why did Jeanne fake her death?"

Stern said, "The man she did go with shot you."

Donne's felt the tarantula climb up the inside of his chest into his throat.

Stern shook his head. "Don't play games with me."

It felt like there were pieces of a puzzle scattered about in front of Donne, but he couldn't find the edges. But it appeared he was going to have a lot of time to sort through them. Despite the urge to get up, lying here would at least give him some time to sort things out. It felt like Stern was leading him somewhere, but Donne would have to get there himself.

Stern looked at his watch. "Remember, I'm going to help you."

"Keep resting," the doctor said. "You're doing really well."

They left, and Donne was left with Jersey Shore incessantly dribbling a ball. His name was Luca.

CHAPTER
THIRTY-FIVE

Donne couldn't even wait until 9 AM. He'd kept oatmeal down the previous evening and did so again this morning. With a full stomach and no TV, he got sick of waiting. He let the second hand count and extra five seconds, and then he called for Luca.

"We're going to walk today," Donne said.

Luca nodded. "Uh-huh. Maybe one of us."

They went through the same routine again, Luca getting his arm around Donne. Donne pivoted off the bed and his feet hit the floor. He didn't need the IV anymore, so the position was less awkward, but if he lost his balance, he only had Luca to grab on to.

"You're pushing it," Luca said.

Donne grunted in response.

He knew Luca was right. But he had to heal fast. People don't let you heal in an old abandoned church if they think you're going to be hunky-dory. Donne didn't want to be confined to a bed waiting.

It was warm in the church, but not warm enough to make him sweat as much as he was. They were letting him wear a T-shirt now, a white Hanes undershirt that it had gone gray and damp. Beads of sweat dripped off his hair into his eyes.

His abs and ass tightened. He did everything he could to balance himself. Again, he focused on making just one step. Pick up your left foot and put it forward. Then move the right one.

His leg twitched underneath him. Something that had always been instinct now took his full concentration.

"Pick an area you want to go to," Luca said. "Where do you want to be?"

"Away from this bed."

Luca shook his head, and Donne could feel it scruff against his arm. "You have to set a goal. Something specific."

"The basketball net."

Luca nodded. "And you want to beat me."

"I will beat you."

Luca chuckled. "You better get walking then."

Donne blew out air and smiled. It was as close as he was going to get to a laugh. His muscles were screaming at him, like being heckled onstage. His face was drenched. He stared at the basketball net, the twine starting to fray just a bit on the bottom left side. He imagined putting up a free throw and it swishing. A lot of steps between then and now.

Now all he needed to do was take one.

A deep breath. His left foot slipped just a bit against the floor. He could feel dust particles digging into his toes. His feet twitched. Donne shut his eyes. Sweat burned underneath his lids.

He lifted his left foot.

His right knee started to buckle.

He put his foot down just a few inches in front where it had just been and let his weight settle.

"Nice," Luca said. His voice was even.

Donne exhaled.

"One more."

"You should rest." Luca sounded bored.

"One." He grunted. "More."

Now he forced all his weight on to his left side. His right foot slid against the dust, and Donne pulled. His thigh muscles protested. The foot was off the ground. He swung his leg beneath him. Toes grazed the tile. He put it down in front of the left.

He screamed as if he'd just completed a marathon in less than two hours. His full weight collapsed into Luca. He felt Luca give way just a hair before steadying them against the momentum.

"Okay," Donne said, trying to catch his breath. "Back to bed."

"Yeah. Nice work." Again, his voice was even, disinterested.

Luca turned them around, and Donne was surprised to see the bed was still within arms reach. It felt like he'd travelled miles. He leaned at the waist and put both hands on the edge. Took a few breaths. His heart was pounding.

Donne was back in the bed. The memory of walking just moments earlier was a blur. He couldn't even picture it. His biggest accomplishment in weeks, and he could barely remember it. Somewhere else in the deep recesses of his mind, he realized he'd missed his exam.

"How are you tied to the senator?"

"Shut the fuck up," Luca said. "Just be cool."

"What is Stern tied up in?"

"Are you delirious?"

Maybe.

But Luca was also right. Donne needed more sleep. He grabbed the water bottle on the table next to his bed and drank some. The cold liquid spread through his body. His wounds weren't throbbing. That was something.

"I want something to read," Donne said. "Can you run out to a bookstore?"

Luca shook his head.

"Of course," Donne said. "You can't leave me. Because you have to make sure I don't leave."

"Far as I can tell, you can barely get two feet underneath you."

Luca shook his head and walked away. He crossed the pulpit and went into a room behind the altar. Seconds later,

Donne could hear a TV.

He leaned back into his pillow and tried to listen to whatever sitcom it was. All he could hear was the laugh track.

CHAPTER
THIRTY-SIX

On the fifth night, the nightmares came.

He woke up screaming and thrashing in the bed. The thrashing sent pain shooting throughout his body. He could feel the gauze and tape tearing from his skin. The sound of his voice echoed throughout the church, and Luca would be rushing to him soon. Donne knew the drill.

Jeanne in the chair. Donne reaching for her, freeing her. Bill Martin raising the gun. Flashes of light.

A coughing fit racked through him. He fought for air, fought to calm his body. Jeanne had been so close. He almost had her.

Outside waves crashed.

Where the hell was he?

There were too many questions, but only one thought tore through his skull. He'd almost had Jeanne. She was alive, she was in his arms, and then she was gone again.

Donne stopped coughing, but instead began to shake. A full-on earthquake broke out across his body and he couldn't get it to stop. His muscles spasmed, his teeth chattered, and his wounds felt like they were tearing apart. It was like going through withdrawal.

He brought his knees up to his chest and wrapped his arms around them. The doctor had been to see him again today and said he didn't have to be hooked up to any more wires or tubes.

That was the good news. The bad news was he was healing so well, his mind was clear again.

And that brought Jeanne's face back full-force.

Luca was rubbing his eyes when he came in the room. "Jesus," he said. "You're like a little baby. Screaming in the middle of the night?"

"Go away," Donne said.

"Can't. If I know you're awake, I have to check on you." Luca pulled up a metal folding chair and sat in it. Wiped his eyes again, and yawned. "So what the hell is the matter with you?"

Donne clenched his teeth and stared at his toes. He was not going to give this guy what he wanted. Without knowing what Senator Stern was after, it was not a smart move to talk. His mind wanted to let it all out, though. Stories of Jeanne, of chasing her down, and watching Bill Martin shoot Nick and Calvin.

And then having her so close. He only wanted an hour with her. To talk to her and find out what happened. Where did it go wrong? Why did she have to run? His eyes felt wet. It was only sweat, he told himself.

The shaking started to subside, but he was still wary of aftershocks. She was in his arms, even if only for seconds.

Luca leaned back, the chair rising up on two legs. He put his hands behind his head and exhaled.

"You said her name," he said.

Donne shut his eyes and saw Jeanne again. His concentrated on her face, and it morphed in to Kate.

Oh God, Kate.

She probably thought he had run off, freaked out by licking invitations. Maybe she thought he was dead in a gutter somewhere. His heart beat faster and some of the pain in his chest subsided. He felt hollow.

He unwrapped his arms from around his knees. Looked at his hands. Closed and then opened them several times.

"She lied to you, man." Luca picked at one of his nails. "You thought she was dead. She didn't want you."

Waves crashed outside.

"I can't figure it out," Donne said. "We could be anywhere in New Jersey. After the storm, this could be anywhere."

Luca said, "But you're still worried about her. You said her name in your sleep."

Donne ignored him. Kept focusing on the waves.

"Here's the thing," Donne said. "This place never flooded. There's no visible water damage."

All four legs of Luca's chair clanked back on to the tile. "Interesting, huh?"

The puzzle pieces were coming into focus just a little more. Donne's brain tickled, as if he was on to something.

"What are they going to do with her when they find her?" Donne exhaled. He hated saying her name. "Jeanne."

Luca said, "Maybe we're not looking for her."

"I doubt it."

Luca shrugged. Then he leaned over and poked at Donne's shoulder. Fire ran down Donne's arm.

"You're going to have scars."

Everything was obtuse. Donne felt like he knew what was going on, but couldn't grab it with his fingers. Jeanne. Bill Martin. Senator Stern. For not the first time, Donne felt a rock settling in his stomach. If only he hadn't drank and snorted so much. If only he'd paid more attention. Being a twenty-five-year-old narc cop was too much for him to handle. It was like being a rock star, and he didn't know how to manage it.

Even when he thought he was doing the right thing. The day he walked into his boss's office with names and a pile of evidence of what they'd been doing. He still never got it exactly right. He'd kept Bill's name out of it. They were partners, and you don't do that to your partner. Five other guilty men went to jail, but Martin and Donne stayed free.

And for the longest time, he'd thought Jeanne's death was karmic payback. But now she was alive and he didn't know what to think. He was thirty-four years old. He should have had a real job with benefits. Instead, he was battling back from another gunshot wound.

Talking to another thug who wouldn't give him answers.

Donne took a deep breath. "Why are you keeping me here?"

Luca shook his head. "Your color's coming back, so that's good."

This wasn't what he wanted for himself anymore. He needed to get back to Kate. Start over. Fix things.

He had to find Jeanne, end whatever was going on here, and get back to his life.

The longer he stayed here, the longer he rotted. The closer Senator Stern was to screwing everything up.

"I'm going to try and sleep some more," Donne said.

"Best news of the night."

Donne lay back and closed his eyes. He didn't see Jeanne this time. He heard Luca's footsteps, and timed how long it took for them to disappear.

CHAPTER
THIRTY-SEVEN

Google brought people to interesting places.
Kate's luck was no different. She'd been searching Luca's name, clicking through newspaper articles, blogs, and photos looking for more information on him. For an hour she had no luck. Beyond the blog she found — one that was all too brief with information — she couldn't find anything on Luca Carmine.

Until she got to the eighth Google page. A short news article link from a local Bergen County paper was there, and Kate almost missed it. The headline and summary didn't mention Luca's name. Instead it was about a woman named Marie Rapaldi. Kate clicked the article because the headline mentioned her original hometown, Bogota, New Jersey. It read "Marie Rapaldi Runs the Bogota 5K for Her Mother."

With the article was a picture of Marie with Luca, and a caption: "Marie, seen here with her boyfriend, Luca Carmine, ran the Bogota 5K in honor of her ailing mother." Kate didn't read the rest of the article, instead backing up to the Google page. She typed Marie's name into Google, along with Bogota. The third link was a Yellow Pages link with her address.

Clearly, Marie wasn't a private person.

Kate was in the car five minutes later.

WHENEVER HER father was prepping a trial, Kate took the first step in collecting witnesses. She hit the road, tracked people down, and talked to them, gathering evidence. She'd gone in the most dangerous parts of Paterson, Jersey City, and even New Brunswick to track down people who the police had investigated in crimes. Nerves rarely got to her, and in fact, part of her enjoyed it. It was why she was able to approach Jackson cold in the Olde Towne Tavern what felt like ages ago.

But now, as she buzzed the intercom of the brick apartment building in Bogota, electricity buzzed through her stomach. Her breath was short and she kept blinking.

The intercom buzzed back. "Yeah?"

"Hi, Marie Rapaldi? My name is Kate Ellison, I'm a paralegal with—"

"311."

The intercom buzzed again, and this time the front door lock clicked open. Kate pulled the door, walked into the musty hallway, and located the staircase. When she got to the third floor, she found 311, the door open a crack. She approached it and knocked. The door creaked.

"Come in."

Kate entered the apartment. It smelled like a Yankee Candle Shop. The front room was painted bright pink and had a pink shag throw rug on the floor. There was a brown couch next to it. A woman in an orange tracksuit sat on it, filing her nails. She glanced up at Kate, showing off a load of eye makeup and purple lipstick, then back at her nails.

"Can I help you?" The Jersey accent was thick with this one.

"Like I said, I'm a paralegal with—"

"Yeah, yeah. This about my brother?" The *er* sound came out like an *uh.*

Kate stood in the middle of the living room. To her right, a cat rubbed its back against the edge of a door jamb.

"Actually, I'm here about your boyfriend."

The nail filing stopped, but Marie didn't look up. "Luca?"

Kate said, "Can you tell me about him?"

"What's this about?"

NOT EVEN PAST   149

"What was his connection to Tony Verderese?"

Now Marie looked up. Kate thought she'd fit right in on the boardwalk, chomping gum and trying to win a bootleg iPod when the wheel spun.

"They were cousins. Why?"

Kate took a deep breath. "His name came up in a document I was going through, and—"

"Bull. That ain't Luca. That's not who Luca is." Marie hopped off the couch. She was nearly a foot shorter than Kate.

Kate spread her hands. "I'm just telling you that I have questions."

"About what? What are you asking about Luca? He's a good man." Marie was inches from Kate. Her voice could have been heard from Leonia.

"Ma'am, calm down. This is all very routine."

"Routine? You know he's got a deal with Senator Stern?"

I did not know that.

"He's a good man, and when all is said and done, we are going to get married." Marie shrugged. "Maybe they'll give us a TV show."

"What does he do for the senator?"

"None of your fucking business. Come here, Percy." The cat sprinted from the door and leapt into Marie's arms. Marie caught it like a football, then stroked its neck.

"Please."

Marie shook her head. "I don't have to talk to you. It doesn't matter anyway. A few weeks from now, Luca will be golden. On his own again. You'll know who we are."

"So why don't you tell me now?"

"Get out!" Marie pointed toward the door and swore in Italian.

Kate thought about pressing the issue some more, but didn't want to leave too much of an impression. She put her business card on the table and left.

CHAPTER
THIRTY-EIGHT

Each time he called in sick, Bill Martin boss's voice got grumpier and grumpier. Martin wasn't happy about it either. He missed harassing students who didn't pay a meter. Pulling over a businessman trying to get back to work after a late lunch.

Now, though, it felt like he was treading water.

The worst part was he was no closer to finding Jeanne. Despite the fact he was convinced she hadn't gone far, there was no trail to track. She came back to New Jersey, showed her face to her captors, for a reason.

Two state troopers found the Bakers' car in a strip mall parking lot out west, off Route 78 somewhere. Martin wondered if she'd gone into Pennsylvania and found a motel there.

Martin decided it was time to be proactive. He was going to visit the one name he had, Senator Henry Stern. The office was in Manchester Township, New Jersey. The town was about an hour south of New Brunswick. Bill Martin never had a reason to go there. Today, he wished he still hadn't.

It was the definition of small-town. The senator's office was on the second floor above a bakery and a doctor's office. On the street, four or five people stood with various signs protesting Stern's school policy and the merger. DON'T CLOSE OUR PUBLIC SCHOOLS. UNJ IS A PUBLIC RESOURCE. They grunted at Martin as he passed, as if he was the enemy. He smiled in return.

Martin had to get buzzed into the office like he was visiting someone's apartment. When he announced himself, there was a long pause before the door buzzed. He climbed a rickety set of stairs to the second floor. The door at the top of the stairs had Stern's name etched in it. Martin wondered how long it would take to scratch that off if he ever got voted out of office.

A receptionist sat behind the desk. Her lipstick was smeared and her hair was a bit out of sorts. She had tried to pull it back into a ponytail, but some of the strands were free from the band. Martin waited for a welcoming smile that never came.

"May I help you?" she asked. Her nose was suddenly buried in a stack of papers.

"I'd like to speak to Senator Stern, please."

"Do you have an appointment?"

Martin presented his badge.

"You're well out of your jurisdiction, officer."

"Detective, and I still need to talk to him."

"What's this in regard to?"

Martin had mulled this question over as he'd driven this morning. No lie seemed like it was going to work. The best he came up with had to do with the merger.

"I want to know how New Brunswick and Rutgers are going to benefit from this merger."

"I believe I can answer that," the receptionist said. "It doesn't have anything to do with Rutgers."

Martin sighed. He didn't want to do it this way. "Go back there and tell him I know Jeanne Baker."

"Detective, he's very busy. And he doesn't take unannounced visitors."

"Just tell him."

She rolled her eyes and reached for her intercom. Then stopped. Instead, she stood up, smoothed her skirt, and walked through the door behind her desk. Martin could hear muffled voices going back and forth. The deeper one spoke very quickly. Her voice came in short, clipped sentences.

The receptionist came back out and pulled the door closed.

Her smile was tighter than the band holding her hair back.

"He's on the phone. He'll be with you in a few minutes."

"Great," Martin said. He would wait this out.

He sat in a plastic chair, like the ones kids sat in at grammar school. Taking out his phone, he texted Leonard Baker, asking if he'd heard from Jeanne yet. It was a daily ritual now. The first two days he'd done it, Leonard responded with "I wouldn't tell you that." Now he didn't even respond at all. But it made Martin feel like he was doing something, so he kept it up.

Fifteen minutes passed. Martin said, "Long phone call."

The receptionist didn't look up. Said, "Politics. Important work."

"That your stock answer?"

She didn't respond. It'd been happening to Martin so much lately, he thought he should be getting used to it. The hair on the back of his neck still stood up.

He got through level 147 of Candy Crush on his phone. One of the young cops busted his balls about that game every day. "You can't figure out your email, but you can play Candy Crush."

"Go be an Angry Bird somewhere else," was Martin's reply.

The response was met with mostly silence. Someone used an app to play a cricket sound on their phone. He couldn't banter with the young kids anymore. Didn't mean he was going to stop trying.

His phone buzzed. It was a text. He checked the ID, it wasn't Leonard Baker. It was his boss.

I need to see you in my office this afternoon. Then a second text. *I don't care if you have Ebola. Get here.*

His cheeks burned red, and he gripped the phone tight. The shaking returned hard. And he thought he was over that nonsense.

The receptionist's phone rang. She picked it up and said no, then paused. Then she said yes. The smile wasn't as tight now.

"The senator will see you now," the receptionist said.

"Of course he will."

Martin stood up and walked to the office door. He stopped,

his trembling hand on the doorknob.

"Do you like your job?" he said to the receptionist.

"I do."

"So did I."

"That's nice."

"Don't dip your pen in the company ink," Martin said.

"Excuse me?" There was a bite in her voice.

"Your hair is all out of place. Your lipstick is smeared. I'm surprised all your buttons are correct. And you boss left you out here to dry. He wasn't nice enough to tell you. And isn't Senator Stern twice divorced? Must be a great guy. The *Star-Ledger* would love a story like this."

The receptionists hand went to her lips. "How dare you?"

Martin shrugged.

Before she could respond, Martin opened the door and walked into Stern's office. The senator was sitting behind his desk, hands folded in front of him. He looked like a schoolmarm.

"How are you, detective?" Stern's voice was the epitome of ice.

"Not as good as I was twenty minutes ago."

"That's a shame."

"Let's chat."

Stern nodded. "I understand you're friends with a former colleague of mine."

"According to her, you've caused her some stress."

"If we're talking about the same person, I'm pretty sure she passed away some time ago."

Martin shook his head. "Let's stop this crap and get down to it."

The senator laid his hands flat on the desk. His ear twitched.

"What are you getting at, detective? Come out with it."

Martin walked over to the couch against the wall. He sat.

"I think you're the one who has to do the talking. Tell me all of it."

CHAPTER
THIRTY-NINE

Baby steps.

That's what Donne's life was now. Baby steps. He could push himself, covered in sweat, to cross a room. But it took twenty minutes. And Luca had to help him back to bed. His legs felt like sandbags, barely getting off the ground and then smashing back into the tile as he tried to keep his balance.

His shoulder was stiff, but the chest wound hurt. Hot iron seared across his pecs and barbs dug into his abs. It made air hard to come by, and breathing was the worst part of his day.

Donne still couldn't get his left arm over his head. He was able to lift it about six inches off his hip. The doctor hadn't come to see him in what seemed like forty-eight hours, and that was bothersome. Maybe Stern and company just wanted him healthy enough. But Donne knew if he didn't get help and physical therapy, he might never have movement again.

The first time Luca saw Donne try to lift his arm, he said, "I don't know how you're going to beat me one-on-one if you can't keep your hands up."

Donne grunted in response. He was curious about Luca. His reaction to Donne's accusations were minor. Yeah, he acted pissed at first, but now he had calmed to the point where he was acting like nothing had happened.

That didn't sit well with Donne. It's tough to plan an escape when you can barely walk. It's tough to plan an escape when you don't know where you are. Donne thought he could get outside no problem. But after that, what next? There was enough traffic passing by that he thought maybe he could flag down a car.

After Luca helped him back into bed, Donne asked, "Do you have my cell phone?"

Luca laughed.

Donne said, "Worth a shot."

"You don't get reception down here anyway."

"Then how are you in touch with Stern?"

"I said *you* don't get reception. iPhones suck. I have a Droid. I can talk to anybody anytime."

Donne exhaled. "Can I borrow your phone?"

"I think you're delusional."

"Probably a sign I'm getting better." Donne settled into his pillow. "Let me ask you something."

Luca shook his head. "You already asked enough."

"Are you married? Girlfriend? How the hell are you able to stay here, five days straight, never leaving? You just sit around, watch TV, and shoot hoops all day."

"All part of the life," Luca said.

Donne tried to wrap that around his mind. A step slow, he kept reminding himself. He was still a step slow.

"Gangbanger?" That didn't seem right.

"Give me a break. No class there. No class." Luca waved his hand at him.

"Who are you, Luca?"

"If I had my way, you wouldn't be here right now. I don't want you to know me. So shut up, before you get yourself in more trouble."

"All right, all right. I'm sorry," Donne said. He didn't want to take it too far and set off Luca's inner alarm. The guy was willing to talk a bit. Donne needed to allow that. "Let me sleep, then."

Luca nodded and Donne shut his eyes. There was no sound for what felt like a few minutes. Donne tried to regulate his breath and make it seem like he was sleeping. He felt like a kid trying to get out of going to school.

Donne heard footsteps that faded. When he opened his eyes, Luca was gone. Probably to the TV room in the back.

Donne lay there, letting it all roll through his head. After a moment, he heard talking. Not TV talking, but Luca. Donne tried to focus in on the sounds, make out the words. Luca was clearly using his superior Droid. He hadn't heard conversations before, and had assumed Luca had been communicating with Stern through texts.

"Hey, baby," he heard. It was like trying to eavesdrop on someone in a library.

"No, no. It's gonna be okay."

Come on, Donne thought. Give me something.

"Marie, I told you it's going to be fine. This is going to pay off, I promise."

The gears started to link up and click together.

"If I do this, we're gold, baby." Luca coughed. "Uncle Tony would be proud of me."

There was silence for a few minutes. At first, Donne thought Luca had hung up.

"I'm not my uncle. I'm not stupid, babe. Keep it small. I'm not going to try to blow up New York just so I can be the boss. This is enough."

And finally, Donne got it. It took him way longer than it should have. The Italian mob of New Jersey had been a black hole for the last year or two. Donne tried to follow some of it, but the news was scattered.

After the lead New Jersey guy—Tony Verderese—tried to take a run at New York last year, and then died in the process, the FBI was happy. The mob was shattered in both states. A power loss. Donne wasn't sure who stood up to fill that void, but someone must have.

"What do you mean 'asking about me'?" Luca's voice echoed off the high ceilings. "What did you tell her?"

Get some sleep, Donne told himself. *Rest now, you're going to need your strength.*

"I knew Stern was wrong. We should have killed her. He *let* her ride in the van. And then he *let her go.*"

Donne's eyes snapped open. He was talking about Kate. The barbs in his stomach morphed into butterflies and acid. He needed to sleep, now.

"I'll take care of her."

The room tilted left, and Donne felt like he was drunk. He squeezed his eyes tight and tried to right himself. He dug his hands into the mattress and his shoulder lit up again.

"No. No, you did the right thing. I love you, babe."

Donne realized, through the blinding pain in his shoulder, that he had no other choice. Whatever else happened, he needed to get out of here.

Tonight.

CHAPTER
FORTY

Usually, the "Tell me all of it" threat worked. Of course, for Bill Martin, it worked on junkies and scared college kids. The tension in his voice, the unflinching stare, the fact that his targets had been sitting in an empty room for nearly three hours before he finally got to them.

They were ready to spill the beans.

But not Henry Stern, a politician long practiced in the art of, well, politics. It was Martin who felt strung out, still thinking of the text from his boss, the timing of it.

"There's nothing to tell," Stern said. "I haven't seen Jeanne Baker in a long time."

Martin leaned back in his chair and tried to think of the right question. A subtle one that would lead Stern to say too much.

"Six years ago, Jeanne Baker died in a car accident."

Stern nodded. "I believe the police report said her body was burned so badly, they were unable to recover it. They had to get DNA from a tooth."

"Dental records," Martin said. "How do you know that?"

Stern spread his hands. "I had just become a state senator. I had friends in the department. I asked around."

"What did you and Jeanne work on together at Rutgers?"

"We were in different departments."

Outside the protesters had started up a chant. It was said

in a sing-song, but the words were muffled by the walls of the building. If Stern heard them, he didn't react.

"So how did you know each other?"

"We worked on the same campus. We crossed paths." Stern looked down at his desk, then back up.

Martin sighed. "Come on, Henry. We're talking one of the biggest colleges — excuse me — universities in the country. You don't just 'cross paths' with people."

"You're right," Stern said. "We did work together on a few projects."

"Like what?"

Stern pursed his lips, and his nostrils twitched. "We worked on how public education ties into political science. Local governments, taxes, and whether the public education system works."

"Oh. Is that all?"

Stern leaned forward. "You can find our research in the stacks of Alexander Library. Do you want directions?"

The senator's phone rang, and Stern held up a finger. He picked it up and told his receptionist he was fine and Mr. Martin would be leaving shortly. After he cradled the phone, Stern raised his eyebrows as if to say, "Are you finished?"

"You left Rutgers shortly after working with Ms. Baker, didn't you?"

"I ran for office."

"What prompted that decision?"

"I've told the story many times."

"Once more would be great," Martin said.

"After Jeanne and I completed our research, I decided I want to effect real change. I wanted to end the waste of taxpayer money in our state."

"Uh-huh," Martin said. "If I remember correctly, you worked with our esteemed governor to cut pensions and health care in education."

"Right. One of our finer accomplishments."

"I'm sure some people would disagree." Martin didn't mind when they went after education. But when they went after cops, it got annoying. "And now you're embroiled in this University of New Jersey and Ben Franklin College thing."

"Rutgers is New Jersey's big public research university. Every state needs one. But now, if we can merge UNJ with Franklin, and create a larger private university, think of what it what it can do for our budget. Your taxes."

Martin nodded. "I'm sure you'll find a use for the money. I'll ask you flat out: What does Jeanne know about you?"

"I don't know what you're talking about." Stern looked at his watch. "I'm afraid I gave you a good chunk of my time, but I have appointments to keep."

"I don't like you, Mr. Stern."

Stern nodded. "That's a shame. I shouldn't have to answer your questions."

"I'm a cop." Martin stood up and pushed his chair in.

"Are you?"

Martin shook his head at the strange question. "For the record, you didn't really answer my questions anyway."

"I'm good at what I do," Stern said.

He reached across his desk and shook Martin's hand. The grip was limp and sweaty. Martin then noticed a bead of sweat on Stern's lapel. The air-conditioning was pumping in the room, but this guy was sweating.

Martin winked at him before leaving the office.

CHAPTER
FORTY-ONE

The drive back to New Brunswick was gridlocked with slow traffic, which did nothing for Martin's trembling hands. But he got to the station eventually, even hitting several green lights in a row on Route 18 in East Brunswick.

He needed a break in this case. He needed to find Jeanne. There wasn't time for a meeting at the station, but he couldn't come up with a good reason to skip it. He missed the office anyway, the bustle, the jokes—hell, the coffee. He needed to stop in and check his mail, check his files. Maybe see Russell Stringer, especially after the Ebola text.

He could explain his absences.

As he hit the button on the elevator, he took a deep breath. After this was over, he was going to a doctor. Time to get the shakes checked out. It had to be nothing, just too much caffeine for a guy his age. He wasn't sleeping well at night either.

That was it.

The elevator doors opened and two of the younger cops stepped out. They nodded his way.

One said, "Hey, look who it is."

Martin nodded back, but didn't retort. Thirty seconds later, he was walking down the hall toward Stringer's office. His hands were in his pockets, and he felt like a kid on the way to the principal's office.

Stringer saw him coming and got out of his chair. He stepped around his desk and went to the door.

"Get in here," he barked, though the volume was low.

Martin obeyed.

"You're late," Stringer said after he closed the door.

"I didn't know I was expected at a certain time."

"As soon as possible."

Martin debated bringing up the traffic, but decided it wouldn't help. Even with his hands in his pockets, he was sure Stringer could see the shakes. Probably looked awkward. He went to the chair across from the desk.

Stringer said, "Don't bother. This will be quick."

Martin sat anyway. The sounds of the office, a TV playing, phones ringing, and some chatter were muffled by the shut door. He was on the outside of it all.

"We're cutting our budget. Dead weight," Stringer said. "We're letting you go."

"You can't do that," Martin said. "The union—"

Stringer shook his head. "You can talk to the union, but they're not going to help."

"I—" Martin wished his hands weren't shaking so hard. He wished his cheeks weren't burning.

"The union really stuck their neck out for you back when Donne turned everyone in. You were the only one who *kept* a job. Not this time."

"I worked in parking and transportation."

Stringer leaned against the wall and crossed his arms. "It was a job. But now it's time to move on."

"I'm not ready." Martin's heart could run a mile in four minutes. "I'm two weeks away from a pension."

"You've been out a week. No doctor's note. You don't even look sick. You've just been out." Stringer crossed his legs at his ankles. "If this job is so important to you, why aren't you here?"

"You don't understand."

"No," Stringer said, shaking his head. "I don't." He walked over to his desk. After leaning behind it, he came up with a cardboard box.

"Layoffs?" Martin asked. "Who else?"

Stringer slid the box across his desk. He didn't say anything.

"Who else?" Martin asked again. "I want to know so we can all go to the same bar and talk trash about you."

"None of your business."

Then the pieces started to click together. Stern said something about him not being a real cop. The receptionist kept telling Martin that Stern was on an important phone call. The incoming text from Stringer just seconds later. Too coincidental.

"It's just me, isn't it?"

Stringer's eyes darted toward his phone and then back to Martin. "Listen, Bill, there's nothing we can do."

"Were you ordered to do this?"

"You need to get your stuff and leave. I'll have Cantrell escort you."

"God damn it, Russell. Be straight with me. Henry Stern put you up to this, didn't he?"

Stringer shifted his jaw back and forth. His gaze met Martin's. As he stood, he opened and closed his hands.

"You have an hour."

"Jesus Christ, Russell. Don't you understand? That guy is a piece of garbage. I'm working on something big."

Stringer's eyes went wide. "Working on what? Henry Stern is not in your jurisdiction. That's a fireable offense."

"Damn it."

Martin wanted scream and shout. He wanted to cause a scene. Instead, he reached out and grabbed the cardboard box and pulled it into his lap.

"Severance?" he mumbled.

"HR has it set up for you."

"Already? I'm just finding out about this now."

"You've been out for five days."

Stringer hit the intercom buzzer on his desk. Behind them his door opened. Martin turned to see Officer Cantrell waiting. When he met Martin's eyes, he shrugged.

We do what we gotta do.

"It's fair, Bill. You'll get by with it." Stringer's voice was soft. "And go see a doctor. Christ, Bill. You have to take care of yourself."

"Fuck you," Martin said.

He got up and went out the door. Without waiting for Cantrell, he walked to his office. Two people said hi to him, but Martin ignored them. If he felt like he was on the outside while sitting in Stringer's office, he felt like he was miles away now. The chatter—the din of the office—was an echo.

The feeling was familiar. When the Donne trial was going on and the New Brunswick PD was shutting down the NARC department, Martin thought he'd thrown his career away for sure. At the time, he didn't know Donne was trying to save Martin's job, keeping him out of the case. And he had thought the union didn't give two shits about him.

Turns out they had, and were able to keep him a part of this thing.

Now, though, it was over.

And he didn't have Jackson Donne to blame.

No, Donne was dead.

Now Martin had to turn his hate toward Henry Stern.

CHAPTER
FORTY-TWO

Luca was asleep.

At least, as far as Donne could tell, he was out. The TV had been turned off, and he'd called his girlfriend one last time to get her to go over the conversation again. Donne didn't pick up much more. The church was dark. Some moonlight sprinkled through the stained glass windows, but that was it.

It was now or never.

He guessed it was after midnight, but time had long changed from actual numbers to "night" and "day," his inner clock lost to sleep and haze.

Donne pushed himself up, and was excited to feel no pain. Stiffness he could deal with—it would slow but not stop him. The pain would halt him in his tracks. He got to his feet and looked around to regain his equilibrium. He found his center, and then eyed up the basketball net. The exit was on the complete opposite side of the room.

After turning, his chest and shoulder whined at him. Clearly, they wanted him to stay in bed. One foot in front of the other. Walking across the church wasn't going to be easy. He'd gotten used to leaning on the bed or Luca for help. This time it was all on his own.

As he stepped, dust kicked up around him. His nose itched and he wiped at it to keep from sneezing. That would be the worst way to get caught, a sneeze. Yesterday, some dust got to him, and after the sneeze, he thought he chest wound would tear back open.

His foot landed awkwardly, and he tightened his muscles to keep from falling. Suddenly, amid the cloud of kicked up dust, his chest was on fire. His shoulder tightened when he tried to reach up and rub his chest wound, and he felt paralyzed.

Donne regained his balance, gritted his teeth, and tried to think the pain away. The more he moved, he thought, the more it would fade.

Another step.

The large wooden double doors had to be close to 100 yards away. At the pace he was moving, he'd get there by dawn. By that time, Luca would be up and Donne would be dragged back to bed.

Maybe it was better to stay. Heal.

No.

Could not stay here any longer.

Luca was going to kill Kate before he could get better.

The doctor hadn't shown up in days. They were just going to let him rot here. Senator Stern said they needed him, but never told him why. They kept Donne alive though, so there had to be a reason.

Just not one that was important enough to stay here and figure out.

Donne kept walking. He was starting to find his rhythm. Maybe it was like running. The way sweat seeped from his pores, they seemed to have a lot in common. Find a rhythm and even someone injured could get moving.

The doors looked real now, thick wooded frames with big iron handles. The dust cleared, and it was like someone changed the channel to HD. They were closer. Donne reached out with his good arm, but still couldn't touch them.

Keep moving, keep pressing.

His body was soaked, and he realized he was still shirtless and shoeless. His feet were dry and crusty, covered in dust. The way this place hadn't been cleaned, it'd been sheer luck he fought off that infection.

The light at the end of the tunnel. The doors were so close, he almost allowed himself to believe he was going to make it. How long had he been walking? The glimmer of the moon had certainly moved, illuminating different areas of the church floor.

His chest throbbed, a bass drum beat of a marching band tune. Donne tried not to groan or grunt, but he was sure some sounds slipped out. Every time he made a noise, he paused, waiting to hear Luca's panicked footsteps headed his way. They never came.

Reaching out, his fingers grazed the metal handle. One more step, that's all that was left. His breathing was ragged. He took that step and wrapped his right hand around the handle.

And for the first time, he realized the door might be locked. This effort was for naught. He pulled. The door gave way. A salty summer breeze wafted into his face. He stepped out on to the stairs and eased the door shut behind him. It clicked closed, didn't slam.

Fighting to catch his breath, Donne looked around.

The pain was background noise now. He was free. In front of him, across an empty street, were large beach houses. If he looked down the road, he could see sand dunes. He was two blocks from the ocean.

Leaning on the handrail, he took the concrete stairs. One. Catch his breath. Two. Catch his breath. Three. He was huffing and puffing by the time he reached the sidewalk.

The hint of sunshine came up over the ocean. Morning was here.

He took more steps, trying to get to the street corner, trying to see the street sign. Figure out where he was and how he could get home.

The corner wasn't far, and he stumbled to it. He caught himself on the street sign and looked up.

Baltimore Avenue.

He ran the street through his head, trying to figure out why it was so familiar. A childhood vacation with his sister and mother. Sunset Beach.

Cape May.

Untouched by Hurricane Sandy.

And about as far from northern Jersey you could get without leaving the state.

He leaned on the street sign, trying to hold himself up. His muscles were tight and sore, and he was soaked. Breathing was hard. His wounds played a rock song. Tears stung his eyes.

A car screeched to a halt in front of him. Donne looked up, hoping to see a police car or a friendly face.

But when the door opened, he saw neither.

Instead, he faced Henry Stern.

He smiled at Donne.

"Little early to be out for a walk, Mr. Donne?"

Donne let go of the street sign and dropped to the grass at his feet.

CHAPTER
FORTY-THREE

Gravel shards dug into his stomach as Luca pushed him forward. Warm red liquid mixed with sweat and ran down his chest. Needling pain pierced up and down his skin. The breeze cooled his back until Luca gave him another slap, the hand burning him on impact.

The morning sun peaked, illuminating the grass and sidewalk. Lawn sprinklers sputtered in the distance. No one was on the road this time or morning, no dog walkers, bikers, or joggers. Or, if there were, Luca and Stern didn't seem to care.

Donne was pushed back into the church. The smell of sea salt gave way to soaked wood.

His body was on fire. Nerve endings screamed for relief. He tried to catch his breath and will his body to relax, but he couldn't. As soon as he hit the church floor, he curled up into the fetal position. Someone kicked him in the ribs, and he screamed out. His eyes went wide, and he caught an image of Jesus reaching out from the stained glass window. The imagery and timing would have made him laugh if it didn't hurt so much.

"You goddamn prick," Luca spat. "I knew you were trouble."

"Shut up, shut up, shut up," Stern said.

Luca kicked Donne again. Air left his body in a rush. His

vision blurred and he tasted copper in his mouth. The dust that had slowed his escape earlier, now spread along his right side.

"I said let me talk to him." Stern pushed Luca out of the way.

The senator crouched down in front of Donne. His ankles were tanned, but when the hem of his pants lifted, it revealed pale skin.

"Is this worth it?"

Donne tried to nod and say yes. Instead he blinked and coughed.

"Should I give you a minute?"

Rolling on to his back, Donne stared at the Tudor ceiling. Wooden braces held it together. They were decorated with twisting golden designs. Donne wondered if they were supposed to represent the crown of thorns, but more regal. Still, he tried to will the pain away.

"I apologize for Luca acting a bit rash," Stern said. "He's overreacting." Luca grunted something, but Stern held up a hand. He rolled his hand at his wrist while he searched for words. "He's a go-getter. This is a big opportunity for him. You don't find that much in the younger generation anymore. They feel too entitled. Luca wants it."

Air came a bit easier to Donne now. It felt like the muscles in his chest were being untied. He reached for the wound in his chest and put pressure on it. The pain spread away from the wound like ants after their hill had been kicked over.

"Feeling better?" Stern scratched at the mole on his right cheek. "Let's talk."

"About?"

"Why you don't trust us. I saved your life." Stern words were conversational, as if they were at a Sunday afternoon barbecue.

The ants now crawled under his skin, skittering up and down. Donne tried to picture the last time he spoke to Jeanne before she "died." It was a moment he tried to bury deep within himself, push away into the dark recesses of his mind. Alcohol helped that mission.

"What about Kate?"

Stern rolled his eyes. "You dumbass romantic. I promised you she's not in trouble."

Luca replied, "You're making a mistake."

Donne was too busy fighting the pain through his body off to ask what he was talking about.

Stern turned toward Luca. "What are you talking about?"

Luca adjusted his jaw before speaking. "His girlfriend is asking around about me. You let her go free."

Stern shook his head. "I'll take care of it. Don't you worry."

Donne coughed. Changed the subject. "If I can help you, why is he beating the crap out of me?"

"You tried to escape," Stern said. "Cost of doing business."

"Listen," Donne said.

"Get back into bed." Stern tapped Donne's head with his forefinger. "I'm sure you're going to see my side of things."

Donne exhaled and tried to sort out what the hell he was talking about. The sound in his ears was funny, sometimes fast, sometimes slow, like someone was fiddling with the fast-forward button in his skull.

"Then again," Stern said, "you have been through a traumatic event. You need to rest." He grabbed Luca by the arm and dragged him away. "Don't talk about this sort of thing in front of him."

But Luca looked over his shoulder at Donne and yelled, "She should be dead. I won't let you make this mistake. The other girl too."

"Come with me," Stern growled.

Their conversation faded. Donne lay on his back, trying to catch his breath, willing the pain to go away.

It took a long time.

CHAPTER
FORTY-FOUR

M artin didn't have a headache from drinking. He stopped in Tumulty's for one tumbler of scotch and then went home and went to bed. The headache he woke up with was different. It wasn't pounding at his temples, instead stretching up the back of his neck to the top of his head.

After showering and dressing, he popped four Advil, poured coffee into his travel mug, and hit the road. By the time he reached Union Beach, the headache still hadn't passed. It felt like someone at the small of his back was tugging on a string attached to his skull. He rubbed his eyes and got out of the car.

Eileen was waiting for him at the front door.

"You should have called me about this days ago," she said. She exhaled. "You should just call me."

Martin scratched his chin. "I've been preoccupied."

He didn't want to admit it had slipped his mind. Maybe Stringer was right and something was wrong with him. The world was fuzzy around him; everything felt a hair off. The only thing in focus to him was Jeanne, but he was making too many mistakes, not following trails correctly.

Making too many mistakes.

Stress was leading to distraction, and that brought him too many mental errors.

They went into Eileen's computer room. She took a seat

behind the desk; he leaned against the wall. The room smelled like burnt toast.

"I started checking out the Bakers' phone numbers and Internet reports. I went all the way back to the beginning of the week." Eileen shook her head. "Nothing jumped out at me. They get a ton of telemarketer calls and spam email. A cousin from Texas emailed them."

Martin stepped away from the wall. "I didn't know they had a cousin from Texas."

Eileen clicked the keys, and an image of a man Sarah's age popped up on the screen. "This is him. I searched the IP already."

"Could it have been Jeanne writing the email?"

Eileen clicked a few more keys and brought up the email. "They don't do a good job protecting their account."

The email was vague and filled with Texas references. The barbecue he'd eaten the night before sounded good. If it was Jeanne, she had disguised an update with banality. For an instant, he thought about searching Travelocity for plane tickets. Dismissed the idea after thinking about the risk. A trip to Texas takes time, and if Jeanne wasn't there, that time would be spent while she was getting farther away.

Less than a week since she disappeared. But still, in that time, they could be anywhere.

"Did you check airports?"

Eileen nodded. "Do you think I'm incompetent?"

"For the money I'm going to be paying you, you better not be."

"This was what I was able to track down after two hours last night. Give me some time and I'll come up with something."

Martin patted Eileen on the shoulder. He left the room and went into the kitchen. The string attached to the back of his head kept pulling tighter. Finding a bottle of water in the fridge, he unscrewed the cap and took a long sip.

"Why is she so important to you?" Eileen was standing behind him.

"Because she's supposed to be dead." Martin finished the

water. "And she's not. And for a few hours, I had her in my arms. Things were different. The future looked different. And now she's gone again."

Martin could picture William playing with Jeanne at the kitchen table. But it wasn't her parents' table. It was his. They were both laughing so hard, Jeanne had to wipe a tear from her eye.

He had this scene playing through his head for days. He dreamt about it. He needed it.

"I'm sorry, Bill. But there's time. We'll find her."

He threw the bottle at her recycling bin. It rattled around the rim and fell off to the side.

"Leave it," she said.

"You should take care of this place."

Eileen shrugged. "I'd rather earn my money."

They hugged, then Martin wrote out a check. She reminded him not to make it out to Eileen Schaeffer, instead using her fake company's title: Toadstool Cooking. It sounded disgusting, but he did it.

She took the check and looked at it.

"I burnt toast this morning," she laughed. "Toast. But hell, people like to believe an old lady like me can cook. You know, I used to do this for you for free. Back when—"

"They probably think you can barely use an iPhone."

Eileen nodded. "I will be in touch. Promise."

Martin walked to the front door, and pressed the button on his key chain to unlock the door.

"You're a good cop, Bill," Eileen said. "Chasing this girl is a mistake."

He smiled. "Are you jealous?"

Eileen shook her head. "It's not that."

Martin shrugged. "We used to have fun, Eileen."

"We still could … if you were smart," she said. "I'll be in touch."

Martin walked to his car. As he drove up Route 18, he kept waiting for his phone to ring. For Eileen to tell him she found Jeanne. That call didn't come.

Not that day. And not the next.

THREE WEEKS later, Martin had all but given up. He'd tapped out all of his contacts, made enough phone calls, and received too many "I don't know"s. The tension headache and the shakes had gotten worse.

Still, he didn't make a call to the doctor. Instead he played the boring retiree.

Each morning he took a walk, then spent the rest of the day doing the crossword puzzle or watching SportsCenter. He was sick of hearing about the Yankees, about steroids, and about NFL training camps. But he kept it on anyway, mainly just to pass the time.

When his phone rang, he almost didn't catch it. He'd had it on vibrate, and it was muffled by the couch pillow. He grabbed it just in time, spilling coffee onto his carpet.

He picked it up, only to hear Eileen on the other end of the line.

"I think I found her."

PART III
STRONGER THAN THE STORM

Three Weeks Later

CHAPTER
FORTY-FIVE

Kate looked at the dresser in Jackson's apartment. The landlord had been in touch, asking if Jackson was going to pay his rent next month. That was when she dropped the "out of town" bit. Jackson was probably dead. She told the landlord she was going to start moving Jackson's things out.

After the meeting with Luca's girlfriend, everything dried up. Word must have gotten around. No one would speak to her. She'd call Stern's office and was told the merger was at the end of the week. Kate had absolutely no shot of being able to speak with him.

Monday night, after a 3 AM mental breakdown with full-on weeping, chest tightness, and muscle spasms, she wanted to give up. But, if Jackson was somehow alive, she couldn't. She'd keep calling, keep googling, keep pounding the pavement, as her dad liked to say.

But that wouldn't pay his rent in a week. And Jackson's landlord was ready to give up, find a new tenant.

With an army of garbage bags, three boxes of tissues, and the phone number for the Vietnam Vets clothing pickup, Kate climbed the stairs to Jackson's apartment. It would be at least two days of this. Her dad had given her the time off, as much as she needed.

But now, standing in front of his dresser, the smell of his

aftershave wafting in the air, she wondered if she could move on. Jackson had been murdered, and his body disappeared.

It wasn't supposed to be like this—no. They were supposed to be married in August.

Now she was trapped in his apartment with a pile of memories. She looked at the bed and remembered the first time they made love. He wasn't sure if they should; they'd only been on three dates. They were sitting on the couch making out like a couple of teenagers. He slid his hand under her blouse, hesitating at her navel. She groped for his belt. He stopped.

"Are you sure?" The words were a breathless whisper.

She laughed, kissed his neck, and brought him to the bed. Clumsily, he fumbled with her blouse and then her bra. She wasn't sure if it was the beer or the situation. But it got better after that.

The flash brought Kate to her knees. The sobs came in hard hacks, shaking her body to the core. She'd been here before, and she let it wash over her. When she was finished and caught her breath, she lay on her back and stared at the cracked paint on the ceiling.

The ceiling she awoke to as he made her scrambled eggs in bed on Easter. The ceiling she'd been bugging him to fix for months because he didn't need to lose his security deposit.

Sit up, she told herself. *You knew what was going to happen when you came here. Fight through it.*

Kate listened to herself.

Everyone around her told her it was too soon. That she needed to grieve and take her time. She didn't need to move on immediately. But Kate felt like she needed to continue going. To her, that was part of the process. Cleaning up was what you did when someone died. And the landlord had left her no choice.

The first thing to go into the garbage bags was the underwear. Boxer shorts and briefs for when he worked out. Socks that hadn't been balled together lay in his drawer unmatched. She tossed them all.

It was easy to get rid of his day-to-day clothes first. College and beer T-shirts, polo shirts. Jeans and shorts. Nothing that brought back strong memories. Kate tried to remember what Jackson was wearing the last time she saw him, but the details wouldn't come. She only remembered the blood.

Closing her eyes for a moment, she shook it off.

Once the vets came to pick up the clothing, she would have room to start setting aside what she wanted to keep and what needed to go. An hour and a half later, she had six trash bags full of clothes. She'd gotten rid of everything except his suit.

The paper she'd printed off the Internet was back in the living room, the instructions from and phone number for the vets. Her father used them all the time, like when he'd cleaned out the attic of stuff her mother said she wanted to keep but would never realize was gone. The vets were quick, her father said. Got rid of things before her mom was even home from work.

It felt like so long ago.

She fetched the paper and unlocked her phone at the same time. Before she could dial, she heard a scuffling sound outside the door. Footsteps maybe. The hair on her arms stood up.

The doorknob jiggled.

Instead of the vets' number, she punched in 911.

She saw the lock turn. Who the hell had a key to this place?

"Who's there?" she shouted.

Maybe it was the landlord. Maybe he'd heard her come in and was coming up to check if she was okay. If she needed help. Her finger hovered over the Call button.

"Who's there?" she said again.

The doorknob turned and the door swung open. And then, Kate almost fainted. Stars clouded the corners of her eyes and the blood drained from her face.

"I'm sorry. I should have called. But I couldn't. I'm sorry."

Kate was on her knees again.

Jackson Donne rushed through the doorway to her. He tried to catch her as she went down, but missed.

"I'm—I—what?" The words wouldn't come. The tears did, though.

He kneeled in front of her and pulled her into him. She

couldn't smell his aftershave, but the scruff on his face scratching against her cheek was familiar. He kept apologizing.

"You're not dead. I prayed and searched, but—" she said. "How are you not dead?"

"I got better," he said.

They stayed there for a long time. Questions and answers would come later. For now, she just wanted to hold him.

Kate didn't want to let him go. Her tears mixed with his on her cheek. They both pulled each other tight.

The room was silent, and that was exactly what Kate needed.

CHAPTER FORTY-SIX

"You've lost a lot of weight."

Donne shrugged. "Three weeks, no beer."

Kate leaned against him on the loveseat. Donne had his arm around her. They both let the silence sit. He was sure she had a lot of questions, but he liked that she wasn't firing them off rapid-fire. He hoped she wouldn't ask anything at all.

She kissed his cheek, and he pulled her in tighter. The smell of apple shampoo filled his nostrils, and he felt a tear drop onto his skin.

"I tried looking for you," she said.

"You can stop."

There were too many questions he didn't want to answer, too many he *couldn't* answer. Not yet, anyway. If he did, she would try to stop him, and that couldn't happen.

The apartment smelled like Lysol, the lemon freshness mixing with the must. The apartment had been closed up for nearly three weeks. If he had to guess, this was probably the first time Kate had been in it in that time as well.

"I got shot. My old partner shot me. But some people found me. They helped me."

"I found you in the warehouse," she said. "Then I lost you again. I tried, Jackson."

The words hung in the air. His apartment felt foreign to him, a relic. The garbage bags of clothes decorating the living room reminded him of a tomb. Except these things were waiting for him like the pharaoh's were. Kate had been packing him up. She was ready to move on.

"You can stop what you're doing. Stop asking around."

Kate sat up, and resting her hand on his chest. Right over the wound. It didn't hurt any more; all that was left was scarred flesh. He wondered if she felt it. Using his good arm, he took her by the wrist and slid it off of him.

"Jackson …"

Before she could go any further, he said, "I promise, I will tell you everything, but not now. Not yet."

The sentence fell flat. Her body stiffened, and she leaned back onto the couch.

"You can't do that. I thought you were dead for *three weeks*." She shook her head. "You're not going to do this to me. You didn't tell me about Jeanne, you just ran out. And now this?"

Donne pushed himself off the couch. His shoulder whined in protest, as it always did. He went into the kitchen and got a glass of water and chugged it down. Back in the living room, Kate now had her knees to her chest, hugging them.

When he returned, he said, "You're right. It's not fair."

"Then tell me." Kate didn't look at him. Instead, she stared at the TV. It wasn't on.

"Kate, I'm going to have to go. This isn't close to over yet."

She slammed her palms on the cushion of the couch. Dust motes exploded. His feet felt rough suddenly. He wanted to shower.

"You aren't leaving. This is not how a relationship works."

"Not tonight. I'm not going anywhere tonight. But tomorrow morning …"

Kate's eyes went wide. She turned her gaze, and he felt it slice through him. "Jesus Christ," she said. "You didn't even expect to see me. You came here to your apartment."

"I have important things to do."

"Did you call your sister? You professors? Anyone?"

Donne's stomach knotted up. If he told her, she'd be a part of this too. And he couldn't do that to her. He wasn't going to put her at risk.

"No one knows, Kate. Not yet."

"Why not? How many times can I ask?" She spoke as if her jaw was rusty. He neck was tense. Her eyes were red, but there were no tears.

The apartment felt cavernous. Had she taken down the pictures, or had he just never hung any? The usual beer bottles, dirty dishes, and old magazines were gone. His schoolbooks had been put away. Every piece of himself was gone, wrapped up in trash bags.

She caught him looking around. "Casper didn't want to wait anymore. I didn't know what else to do. "

"You needed to keep moving," he said.

Kate didn't answer. She didn't need to.

When he thought Jeanne was dead, how long did he wait to clean up? Her parents helped throw everything out. They decided what to save and what to destroy. All he did was drink beer and watch. Occasionally, he'd fold some clothes and bag them, but even that hurt.

This wasn't Kate's fault. And he couldn't blame her for being angry.

"Tell me what's going on, Jackson." She stood up.

Donne stood there, fighting the urge to speak. He blinked once. Twice.

"I'm out of here."

She turned and headed to the door. Her hand froze on the knob.

"There has to be a reason for this, Jackson. A damn good one. This isn't who you are." She shook her head.

"It's who I've always been," he said.

"You can change. I've seen you change."

He didn't speak.

"Last chance," she said.

Donne didn't stop her from leaving. It was better this way. A relationship could be mended, but what he had to do couldn't wait. Kate would understand. When it was all out in the open, she would understand. And she would come back.

But there wasn't time for that now. Time was short. He had to get back to work.

CHAPTER
FORTY-SEVEN

"Man, dead looks good on you, yo," Jesus said.

Donne, hands in his pockets, stared at the sidewalk. A few college kids walked by, passing a forty of Bud. It was that time before they had to be out of their off-campus apartments, but well after finals were over. He wondered how he would have done on his last final.

"I just figured, you know, since you ain't takin' my advice, you must be dead."

"Almost," Donne said.

Jesus pointed his chin at Donne. "Why you here?"

An elderly couple walked by, mumbling to each other. They were trying to read a computer printout. Donne got a glimpse of the Google Maps logo.

"How's Tracy?" Donne asked.

Jesus shrugged. "Why you here?"

Donne took a look around. There weren't any people around. Cars buzzed by them, heading toward the theater district. No one stopped to eye them up.

"I need a gun," Donne said. His chest burned as he spoke. The image of Bill Martin, arm around Jeanne, firing his gun, flashed through Donne's brain. He took a deep breath.

"No. You don't." Jesus turned and started walking away. "Go home, Jackson."

Donne jogged after him.

"Enough of this," he said. "I have money, and I'm not playing your games."

Jesus stopped walking. He shook his head. "No, man. This ain't you."

Donne felt his jaw working overtime, pressing his teeth together. "You have no idea. When I was a cop, I was the first one in the building."

Jesus laughed.

A cop car sped down George Street, sirens wailing. Donne froze. Jesus didn't even flinch.

"How much you got?" Jesus asked.

Donne showed him a stack of cash he'd retrieved from his apartment. Kate hadn't found it, and Donne was glad. She would have asked him what it was for. He never wanted to explain a situation like this to her.

Jesus flipped through it. Once it was in Jesus's hands, it didn't seem like as much as Donne had thought.

"I'll get you something." Jesus walked off again. This time, Donne didn't follow.

Fifteen minutes later, Jesus was back with a soft lunch cooler. He handed it to Donne, who almost dropped it because of the weight.

"Close-range revolver. Don't try to kill anyone from a block away." Jesus sucked his teeth. "You gotta look in their eyes."

Donne chewed on the inside of his lip for a moment. Then said, "That won't be a problem."

No one answered the door at Martin's apartment. He buzzed and buzzed before finally hitting all the buttons on his floor. Someone called down and asked who it was. Donne said he was UPS. The person told him to leave the package at the door.

No luck.

A rash of fall-type weather had broken out around New Jersey, and a cool breeze funneled down the street. Donne enjoyed it. After being trapped in a church for weeks, healing and training, the outdoors felt like a blessing. The sun filtered through the tree leaves, speckling the sidewalk. The air wasn't humid, a miracle during New Jersey summers. He wished he could stay outside all day and enjoy it.

There was, however, too much to take care of.

Back in his car, Donne watched the front door. Martin would have to return sooner or later. How long had it been since he'd staked something out? Three years? More? The world of private investigation still felt foreign to him. He was sure he was wide out in the open and would be spotted the second Martin got home. Didn't matter, though — he had to be here.

He needed to see Martin. It probably wouldn't be much of a wait anyway. This time of the morning, Martin was probably just out getting coffee.

Until then, Donne played with his iPhone. He checked Twitter, but found nothing interesting going on in the sports world. He played a game of Angry Birds, but got stuck. Then he checked his email.

They had sent him one. The hair on his arms straightened.

How is the real world treating you? Friday is coming.

Donne hit reply and sent a quick acknowledgment email. Things were moving quickly. It was already Wednesday.

The press conference to announce the merger between UNJ and Ben Franklin was going to happen, and there was no way to stop it. If someone had told Donne he was going to play a role in it three weeks ago, he wouldn't have believed it. But now, it was his only way to get back at them.

Donne opened the console in between the seats of his car. The snub-nosed revolver, serial number scratched off, gleamed in the sunlight.

By Friday, Donne would take care of everything.

CHAPTER
FORTY-EIGHT

Twice weekly phone calls. Each one from a different disposable phone, and lasting less than a minute. She hadn't heard them, but Eileen guessed they were check-in calls. Just Jeanne telling her parents she and William were okay. Bill believed that.

At first, Eileen didn't think much of the calls. Wrong numbers, pranks, that sort of thing happens all the time. But there was a pattern. The calls kept coming from one of three motels along the Pennsylvania–New Jersey border. There was one just outside of Clinton and two in towns Martin didn't recognize. They all circled around Route 78—the interstate highway that connected New Jersey to the Keystone State.

That's where Martin drove after getting the information from Eileen. He wondered why Jeanne wasn't being a bit cleverer. She switched motels every couple of days, but seemed to only vary it among three stops. Eventually someone would track her down.

Martin drove to the farthest hotel first. It was a Days Inn, ten miles over the border, just off the exit, and the last place from which the Bakers had received a call, according to the records Eileen had pulled up. He parked in the lot after circling it and seeing nothing suspicious, except a pool that needed to be cleaned. Leaves and dead bugs pocked the surface of the water. If the pool was that dirty, he dreaded seeing the sheets on the bed.

Jeanne had to be renting a car, though he was unsure how she got the money. It would be impossible to know if she was staying here without going inside.

The lobby was sparse. A long desk with an employee behind it. Tiled floors, a couch, two plants, and a setup for complimentary coffee. The receptionist smiled at him, and it was at that moment Martin had no idea what to say. Without a badge, he'd lost his most powerful weapon. There was no reason for this woman to talk to him, no question he could ask to get her to hand over information.

He pulled out his cell phone and brought up a picture of Jeanne. It was one he'd taken of her in the hotel room on Route 9, weeks ago. He pretended to be playing with an app but snuck a shot of her instead. It was blurry but would do the job.

"I'm looking for this woman. From what I understand, she's been staying here."

The receptionist looked at the picture for a moment, then said, "And who are you?"

Martin shook his head. "I'm a friend. She's been missing and I'm worried about her. Her parents got a call from her from this motel the other night. They asked me to drive out here."

The receptionist looked at the picture again and frowned. "I'm sorry. I don't think I can help you."

"Can't help me because you haven't seen her or can't help me because you don't want to?"

"Company policy, sir. I can't tell you anything."

"Listen, I'm a retired cop. That's why her parents asked me to come. She has a small boy with her."

"Sir, I—"

Martin held up his hand. As he spoke, his stomach curdled. "She is a drug addict. They're worried about the boy. They want to get her some help. It's almost kidnapping."

"I'm afraid you'll have to get the authorities involved."

The coffee was burning and the smell was nauseating.

"Didn't you hear what I said? I'm a cop."

"You said you were *retired*." The receptionist leaned in closer. "I'm sorry, sir. I would love to help, but this is my job. My only job. If I get fired, I'm not finding another one."

He blinked. The word *fired* brought him right back to Russell Stringer's office.

"Please. They don't want her arrested. They just want to know she's safe. That's why they asked me to come here. My experience. I'm a friend of the family. Just need to talk to her."

Leaning back, the receptionist looked at her computer monitor. She typed a few things. Martin waited, and hoped his begging worked some magic. It would make him feel better about pleading.

"I'm sorry, sir," the receptionist said.

"She's here, isn't she?" Martin nodded as he spoke. "And that's why you're not denying anything."

The receptionist took a deep breath. "If you'd let me finish, I haven't seen her in days. The kid is cute, though. And if it makes any difference, the last time I saw her, she didn't seem stoned. They were happy. Playing in the pool."

"Do you know what name she used?"

The receptionist paused, and Martin realized he'd pushed too hard.

"That's all I can tell you, sir."

Martin smiled. "That's enough."

THE SECOND hotel was more of the same. Tile floors, coffee, a receptionist who wanted nothing to do with him. He didn't get much in the way of a response this time. The receptionist wanted to call the cops the moment drugs were mentioned, but Martin stopped him.

"We only need the police if she's here," he said. "If you haven't seen her, there's no reason."

She hadn't been there in two weeks.

MARTIN'S HEART was hammering when he pulled up to the third motel. The Amaker Motel was about two and a half miles off 78, on the outskirts of Clinton. The town was known for its historic downtown area with small shops and boutiques. Great place for a walk on a warm summer evening.

But the motel wasn't even close to capturing that culture. It was rundown, with a crumbling parking lot. The building was two stories high, and you had to walk outside to get to your room. There was a pool that appeared to be clean. Only six or seven cars in the lot. Martin tried to guess which one was Jeanne's. None were marked as rentals, so he was out of luck on that account.

He wiped sweat off his brow before entering the lobby. A man in overalls stood behind the desk. There wasn't any complimentary coffee. A sign offered hourly rates. He took a deep breath. If Jeanne was here, she was desperate.

Again the phone, again the picture, again stonewalled. This guy didn't care that he was a former cop, and he didn't care that Jeanne could be a drug addict.

He shook his head and said to Martin, "I don't care what people do as long as they don't destroy the furniture."

"She's here, then?"

"Didn't say that. I'm just informing you of my policy."

Martin moved his jaw back and forth. "I'm a former cop."

"You said that."

"She has a kid with her."

"I know."

Martin wiped his face, then put his phone away. "I'm trying to help her."

"I've been in this business for a long time," the man behind the desk said. "Almost forty-two years. And one thing I've learned, a guy like me does not beat out Holiday Inn and stay in business if you don't take all comers. What do you think would happen to me if word got out that I'm talking to former cops and telling them about people who stay in my hotel? Hell, even if they're not staying, I can't give you any information. People will find out, and I will go out of business. And in this economy? That's just not going to happen."

Martin tried one more time to ask a question. He opened his mouth and was ready to beg, play the family card. Before he could get a word out, the man held up his hand and shook his head. Then he pointed toward the door.

"Let people do what they want to do," he said.

Martin slapped his thigh hard. He thought about cursing, swearing, and making a scene. This guy wouldn't call the cops on him. Whatever or whomever he was hiding was too important. But Martin was also pretty sure the guy would take steps to keep Martin from knocking on every door in the motel.

"Thank you for your time," he said through gritted teeth.

The man kept pointing at the door.

The parking lot was treacherous. He had to step over crumbled stone and potholes to get back to his car. Instead of walking over the broken asphalt, he decided to take the sidewalk that swung close to the pool. It wasn't perfect, but at least it didn't break under his feet as he stepped. He wondered how he didn't drop his suspension driving into the place. Maybe there was an easier exit.

As he walked, he heard a squeaking gate open and close. He looked up when he heard the voice—a familiar, feminine one—say, "Okay. But you can only go in for fifteen minutes. Then back inside for lunch."

"We've been inside all day, Mom."

"It's for our own good. Just for another week, I promise."

Martin looked toward the pool. She looked up at the same time. Jeanne and William were standing on the pool's edge, towels slung over their shoulders.

As soon as she and Martin made eye contact, she said, "Oh no."

"**W**hat the hell did you do?"

Marie Rapaldi stood at the door of Kate's apartment building and started screaming the minute Kate got out of her car. Marie took a step forward and almost tumbled into the shrubbery next to the door. Kate glanced around, expecting to see a crew of reality TV producers to storm the building.

Kate said, "What's the matter, Marie?"

"You're destroying my life!"

It had been weeks since Kate had visited Marie. Before Kate could get any closer to her apartment building, Marie regained her balance and shuffled over to Kate.

"I don't know what you're talking about, Marie," Kate said.

The woman jammed her index finger into Kate's chest. When she spoke, he breath could have melted tree bark.

"Luca and I were happy. We're on the verge of big, big things."

"What big things?" Kate asked.

"What big things?" Marie's voice was high and singsong. The attempt at mocking missed the mark when the s dragged out too long. "He was going to be in charge of this st-state. I was going to be Mrs. Gotti."

Oh.

Kate's fingertips tingled. "I—"

"Then you come along and he stops calling me. Tells me I'm a liability, and when things are copa—copa—copacetic, he'll call me back. I haven't talked to him in three weeks. I keep calling and he keeps hanging up. Won't even let his voice mail pick up." Her eyes welled up. "I miss him. My boo."

"Marie, I'm sorry. I was just doing my job."

Marie wobbled, then decided to sit down on the sidewalk. She wiped at her eyes, and makeup smeared across her cheekbones. Kate dug out a small package of tissues from her purse and handed them to Marie. It took her a few seconds to dig out a tissue because she had trouble with the little piece of tape that kept them in the plastic.

"You might be a nice lady," she sniffled. "But your job is ruining my life."

"If you tell me how, maybe I can help." *Come on, you drunk. Give me everything.*

"I don't know how." Marie wiped her nose. "All I know is Friday is circled on Luca's calendar. I asked him why once. He said then we're home free. This was just after Uncle Tony died. Luca was always on the phone. I thought it was people saying they were sorry. We're supposed to go to Seaside on Saturday."

And, with that, Marie turned her head to the left and vomited all over the sidewalk.

KATE CALLED Marie a cab and went inside. She hoped the cab would get there before a roaming cop found her. Kate wasn't ready to involve the police yet. Because what Kate was beginning to suspect meant anyone could be involved.

She opened the web browser on her computer again, brought up the UNJ website, and typed Luca's name into the employee search. Nothing. Kate tapped her nose for a minute.

She tried the Ben Franklin College site next. Again, nothing. Kate exhaled and gave herself a moment to think. Marie's drunken ramblings had laid the pieces out there. Kate just needed to put them together.

Friday was the merger press conference. Kate googled that.

The first lesson of law school, the first lesson her father gave when he hired her: Google is your friend. It was paying off these past few weeks.

There were several articles about the merger and the press conference. Most of them were about Senator Stern or the protests against the merger. There was one regarding the actual itinerary for Friday.

She scrolled through it. And then she decided it would be better to talk to someone at Ben Franklin College.

There was still a chance to save Jackson and bring him back to earth.

CHAPTER
FIFTY

Jeanne put her arms around William and started to turn back toward the hotel, but not before he saw Martin. He started to wave.

"Hey!" he shouted. "We're going swimming."

Jeanne shot him a look but relented.

Martin ambled up the way and opened the gate to the pool. By the time he got to them, William had already jumped in. Jeanne told him to stay in the shallow end, which elicited a groan, then some splashing and a giggle.

Martin sat in one of the vinyl chairs and waited. Jeanne joined him, brushed the hair out of her face, and said, "You found me."

"Way to state the obvious. Took three weeks."

"They didn't find me, though."

Martin shook his head.

"Unless you brought them."

Martin shook his head again. "I'm not sure how hard they're looking."

Jeanne cocked her head in his direction, then glanced at William. He was at the very edge of the shallow end, his back to them, staring off into the deep end. The sun reflected off the water into his eyes, so Martin turned back to Jeanne. He shouldn't have left his sunglasses in the car, but he was always misplacing them otherwise.

"Why wouldn't they be looking for me?"

Martin shrugged. "I'm not a cop anymore."

Jeanne started to say something, but he held up his hand.

"That said, I still found you. It took three weeks, but I tracked you down." Martin scratched his wrist. "Now imagine someone with the power of a state senator, with ties to people everywhere. He either knows where you are and doesn't care, or doesn't need to look."

A vehicle rumbled into the parking lot, and Jeanne visibly tensed. Her back went straight, and she quickly turned to look into the lot. Martin looked over his shoulder. It was a Coca-Cola delivery truck.

"That doesn't make any sense," she said. "As soon as I came back, they captured me. I went to confront him, in his office, and the next thing I knew —"

Martin smiled. "You went to confront him at his office. Why? Why now?"

"No, Bill." She looked at her watch, then at William. "Ten more minutes, buddy."

"Mom … you're busy. Twenty more." He disappeared under the water and then popped back up. A six-year-old with no fear and no swimmies; not bad, Bakers.

"Nine. More. Minutes."

Another groan, then again under the water.

"Did you tell him yet?" Martin leaned forward.

"You're not staying with us, so no. In fact, I think it's time you leave." Jeanne rubbed the corner of her eye. "I don't want to hurt him anymore than he's already been hurt. I don't want to confuse him."

"So you're just going to keep secrets the rest of your life."

The Coca-Cola guy opened the rear of the truck and started to pile boxes on to a hand truck. After each box, he tapped buttons on a scanner. No clipboard. Martin looked back at Jeanne.

"I'm not leaving until you tell me what's going on. Jackson is dead. Henry Stern or whoever clearly doesn't even think you're a threat anymore. Might as well just tell me. If it's a problem, I can take care of it. And then you can go back to a normal life."

"Why are you bothering, Bill?"

Martin ran through all the answers he could give, as if there was a Rolodex in his head. Ninety-nine percent of the answers weren't even true anymore. He picked the one that was.

"Because it's all I have left," he said. "No job. You're supposed to be dead, and at the very least you're off the grid. I have coffee and a crossword puzzle each day. That's it. I need to know what's going on here. Whatever it is cost me my job. It cost me you." He looked out at William. "And it cost me him."

"Bill …"

He raised his hand again. "Humor me. Please. This has gone on too long. Maybe we can still stop it."

Jeanne took another look at William. It was as if the kid had no idea they were even there. He'd submerge in the water, touch the bottom of the pool, and pop back up again. Then he'd swim over to the wall and kick off of it, leaving a small wake behind him.

"Henry Stern is about to become the most powerful man in the state."

"More than the governor? I find that hard to believe."

Jeanne said, "If you want me to tell it, you have to listen. Please don't interrupt. Six years ago, I got put on a project with Stern. Back when we were both at Rutgers. We looked into public ed versus vouchers. If private schools were better. It was around the time that movement was really starting to gain some footing. The research we did was important for the state. At least I felt that way."

Martin wanted to tell her that he remembered, but didn't interrupt.

"What we found was typical: There wasn't much difference between charters, private, or public school test scores. Charters and privates could kick the underachieving kids out and kind of goose their statistics, but that was about it. But Henry didn't take that really well. He thought for sure private schools, charter schools — for-profit schools — were the answer."

"Did that report ever get out?" Martin said before he remembered to shut up.

Jeanne shook her head. "It did, but I had to leak it to blogs and Internet sites. Never got to the mainstream press. Some education blogs picked it up, but no one really cared. Stern tried to bury the report. Got very, very nervous about it. Wouldn't tell me why. It was weird. Once we started to get the data and see the end of our research, he started to have panic attacks. He wanted to bury the report. Find other information, other research.

"One night, about a week before we were going to go live, Stern got a phone call as we were wrapping things up. He left the room to answer it. When he came back in, he was all pale. He excused himself and said he'd see me tomorrow. It wasn't like him. So I decided to follow him. He drove up to Jersey City and met with Tony Verderese."

Tony Verderese, head of the New Jersey mob. He tried to make a run at New York too, and nearly blew up the *Intrepid* because of it. And that play killed him.

"So you came back now? Now that the mob is basically gone in New Jersey?" Martin asked.

"Is it gone, Bill? Really gone?"

"Not really my department, but from everything I've heard—since Verderese died, the mafia stuff has calmed down. The FBI is thinking of saving some money and transferring it over into counterterrorism."

"And who do you think has the kind of influence to make that happen?"

Martin didn't say anything.

"Henry Stern was a big-time gambler. Sports, card games. I used to see him talking to the math professors trying to come up with a way to count cards. To them it was a goof, they laughed when he asked them. But you should have seen him storm out of the room when they wouldn't answer him."

"So he owed Verderese money?"

Jeanne nodded. "Big time. The next day, I confronted him on it. His only reaction? He told me I was dead. That I couldn't stop him."

"And that's when you came to see me. When you told me about William?"

She nodded again, then looked toward the boy. Now he was floating on his back. Piece of cake. Bill Martin still couldn't do that.

"And then I was gone. It didn't take much planning. It had to be quick. My parents knew people."

"They told me."

"I'm so sorry, Bill."

"So am I."

Martin neck burned hot and his muscles tensed. Twice he opened his mouth to say something but stopped. It didn't go unnoticed.

"Say it." Jeanne folded her hands.

"I could have helped you."

She looked up at the sky. "I was young. I was scared. I was pregnant. They would have killed you and me. They would have killed Jackson. I knew who Stern was tied up with. And I knew he wanted to make a run at state senate."

"How? If he was in such debt, how could he bankroll that?"

Martin took a deep breath and remembered the campaign. First the Rutgers merger, then promising to support public school teachers in the state. But Stern also ran on saving taxes, cutting property taxes. Bringing New Jersey back from the brink of bankruptcy. He played both sides of the political fence, and people ate it up. He won by a landslide.

"They did. He's their puppet, Bill."

"What was the first thing he did in office?"

"Open a series of charter schools. Who was in charge of them?"

"No idea."

"Some of Tony Verderese's guys. They ran money through them. He paid off his debt."

Martin didn't say anything.

"For-profit schools used to money launder for the mob."

"And nobody looked into this?"

"People *loved* what he was doing. Why look into a good thing?"

His next move was to support the governor's attack on public pensions. He got it through the senate. And taxpayers applauded. Then he worked on the Rutgers merger. Six years of fighting, and he finally got it through. And that's when, with little pushback, he brought up the new merger.

"What made you come back, Jeanne?"

"Think about it. Tony Verderese died. Days later, Stern announced the UNJ merger. Turning the school private."

Martin shrugged.

"Think what you can do with all the money. The donations, the scholarships. Football. Basketball. A college, if run correctly, is a ball of cash."

"Rutgers isn't. Rutgers is deep in debt."

"If they think they can make UNJ private, they think they can make a profit. And now that Verderese is dead, who is stepping up to make this work?"

"You think he's making a run to fill the hole?"

"I don't know, Bill. He probably has friends. He's a puppet. Has been since he left the army." Jeanne checked her watch. Time for William to get out. "I just know he can make a lot of money with this. Hidden money. Laundered money. It worked at the lower levels. Why can't it work here?"

"It didn't happen when he got elected."

"People would have noticed then. He had to garner more goodwill."

Martin shook his head. "The information you have. It's six years old. It's not going to stop him now."

"I don't care if it does." Jeanne set her jaw and stared over Martin's shoulder.

Martin shook his head. "Mob ties? Gambling debts? It's old news. He's already in office."

"Not my problem anymore."

Martin took a deep breath. "He punished you. Tied you up. Beat you up. He would have kept you there."

"I shouldn't have gone to talk to him, but I couldn't resist.

I thought it was over. He won. So I wanted to show him up."

Martin shook his head. "You fell in their lap. And he panicked."

"Friday's the big day. The merger will be announced. I guarantee at least three mob guys will be on the new board of governors. To keep an eye on the money."

Martin shook his head. "It won't happen," he said.

"Let it go, Bill. He won."

Martin rubbed his face. "I can stop him."

CHAPTER
FIFTY-ONE

When Martin didn't show up to his apartment after an hour, Donne had to move.

As he turned the wheel to pull into traffic, a needle stabbed through his left shoulder down into his fingertips. Physical therapy was still in order, but it had healed enough to move. That's why they let him go. He was functional and could serve his purpose.

Luca said it best, the day before he left. "Thank god you're a righty."

"It didn't help me in my professional baseball career," Donne said.

"And you still haven't played me in hoops." Luca nodded toward the basket.

"I don't even think I can take a shot."

Now Donne made it about ten miles on Route 18 when he spotted the tail. A blue Honda Accord had been about four car lengths behind him since New Street in New Brunswick. He probably wouldn't have even caught it if the driver hadn't changed lanes each time Donne did. He put his blinker on, moved into the left lane and accelerated, passing three cars before pulling right again. The Accord did the same.

Amateur.

He could lose this guy with barely an effort, except for one problem: He wasn't exactly sure where he was going himself. The route was tricky, and he didn't know Union Beach all that well. Circling back and forth would only serve to get him lost. He took the exit off Route 18 and pulled down a side road.

There was a long sheet tied to the picket fence of the first house he saw. In black marker someone had written HEY GOVERNOR, WE'RE PART OF THE SHORE TOO! RESTORE US! Donne slowed as if he was reading it. The car behind him passed him, leaving the Accord directly behind him.

Donne put on his hazards. The car didn't pass. Checking the rearview mirror, Donne couldn't make out the driver. The glare from the sun off the windshield made the glass opaque.

He pulled his car over to the curb, threw it in park, and got out. The Accord stopped and the passenger window rolled down. It was Luca.

"Let's talk. There's a park around the corner." He pointed to the basketball on his passenger seat.

The needles were now poking at his stomach. He got back into his car and followed the Accord around the block to an outdoor basketball court. It was empty. Luca got out. He was wearing basketball shorts, a tank top, and high-tops. Donne was just glad he had shorts and sneakers on.

Donne stepped on to the asphalt court, and Luca bounce-passed him the ball.

"Don't I have more important things to do?"

He took a jump shot from the elbow. The ball rattled halfway down, then popped out. Unforgiving rims. Luca rebounded it, backed out behind the three-point line and swished one.

"I want to make sure you're going to do it."

"Stern brought me back to life. I owe him."

Luca passed him the ball. "You warm?"

Donne shrugged and took another jumper from the free throw line. Swished it.

Luca said, "Your ball."

Donne took it at the top of the key and checked it. Luca got down in a defensive stance, and Donne went left. His shoulder and chest burned at the sudden movement. Luca reached in and tapped the ball away. He grabbed it and took it to the hoop for a lay-in.

"Winners out," Luca said. "We're playing to ten? Win by two. Three-pointers count as two. Everything back."

"Whatever."

Luca grinned. "Come on, you wanted this."

"You need me to do a job."

"Stern wants you to do a job." Luca checked the ball. "It should have been finished weeks ago."

He went right and Donne stepped in front of him, hands wide. Luca pulled up dribbling.

"You think Stern drives the bus?" Luca shook his head. He took a jump shot and swished it. "Two-nothing."

Luca took the ball out again. Donne's breath was ragged and his wounds stung. Sweat dripped from his hair. Luca checked the ball and drove directly at Donne, who stood his ground. They collided and Donne landed on his ass. Luca was down next to him. Donne heard the ball bouncing off to his right and sprang to his feet to chase it down.

He grabbed it at the three-point line as Luca got to his feet. Donne took two dribbles, then took a jumper. *Swish.*

"Nice shot," Luca said.

Donne checked the ball and went right. He drove to the hoop, and Luca stepped aside.

"Can I trust you?"

Donne, in the midst of going for a layup, heard the words and shanked the shot. The ball bounced off the back rim and into Luca's hands. He backed it out and took a two. *Swish* again.

"Four-nothing."

Donne caught his breath and said, "Does Stern trust me?"

Luca nodded.

"That's all you should need."

Luca checked the ball and took another shot from beyond the arc. He banked it in. Six-one.

As Donne went to retrieve the ball, Luca said, "You taste a little bit of freedom, and I want to know how you react to what Stern says."

"He's right." Donne passed the ball back. "Martin and Jeanne tried to kill me. They destroyed who I was for six years."

Luca nodded, then hit another two. "Eight to one."

They checked again. This time, before Luca could take the shot, Donne stepped up with an outstretched left. He blocked the ball and knocked it away. Luca stepped back to get into a defensive stance. Donne went right, and Luca backed up. Donne pulled up and hit a floating shot.

They reset. Donne took a two and swished it. Eight to five.

"Everyone gets a run," Luca said.

Donne was too out of breath to reply. He went left this time. Luca tried to go for the steal, but Donne blocked him with his body. He made a lefty layup.

At the top of the key, Donne took another two, and it rattled in. Tie game.

After the check, Donne tried to go right. Luca stepped up and threw an elbow into his chest, sending Donne flying. Luca grabbed the ball and took it behind the line. Before Donne could even get to his feet, Luca swished the three.

"Game," he said.

Donne brushed a few asphalt pebbles off his knees, and then rested his hands on them. His breath came back in fits and starts.

Luca came up to him, leaned in and whispered. "I guess you're not all the way back yet. Stern likes to leave a lot of loose ends. Do what you're supposed to and you and Kate won't be one."

LEANING AGAINST the driver's side door, Donne took some deep breaths. His shoulders felt heavy, and there was a dull ache in his lower back. Across the street was a convenience store. He went in and bought a Gatorade. He downed it in two gulps.

The last time he felt this way was the last time he was on a bender, just after Jeanne died. That exhausted, dehydrated, dull pain throbbing at the back of his skull. The heaviness weighing on the lids of his eyes, even though he'd gotten a full night's sleep. The dry mouth, to the point where it felt like his tongue was cracking.

But now, he hadn't drunk alcohol in nearly a month. And wouldn't until this was all over. He should call the *Guinness Book of World Records* people.

Luca was still on the court, taking jump shots. The bounce of the ball brought Donne back to the church.

Henry Stern stared at him and smiled.

"How do you feel today?"

Donne leaned back on the bed and tried to push the pain in his muscles away. The breakout attempt couldn't have been that exhausting; he was only walking. But it felt like he'd participated in an Ironman race.

"I need exercise," he said.

"We're going to get that for you." The state senator put a hand on Donne's good shoulder. "We're getting you healthy."

He handed Donne a glass of water. Donne took it and drank deeply.

"The people you aligned yourself with were all wrong," Stern said. "They are the losing side."

Donne didn't ask what he was talking about. Martin's gun erupting in flame flashed through his head. Jeanne had her arms around him when he did it. It was like James Bond movie poster, with Martin so stoic and calm. Three shots, no blinking, and Donne was down for the count.

"Jeanne is not your friend. Not your lover," Stern said. "Not anymore. Maybe she never really was."

Donne sighed and touched his chest. The bandage was wet and sticky. The wound must have reopened.

"Help me," Stern said. "And end up on the right side for once."

BACK IN the car, Donne wound through more side roads, noticing the gutted houses, the construction workers lifting full homes onto stilts and digging up foundations. No matter what the commercials said, New Jersey wasn't back yet. The shore was a lot like Donne: functional.

That was celebration enough, he guessed.

Finally, he tracked the house he wanted. The blue siding

with the white porch and stones on the front lawn. Donne opened the console and pulled out Jesus's revolver. He slipped it in the pocket of his cargo shorts, then got out of the car.

The stones crunched under his shoes as he approached the steps. He expected to feel his heart trying to tear itself from his chest. He expected to be sweating like a runner at the end of the marathon. But everything was normal, besides the caffeine jangling in his veins.

After he rang the doorbell, he could hear movement coming toward the door. Without thinking, he ran his hand over the outline of the gun pressing against his pocket lining. Hopefully, she wouldn't be looking for it.

The woman opened the door and turned pale.

"Hello, Eileen," he said. "I need to find Jeanne Baker."

CHAPTER
FIFTY-TWO

Kate waited in the hallway of Plunkett Hall, outside the office of public relations. She'd called ahead and identified herself as Myron's paralegal. She wanted to look into information about the merger, and invoked the senator's name. Her dad and Stern were friends, she said. They told her they would be with her as soon as they could, but when she got there, could she please just sit in the hallway.

People in suits and ties strolled past her, briefcases in their hands or files under their arms. For an institution of higher education, it sure seemed a lot more like an office building. No one discussed Plath or solved complicated math problems as they walked. There were half conversations about money and press-related discussions. Not much she could pick up from them.

Twenty minutes after she arrived, a woman in a short skirt, white button-down, and black blazer poked her head out the door.

"Are you the paralegal?" she asked.

Kate stood up and introduced herself. The woman, Maggie Chambers, invited her in.

"What can I help you with?" she asked after they sat.

"I'm looking into some issues about the merger. My dad is working a case at UNJ, and he thought you might be able to shed some light on things."

"What kind of light?"

"I'd like to know who's going to be on the board of trustees once this all goes through."

Chambers folded her hands in front of her. "I'm afraid that is confidential information."

She glanced at the computer on her desk, then up at the bookcase next it. Kate checked out the bookcase, only to see binder upon binder of information. The office was spacious, with a big window looking out over campus, but the way the binders were crammed into the bookcase made the room feel cluttered.

"Do I have to go through certain legal channels to obtain it?"

"Yes," Chambers said.

"Do you know who's going to be on the board?"

"I wrote the press release."

"Can I see it?"

"Absolutely not."

Kate tapped her fingernails on the arm of the chair. The fabric was soft and made no sound upon impact.

"Why is this such a secret?"

Chambers sat back in her chair. "Have you followed the story of this merger? It's private business. Everything is top secret. Henry Stern thinks this is some big dog-and-pony show. On the day of the press conference, he's going to line all the board members up onstage and introduce them like they're a sports team. Like he's some sort of showman. Until then, he wants it to be kept quiet."

"Once the names are released, is anyone going to recognize them?"

Chambers smiled. Then shook her head.

"How do you feel about the merger?" Kate asked.

"Off the record."

Kate nodded.

"Once this goes through, I'm out of a job. UNJ is taking over the brand. The salaries of this place are going to plummet because—hell, it's private, and who wants good educators here? This is going to become a profit factory."

Outside, the sun went behind the clouds, and the office was covered in shadows.

Kate took a shot in the dark.

"What if I told you that I'm working on a case that could ruin the merger?"

Chambers rolled her eyes. "I doubt it."

"I'm serious. It involves the mob."

"I would have heard about it."

Kate shook her head. "Not if UNJ is running the show. Does the name Tony Verderese ring a bell?"

"He's dead," Chambers said.

"Yeah, but other people want his position. And they're going to use this place to get it."

Chambers tapped a few keys on her keyboard. "If that's true, this is going to be the biggest shitshow the state has encountered in the past ten years. I might not want to be a part of this place. You thought Xanadu was bad. If you can fix it—"

Xanadu—or whatever they renamed it to—was one of New Jersey's dirty words. It was a plaid—yes, plaid—building erected near old Giants Stadium. It was supposed to be a cross between a mall and an amusement park, complete with indoor ski slope. During construction, the builders ran out of money and never got the place open. Now it sat on Route 3, only to be laughed at by New York commuters.

"I can," Kate said. "And you'll keep your job."

Chambers stood up. "I don't believe you. You should probably see your way out."

"How about I call Senator Stern. I think he'd help." She took her phone out of her purse.

"You're bluffing." Chambers folded her arms. "He wants this to go down."

"Fairly. Who do you think hired us?" The lie came easy. "You know how politics work. It's all about who you know. Now do you want to be responsible for this place having mob ties? Then I wouldn't be able to save your job."

Chamber's hands dropped to her side. She pointed to the computer. "All yours."

Kate gave herself a ten count. Then she got out of her chair and rounded the desk. Chambers got out of her way. On the screen of the computer was the press release announcing the new board of trustees. Kate scanned through the names and didn't recognize the first three.

She did, however, recognize the fourth.

Luca Carmine.

Maggie Chambers pressed a button and asked her secretary for a cup of coffee. Before it was delivered to the office, Kate had saved the file to a zip drive and made her way back to her car.

CHAPTER
FIFTY-THREE

ileen held the door nearly shut and said, "I don't know who that is."

Donne put his hand on the flat part of the door and gave it a little shove. She stepped back. His hand was still slick with sweat.

"It doesn't matter," he said. "I can tell you who she is, and you can find her. That's what you do."

Eileen tried to push the door closed, but it didn't budge against Donne. His shoulder ached at the movement, though. He tried not to grimace.

"It's going to cost you money. I'm not cheap."

Donne took a breath, reached down, and inched the gun out of his pocket. "Today you are."

He expected her to scream and run, or to try again to slam the door in his face again. Instead, she closed her eyes, exhaled, then opened the door. Donne stepped through, and Eileen closed it behind him. The smell of something burning hung in the air. Coffee, maybe. It was an old smell. She needed to open a window.

They stepped over strewn books to enter her computer room. The whine of servers and computer fans was a low rumble. In his head, it was louder the first time they were there. But his mind had been clouded by a lot of static, and that had to be affecting his hearing.

This room smelled like wet paper and ink. Preferable to the smell of burnt food. The only thing on her desk besides computers was a coffee cup and a water bottle. The coffee mug was blank, not even a cute phrase written across it.

"All right," Eileen said. "Do you have a phone number?"

Donne shook his head. "Just her name."

"Could she be using an alias?"

"Likely."

Eileen turned to him and shrugged. She raised her eyebrows.

"I don't know," he said.

"Well, then. Something like this could take days."

"I don't have days. I have minutes."

Eileen laughed. "Then you might as well shoot me. Or leave." She typed something. "I'd prefer the latter."

Donne's hand went to his pocket again. "What about Bill Martin? If you can find him, I bet we can find Jeanne."

Eileen stopped typing and stared at the screen. Donne's hand hovered over his pocket.

"What's Bill's phone number?" she asked.

"You have it."

Sighing, Eileen typed some more. Waited. More typing. Donne tried to read the screen over her shoulder, but the text was scrolling too quickly. He couldn't catch up, and his head ached.

"Damn it, Bill," Eileen whispered.

"You found him?"

"He didn't turn his phone off. The GPS tracker. He left it on."

Donne smiled. "He never was good with technology. Where is he?"

Eileen gave him an address. Donne typed it into the Notebook app on his phone. Then he went into settings and turned off Location Services.

"There. Was that so hard?"

"Don't be an idiot," she said.

Donne didn't respond. He put his phone away and left the

room. She didn't follow him. As Donne found his way out, he made note of the books on the floor. Notebooks full of nearly illegible writings. The shelves were full of how-to type books. And more marble notebooks. He reached down to look at one.

"Don't." Eileen's voice carried from the other room.

He hesitated. Eileen was pushing her luck.

He said, "Why not?"

"You feel like you're safe?"

Donne didn't answer.

"If you look in that notebook, you certainly won't be."

He stepped out on to the porch, the wooden planks creaking beneath his feet. The blue Honda Accord was double parked next to his own. Donne's hand went to the handle of his pistol as the driver's side door opened. The muscles in his neck tensed, and he flared his nostrils.

Luca got out of the car.

Donne bounded down the steps and across the stones into the street. Luca held up two hands to stop him.

"Got what you're looking for?" Luca asked.

"Leave me alone."

"Get out of here."

Donne didn't say anything. Luca looked him up and down, pausing at his pocket.

"Did you?" Luca didn't finish the question.

"You know what this is for," Donne said.

"Then get to it."

Donne walked by Luca, around the Accord, and got into his car. He started the engine and looked toward the street. Luca wasn't there anymore. He wasn't sitting in his own car either.

Luca was on the porch, ringing the doorbell. Donne rolled down his window to call to him. Before he could, the front door opened, and Eileen said something. If Luca responded, Donne didn't hear it. He did, however, hear two quick *pops*.

Luca turned and got out his cell phone. Donne took one last glance and saw Eileen facedown in the doorjamb. Her body held the front door open.

The road was empty, and if anyone heard the shots, they

hadn't reacted to them yet. No one was in the street. No cars were coming. It was a ghost town.

Donne didn't wait to see what Luca did next.

A mile and a half away, Donne stopped the car and caught his breath. Then he took out his phone and typed the address Eileen had given him into Google Maps.

To use the app, Location Services had to be turned back on. He was able to hide himself for all of ten minutes.

CHAPTER
FIFTY-FOUR

"How?" Jeanne asked for the third time.

Martin pressed the bridge of his nose and index finger. They had moved back into the motel room, which smelled of Lysol and mothballs. Housekeeping had been through, so the room was in order, except for a few Marvel action figures strewn across the desk. The shower was running for William.

"I don't know yet. If I can gather enough evidence, I can confront him on Friday."

"There'll be state troopers everywhere. Security will be crawling all over campus. You won't even get close."

Martin shook his head. "But I can get through that."

Jeanne shook her head, then fell back on to the bed. "You're just an ordinary citizen, Bill."

Martin sat down next to her. "When this is over—whether or not I do what I say—will you stay with me?"

Jeanne turned her head away from him. Silence hung in the room like steam after a shower.

"Will you tell William I'm his father?" Martin kept pushing.

Jeanne didn't say a word. Martin reached out and took her hand. He squeezed, gently. She squeezed back for an instant and then pulled it away.

Martin looked at his shoes. There was a white scuff on the

right one.

"Why didn't you run farther? Back to Arizona?" Martin looked at the Hulk toy on the desk. "Hell, even Canada?"

Jeanne rested her hands on her stomach. "If I wanted you to know anything, I would have told you. Haven't you figured that out by now? You weren't even supposed to find me. My dad—"

The shower stopped running.

"Did you use soap?" Jeanne shouted.

There was a pause, then the shower started up again.

Martin exhaled. "I have two days to look into this. You don't have to worry."

"You'll draw attention to yourself."

Martin didn't answer. His blood was pumping hard, and there was a ringing in his ears.

"Thank god for my parents," Jeanne said.

Martin nodded to the bathroom. "How is he handling this? How is he doing?"

A mumbled song came from the bathroom. William was singing something. It sounded educational. With how loud the shower was, the boy must have been screaming the words.

Jeanne turned her head. Her hair was splayed out across the comforter. A few strands fell across her eyes and nose. "He's amazing."

"Did you ever think—"

"I was never going to see him again after he was born. That was the deal. I couldn't call. I couldn't Skype."

Martin rubbed his chin. "He wasn't looking. He thought you were dead."

"And now ....?"

Martin leaned back on the couch. "Why hasn't Stern found you yet?"

"He will."

Jeanne sat up again. She pulled the corner of her shirt up so Martin could see her ribs. And the yellowish bruise that covered them.

"Tell me I don't matter to him."

Something caught in the back of Martin's throat. He swallowed.

"I shouldn't have asked how William was," Martin said. "I should have asked how you were."

Jeanne looked at the motel room door. "I lost."

"The man caused you to fake your own death. When he found out you weren't dead, he beat you and put you on video. And now he's trying to turn the state's education system into the world's biggest money laundering scheme. I have never said, 'This goes all the way to the top' before." Martin tapped the mattress. "Jeanne, this goes all the way to the top. And there's only one way to put a stop to it."

"You don't have any proof. And you won't get any. He's too careful."

Martin smiled. "You had proof six years ago. He'll slip up again."

The shower stopped again, but William kept singing. He was looking for his friends.

Martin whispered. "It's shady business. And once the leader goes, everything becomes a black hole."

"Someone else will step in."

Martin shook his head. "Not immediately. And even so, that person won't have anything to do with you. You can live your life. And you can raise William right."

"You need to leave now," Jeanne said.

Martin looked toward the bathroom. "Let me say good-bye."

Jeanne shook her head, then stood up. She went to the door of the room and turned the handle.

"We are safe here," she said.

"For how long?" Martin got off the bed and approached the door. "How long are you going to move from hotel to hotel?"

Jeanne pulled the door open and Martin stepped out into the hallway. There was a nice breeze, and the sun had gone behind some clouds. It didn't feel like June but the beginning of October.

"We'll be fine," Jeanne said.

She closed the door. Martin stared at it for a long time. At one point, he raised his hand in a fist to knock, but thought better of it. He turned and headed toward the stairs. The sun came out again, and Martin squinted.

As he drove out of the parking lot, it felt like paint thinner was eating away at his stomach lining.

CHAPTER
FIFTY-FIVE

Donne fiddled with the radio as he drove. Phone callers complained about the Yankees, pop radio repeated the same songs over and over, and the news droned on. He turned the radio off and stared ahead at brake lights. His fingers tingled and his seat belt felt too tight across his chest.

He shifted in the driver's seat to try to loosen the belt, but it wouldn't budge. The wound didn't ache too much, but he remembered being stuck in the bed, just after his escape attempt. They didn't tie him down, but he was so exhausted, he couldn't get back up. It felt like there was a band across his chest.

Henry Stern touched his good shoulder. Donne blinked sweat from his eyes, and tried to sit up. His abs ached in protest, and he was forced to remain prone.

"You need to rest," Stern said.

The room was hot and the air was heavy. Donne's skin felt like it was on fire.

"You tried to do too much, and now you have a fever." Stern's voice was like cold water. "Don't worry. We're going to bring you back."

"I have to go," Donne said.

Somewhere behind him, he could hear Luca talking. The words were hard to make out — something about blood and ice.

"Remember," Stern said. "We're helping you. You're going to get

better."

"Jeanne," Donne said.

Stern shook his head. "She's not trying to help you. She tried to destroy you. Her and her cop friend. They don't want you around."

Donne swallowed. His saliva felt like rocks and it stabbed his esophagus.

"Is this the life you want to live? Chasing down ghosts and dying because of it? I've been there, Jackson."

"You aren't helping." Donne's own voice seemed far away. He wasn't as healed as he thought.

Not even close.

Stern nodded. "You and I are very much alike. Jeanne Baker tried to ruin me too. I never thought I'd see her again, but when she showed up at my office – it felt like I lost it all." Stern tilted his head. "I am saving your life. Your 'friends' shot you, abandoned you. Left you to bleed out on a warehouse floor, just another casualty. We have the same enemy, Jackson. Bill Martin killed my friends too."

Stern stood up and walked away. Donne stared at the ceiling. The walls seemed to be moving, blurring together and forming one dark blob. Donne leaned his head back deeper in to the pillow and closed his eyes.

"You were only sent here as a sacrificial lamb, Jackson. You were supposed to die."

Donne didn't speak.

"You know who the real enemies are. Jeanne Baker and Bill Martin – "

"Tried to kill me," Donne hissed.

He opened his eyes and saw Stern hovering over him again. A smiled crossed the senator's face.

"Yes," Stern said. "They're in this for themselves."

"I can help," Donne said. He pictured Bill Martin facedown, blood dripping from his lip. Jeanne crying while kneeling over him.

"You can. You will."

Donne's eyes sagged. Before he could ask any more questions, he was asleep.

THE TRAFFIC broke up just before Clinton, and Donne was able to settle into an easy drive.

He put his blinker on and took the exit, seeing the motel in the distance, hovering over the highway like a beacon.

Stern was right. He couldn't trust Martin, and he couldn't trust Jeanne. The thought had pierced his brain once Stern started explaining everything to him. Three weeks lying in a bed, trying to heal, and each day the senator talked about revenge. How his "friends" weren't anything close to that.

Each day, Donne began to agree more and more. Each day he replayed the image of Bill Martin shooting him as Jeanne draped herself over him.

There was only one thing on his mind. The word Stern has used over and over each day.

Revenge.

Bill Martin and Jeanne couldn't go on. They couldn't start a new life together. That wasn't fair. They thought he was out of the picture?

Not a chance.

Donne pulled into the motel parking lot and parked. As he reached into the console for his gun, he felt like he was back in the church. His heart was hammering, and he was sweating so much, he thought he might have been rained on.

He hefted the gun and again put it in his pocket. Then he got out of the car and headed past the pool toward the lobby.

It was time.

CHAPTER
FIFTY-SIX

Donne walked into the lobby past the coffee stand to the front desk. The woman behind the desk was whispering on the phone and held up a finger to Donne, asking him to wait. She smiled as she did so, and when she stopped talking she lip-synched an apology to him. Donne smiled back and shrugged.

He went over to the coffee stand and poured himself a cup. As he was stirring in cream, the receptionist asked if she could help him.

Taking his cup with him, he approached the desk.

The receptionist smiled. "Maybe you should have gotten a water instead."

"I'm sorry?"

"You're sweating."

"Oh, I—" The gun felt heavy in his pocket. "It's warm out there."

The weather was still October-like.

She shrugged. "Summertime. What can I do for you?"

"I understand a woman is staying here. Her name is Jeanne Baker." Donne wished he had a picture. "I need to see her."

The receptionist said, "I'm sorry, sir. I can't help you. Motel policy."

"Please, I'm her fiancée. I know she's here."

"You're not the only person to be asking about her today. I'm going to have to call management."

For an instant, the words didn't register. Then Donne reached across and put his hand on the phone receiver before she picked it up.

"Sir, please."

"I'm sorry. There was another man here, wasn't there? Salt-and-pepper hair. Claimed to be a cop?"

She didn't answer, but her eyes gave away the affirmative.

"Are they together now? Which room?"

"I'm going to have to call the police."

"No," Donne said. "You're not."

He removed his hand from the phone and dropped it into his pocket. The handle of the pistol was ridged and he could feel the bumps on his fingertips. He pulled the weapon an inch, so it cleared the top of his pocket.

"Oh my god. Please leave," the receptionist said. "Now. I'm going to call the cops."

"Where *are* they?" Donne shouted. The receptionist flinched.

"They're not here!" she screamed. "They're not here. I don't know where they are. The other man came and went this morning."

The receptionist snatched the phone receiver and pressed three buttons. Donne didn't need to see to know which ones. His heart was racing, and he heard buzzing. Taking a step, he knocked over the cup of coffee. As it splashed against the ground, some of the liquid singed his ankles.

"I'm sorry," he whispered. "I'm sorry."

Tears were in the receptionist's eyes. Donne turned and ran from the lobby. He got into his car, started it, and peeled out of the parking lot, praying no one caught a license plate.

He drove ten minutes back toward New Jersey on the highway before pulling over to catch his breath. Sweaty palms, heart thumping, and shortness of breath. His chest felt tight, and his vision blurred. He thought he could hear his own heartbeat.

Counting to ten, Donne took a deep breath. Exhaled. Then another. Exhaled. Both hands on the steering wheel and focus on the horn. He stared at the Honda logo while he breathed. His heart rate was dropping back to its regular rhythm. The air-conditioner felt good on his arms.

He cruised back into New Jersey and hit the Parkway south. He had another destination in mind.

THE BAKERS were listed.

Donne had done what was asked of him the past two years and stayed away from them. He didn't drive past their house, he didn't call, and he didn't look out for them. But, apparently, the Bakers were extremely old-fashioned. And when Donne ran their name into a search engine, their address pulled up.

They'd moved down the shore.

The drive was a quick one, Donne pushing the needle to eighty-five on the clear highway. He made his way through town, winding through damaged neighborhood after damaged neighborhood before his GPS took him to their home.

Donne took the gun out of his pocket and placed it in the glove compartment His temples throbbed, and he almost put the car back into drive. Instead, he turned the key and shut the engine down. As if his mind was outside his body, he floated across the street, and the next thing he knew he was ringing the doorbell.

The door opened seconds later, and Sarah Baker stood in front of him. She didn't blink and didn't speak. She nodded slowly and then stepped out of the way. Donne walked in, turned left, and almost expected to see Jeanne standing there.

Instead it was Leonard. He put his iPad down, took off his glasses, and sat back in his chair.

"Hi," he said.

"I'm looking for her."

Leonard let out a long wet cough, one that racked his shoulders. Once he finished, he wiped his lips and stared at the carpet while he caught his breath. Donne looked for Sarah, but she was nowhere to be found.

The clink of dishes and the sound of a running faucet came from another room.

"How are you, Jackson?"

He didn't expect the question, and his hand immediately went to his chest. He could feel the scar through his shirt, a hard piece of skin that pressed against the fabric.

"It's been a long month," he said.

Leonard nodded. "The last time I saw you, I bailed you out of jail. I told you to stay away from my wife and me."

"And I did."

"But you're here."

Donne walked over to the empty couch and sat. Leonard let out another wet hack. He sat back and stared at the ceiling, gasping for air. Out of the corner of his eye, Donne saw Sarah edge up to the doorway, clutching a towel. Leonard caught his breath again.

"That doesn't sound too good," Donne said.

Leonard shook his head. "Nope."

"Where's Jeanne?" Donne asked.

"Let her go, Jackson. She's safe."

The water in the kitchen started up again. Donne listened to it for a moment. Sarah was humming a tune he didn't recognize.

"That's not why I want to find her."

Blinking, Leonard said, "I don't understand."

Donne patted his empty pocket. The move was becoming second nature. He missed the weight of the gun and wished he hadn't left it in the car.

"Six years, Leonard. Six years she's been alive. My life, my whole life the last six years revolved around that. And now, just as I'm getting it back, getting myself where I want to be, she comes back. Beaten and battered, but she's back. And I'm just supposed to jump back in and save her. I finally moved on."

Leonard spread his hands, but didn't speak.

"Why didn't you tell me, Leonard?" The ropes in Donne's neck tightened, pressing against his skin. He balled his hands into fists. "How could you let me live like this?"

Leonard's face went pale and he brought his hand to his lips as if he was about to cough again, but held it back. "Because it wasn't about you. It never was."

Donne slammed his hand on the tabletop. The iPad bounced off it and clattered on the floor.

"Where is she?"

"Go home, Jackson."

"Where?" Donne's throat burned as the words tore from him.

"You helped her enough. She's free and gone." He reached over to touch Donne's arm. Donne snatched it away. "You did your part."

Donne shook his head. "No. Not yet."

He turned to leave, while Leonard sat back down. As he walked, he opened and closed his hands, digging his nails into his palm. Behind him, Leonard must have picked up and opened his iPad, because Donne heard the familiar click. He stopped.

An iPad.

Donne turned on his heel. "It was you."

Leonard looked up.

"When Bill and I went to that bodega—we were … I saw your Skype name." The images and information were mangled in his brain, and he couldn't put it all together. "We were supposed to be looking for an iPad, but we found a desktop computer. One that had your Skype name on it."

"Jackson, you're not making sense."

"What did you do?" Donne growled.

"You're being crazy."

"How are you involved? Is this about you?"

Leonard started to speak, but Sarah appeared at the kitchen door again.

"Tell him," Sarah said.

Leonard wiped his face. Donne looked from him back to Sarah. She was drying her hands with a kitchen towel. He couldn't read the expression on her face because there wasn't one.

"She came back because I'm dying," Leonard said. "Cancer. I don't have much time. I gave up chemo."

Donne felt cold.

"Sarah needed Jeanne. She's getting old. Can't do what she used to do. So we asked her to come back. But Jeanne—you remember. Stubborn. Went to see the senator, and he took her."

"Why? What did he confront her about?" Donne's chest felt like it was vibrating.

Leonard shook his head. "And when I started getting the messages, they told me not to go to the police. And Bill—she loved Bill. If I had forwarded the video to him, he might have died. I couldn't do that to him."

Despite the cold, beads of sweat formed on the back of his neck.

"So, I—"

"I knew computers, it was my job," Leonard said. "I knew how to make it look live to you. I knew how to patch you in. And I knew you were at Rutgers. I always kept an eye on you. It wasn't hard to find your email address. I knew you would act. And—" Another cough took hold of Leonard. Sarah flinched at the sound.

As Leonard tried to settle himself down, Sarah said, "The senator is dangerous."

Donne shook his head. *No. He's the one who helped me.*

"And you were expendable. We could risk you. We needed Bill, in case …" She trailed off.

It fit. Just like Stern had said. He didn't give them any more time to answer. He left the house and went back to his car.

And his gun.

The senator was right. They were all against him.

CHAPTER
FIFTY-SEVEN

The front door was wide open. That was never a good sign.

"Eileen?" Martin called out.

No answer. The only sound was the creak of the porch boards beneath his feet. The breeze blew at his back, and the door shuddered.

He called out Eileen's name again. Still no response. Instinctively, Martin reached for his holster, only to be reminded it was no longer there. No gun. No protection.

Calling out probably wasn't his smartest idea.

He stepped into the house. It was bare. The furniture was there, but it was all in place. The coffee table wasn't askew. The couch cushions had been flipped. The stain of cranberry juice wasn't visible anymore.

And the bookcases were completely empty.

But what bothered Martin the most was the silence. The hum of the servers was gone, replaced by the occasional distant car horn or bird chirping. He dashed across the living room into the computer room.

They were gone. All of them. The room was completely barren. The desk had even been dusted. Only a tissue box remained. The room smelled like dish soap. Martin grabbed a tissue and used it to open each drawer of the desk. They were all empty.

Every piece of information Eileen had ever tracked was gone. Everything she'd saved, backed up, and written down had been taken. Whoever did this would have needed time and a moving van. And since the door was still open, Martin suspected he'd just missed the culprit.

God knows what Eileen knew, and thusly what her assailants would soon know. National secrets. Suspected terrorist attacks. Barack Obama's cell phone number. It was all gone.

Martin's hands began to tremble, and his mouth went dry. He tracked through the entire house — spotless. Even the dishes had been washed in the kitchen. The bed had been made. It was exactly the opposite of how Eileen would have left it.

And there was no sign of her.

He thought about calling the Union Beach cops, but didn't know what to say. *Hi, my friend is missing, and her house has been cleaned. I suspect foul play.* It didn't have the right ring to it.

Martin didn't want to contaminate the area with his fingerprints, fibers from his clothes, or stray DNA so he walked back to the porch. Before he crossed the threshold, however, something caught his eye on the carpet. It looked like the cranberry juice stain that used to be on her couch. Martin knelt down and saw a dash of thick red liquid. Blood coagulating and stiffening the carpet strands. Not much, though. But it seemed he was right, at the very end of the cleaning project, the assailant had been rushed. He missed the last little bit.

Cool air hit Martin's face once out on the porch. Overhead, dark clouds had begun to roll in — a midsummer thunderstorm. The sky rumbled as if it were clearing its throat. Getting ready for a big announcement. The air was heavy with moisture, so humid he felt like he was swimming.

Of course, maybe that was just the thoughts running through his head.

There was too much cleanliness — military-level. Too much order and organization. Martin's stomach turned. He ran down the porch steps and across the street to a gutter drain. The contents of his lunch: Coffee and two pieces of buttered toast came back up. He then dry-heaved, tasting bitter phlegm.

He caught his breath and wiped his mouth with the back of his hand. Another piece of his life gone.

The timing was too big a coincidence. This had Henry Stern written all over it.

Before Martin could get into his car, the sky opened up. Thick drops of rain shattered off the asphalt like glass. His shirt soaked through as he fished for his keys. Martin looked up and opened his mouth, filling it with rain. He swallowed, and shook his head.

Once he was back in his car, he made a phone call to the private shooting range he'd use on weekends. Scheduled an appointment and told them he would pay extra if they could block off an hour for just him.

When he told the manager how much he would pay, the manager quickly agreed. Martin had to focus and couldn't afford many distractions. There wasn't much time for practice.

But there was enough.

Plus, it'd be better for him if fewer people saw him practicing long-range rifle use. He didn't need any witnesses.

He got back in his car and drove off, setting a course for home. His rifle needed cleaning.

CHAPTER
FIFTY-EIGHT

"I screwed up," Donne said into the phone.

There was silence on the other end of the line for a moment. Donne looked around his apartment. The garbage bags of clothes were still scattered around the living room. The TV had been unplugged. All the clocks blinked 12:00.

"What did you do?" Luca asked, finally.

"I can't find her."

"Yeah, and ..."

In the hallway outside the apartment, Donne heard conversation. The tone was calm, unexcited. However, he felt his pulse begin to race.

"I went to her parents. To get them to tell me. They didn't know."

"More loose ends?" Luca's voice was strained.

The conversation moved on, and the hallway fell silent again. Donne waited for his pulse to slow.

"He's dying. Jeanne's dad," he said. "And he still wouldn't tell me."

Luca laughed.

Donne eyed the gun on his coffee table. It was still unloaded from after he cleaned it. He reached down and spun it "spin the bottle" style. The metal scratched at the wood table. When it stopped the barrel pointed directly at him.

Luca said, "Are you drunk?"

"No."

He leaned over and looked into the barrel without picking up the gun. The light that had been reflecting off the inside metal of the barrel faded as he leaned in. He could smell the oil and the cleaning fluid. It looked brand-new, just off the rack. Jesus had used this gun before, Donne was sure of it. But after an hour of wiping and oiling, it was good as new.

Spotless.

Untraceable.

For the next couple of hours — days? — he had to believe that.

"They sent me to you. Expected me to die."

There was a crackle on the line. Luca didn't speak.

"How long have you known me? Three, four weeks? And it feels like Stern knows me better than anyone else. Even Kate."

Luca said, "Research. Bill Martin, all your old cases. Everything that was in the news. We know. He cares about you."

Donne thought about his time in the church, how Stern was able to pull bits and pieces of his life into context. Use it in conversation. It didn't register then.

Donne said through gritted teeth. "He told me I'd get back at them."

"But you can't if you can't find her."

"They shot me."

Donne didn't realize how tightly he had been holding the phone. The plastic dug into his fingers, and when he loosened his grip, his skin stuck to it. He switched the receiver to his other hand and flexed to allow blood to return to his fingertips.

Donne shook his head. Not that Luca could see it. "Too many years of letting her get to me. Too many years of thinking about her, only to almost die because of her. And Bill Martin. No more of this. You know where they are."

"How?"

Donne thought about it. "The woman. The hacker. Her equipment."

"Good thinking," Luca said. "I'll look."

"Today."

"I'll see what I can do."

Donne stared at the barrel of the gun.

"Today or not at all."

"I'll call you back."

Donne hung up without saying good-bye. He put the phone down next to the gun and leaned back into his couch. The cushions seemed tougher than they were before he left. Stiff with dust and a lack of use.

Exhaustion rolled over him.

He just wanted all this to be over with.

AN HOUR later, Luca called again. Donne picked up, but was barely able to get a greeting in.

"Downstairs. Now." A beat. "Please."

The line disconnected. Donne looked at the pistol still resting on the desk. He reached down and instead picked up the glass of water he poured and gulped it down. Leaving the gun, he went downstairs.

Parked on the corner was a black Volvo with tinted rear windows. Luca stood near the driver's side door, arms folded. His biceps bulged as he flexed them once. Then he reached up and straightened his oversized sunglasses.

Luca approached Donne and asked him to raise his arms. Donne did the best he could with his left hand. Luca frisked him, checking even the most sensitive of body parts.

"Get in," he said when he was finished.

"You never did that before."

"I told you this afternoon, a few days on your own, you never know what you might think. Chicken out."

"I'm all in," Donne said.

Donne went for the front passenger door, but Luca shook his head and pointed toward the backseat. Donne obliged.

Henry Stern sat on the opposite side of the car. He had an iPad open, but once Donne got settled, he closed the sheath it was in. He shook his head at Donne, which caused a tremor to shudder down Donne's spine.

The car pulled away from the curb and headed toward College Avenue.

"How are you feeling?" Stern said.

"I still can't lift my left arm over my shoulder."

Stern waved at him. "It'll come."

"I told Luca, this has nothing to do with you or him. This is on me," Donne said.

Stern smiled, then, after a pause, laughed. "This has everything to do with me. I'm sure Luca has explained that."

"I won't be caught," Donne said.

"For your sake, I hope not." Stern tapped the iPad again. "But you and I aren't connected. There's no proof we know each other."

Donne wiped at a bead of sweat that had formed over his eyebrow. "For six years—longer—they have been a part of my life. Dragging me down to hell. And every time I think I'm over it—every time I'm past it—they come back. Something brings me back to her. Back to him. I'm finished with them, and for the past three weeks, this is all I can think about."

Stern didn't respond.

"And don't bullshit me," Donne said. "You're the one who put me here. All that talk those last three weeks about how I shouldn't trust them. This was *your doing*."

Stern rubbed his chin. "So you're doing this for me."

Donne took a deep breath. Outside his window, he saw Winants Hall. He thought about the days leading up to the Rutgers merger, the excitement on campus, the buzz in the media. The merger had put Rutgers onto the national academic stage more than a football or basketball win ever would.

And now they were going to try it again. UNJ or Benjamin Franklin or whatever they were going to call it would become the next big private university. New Jersey would have two of the best in the country, as the ranking would move the school into Princeton territory.

Or so the scholars said.

Taxpayers would be happy. Henry Stern would be happy. And he would even profit.

But then, stuck in his head, was the image of Jeanne trying to ruin things by coming forward with whatever she had on Stern. The picture of Bill Martin firing the gun kept him up at night.

"I'm doing this for both of us," Donne said.

Stern nodded and opened his iPad again. Donne exhaled and stared out the window. A few students were striding down the street with backpacks slung over their shoulders. They stared at their cell phones, and one strolled into the crosswalk without looking. A campus bus jammed on its brakes.

"You have an iPhone, correct?" Stern asked.

Donne nodded and took it out of his pocket. Stern tapped some things into the iPad, and Donne's phoned ringed with a text message. It had a note attached to it. Donne opened it up and saw three addresses. One of them was the motel Donne visited earlier that morning in Pennsylvania.

"For the last two and half weeks, Jeanne Baker has been staying in one of these motels. She's been moving around, varying her pattern. She hasn't stayed in one of them for longer than three days. I'm not sure which one she's in today, because, well, Eileen ..."

From the driver's seat, Luca didn't react. The blinker clicked, and they made a left turn on to Somerset Street.

The car stopped, and Donne realized they were in front of his apartment building. There was a lead ball sitting in his stomach, pressing against his abdomen.

"Know this," Stern said. "If you fail, if you're brought in by the police —"

"Is this the *Mission: Impossible* speech?"

Stern shook his head. "Worse."

The car doors unlocked, and Donne could see Luca's eyes in the rearview mirror. He'd taken off his sunglasses. They weren't the bright, excited eyes of their time in the church. Instead, they were cold. Donne sniffed, then coughed.

He pulled the handle, opened the door, and got out. Just before he got to the door of his apartment building, Stern called his name.

"There's something else," he said.

Donne walked back to the open window. Stern pressed his lips together and took a deep breath. Donne waited.

Finally, Stern said, "Good luck."

The window closed and the car pulled away.

CHAPTER FIFTY-NINE

Bill Martin stood on the campus of UNJ, just outside of Trenton. He was in the middle of the quad, with the two-story freshman apartment building to his left. He shook his head. They used to have dorms, a single cinderblock room with two beds and two desks. Now these kids got apartments.

He walked over to the entrance and inspected the door. The apartments were empty now with school out of session. He pulled the glass door, but it wouldn't open. To the right was a place to slide a key card to gain access. Martin gave the door another tug, with no luck. That wouldn't work tomorrow.

A guy wearing khakis and a UNJ polo shirt approached him, hands in his pockets. He smiled and said, "Can I help you?"

Martin returned the grin. "My son is starting here in August, and I wanted to walk the campus."

The guy looked around. "Without your son?"

Martin shrugged. "He's working. I'm retired. Thought I'd take a tour."

"An official tour starts at three. You can catch it over at the student union." He pointed over his shoulder. Martin could see the building down far away down the lawn. It was maybe three football fields away, at the end of all the academic buildings.

"Yeah, but what fun is that?"

The guy laughed. "Enjoy your day, sir. I hope your son

enjoys UNJ." He paused. "I mean Ben Franklin University. I really have to get used to saying that. Today's the last day I can wear this shirt."

Martin nodded, and said, "Thanks for your help."

The guy gave a little wave, turned, and left. Martin whistled "Air That I Breathe" quietly. He waited until he was alone again and then crossed the quad to the Robert F. Jenkins building. The name was written across the wall of the building in thick, painted pieces of aluminum. Must have been a hell of a donation.

When Martin tugged on this door, it swung open. Martin entered, and his skin immediately cooled from the air-conditioning. On the wall to his right was a directory, listing the building's science labs. Martin ignored it and found the staircase. The stairwell was the way Martin remembered the dorms. Cinderblock walls painted yellow. The stairs were metal and clanked underneath his feet as he stepped. He reached the top floor and kept going to the roof.

The door to the roof wasn't locked either. Martin pushed it opened and stepped onto gravel. The sun felt warmer—the October-like weather was gone—but there was a noticeable breeze that cooled the heat. Without the buildings blocking the wind, it was actually a pretty nice day. Martin walked to the edge of the roof and looked out on one of the campus's many parking lots. He could see his car, alone in the empty lot. He'd been here once when class was in session and couldn't find a spot, circling for almost forty-five minutes. Today, his Mazda was all by itself.

Seeing the distance between the car and building, he wondered if he'd be quick enough to get up here unnoticed. Probably. Everyone's attention would be on the other side of the building. Security would be light, anyway, nothing beyond the usual state trooper presence. This wasn't a high-priority target. Football games were more worrisome to law enforcement. This was going to be a small outdoor press conference. No longer than an hour.

That's what happened at Rutgers, though that happened

indoors. Martin remembered seeing the itinerary as the state cops were briefing Stringer. Everything was mapped down to the minute, even the press questions. The politicians wanted to get the hell out of there, and academia had little interest in more pomp and circumstance.

Though at Rutgers, at least, they rang the bell. What would they do here? Release white smoke? Fly a kite in a lightning storm?

He switched to whistling "Long Cool Woman" and paced on the roof. In the other direction, Martin could see the setup for the press conference. The stage was set up in front of Clyde Hall, the administration building right next to the student union. He could see a few people milling around before the tour. Some men in overalls were working on the metal stage and bleachers, not unlike something seen at a high school graduation. Speakers were being set up at each end of the stage. Easy and simple. The work would be done in an hour.

Martin knelt down at the edge of the roof, feeling gravel dig into his knee. He closed his right eye and lined up the shot. He gathered it was about six hundred yards, just at the edge of his range. He'd hit eight of ten shots at that distance when he was practicing. The owner of the range—one of the biggest in the state—was impressed, but was smart enough not to ask what the practice was for. Martin had paid him too much money. He hoped tomorrow wouldn't be as breezy as today. The shot would be that much more difficult.

But that wouldn't matter. By the end of the day tomorrow, Martin would probably be heading to prison. He wasn't going to need much money, he'd settle for the public defender. As long as Jeanne and William were safe, he could live out the rest of his days in East Jersey State Prison. He had nothing else at this point.

Still, it bothered him. Why haven't they been tracking Jeanne? She was important enough to tie up and use to get Donne, but now they couldn't find her. It took him three weeks; it should have taken a state senator less than that.

Unless.

Martin felt a knot in his stomach. Maybe they weren't tracking her because they already found her. Martin did keep an eye on the motel parking lot when he was there, but how detailed a job did he really do? It was a quick sweep, because—at first—he was sure he beat out the senator. He didn't see the flaws in his logic until he was actually speaking with Jeanne. Maybe he missed something.

He shook his head. It was likely he did miss something. They knew where Jeanne was. They had to. Henry Stern was too powerful, had too many connections. Someone doesn't get to that high a position without them.

Basically, they were waiting. They just wanted to make sure the merger went through before anything happened to Jeanne. Martin was wrong. Jeanne's information could still hurt the senator, but the merger was his sole focus right now. It had to go through swimmingly; he could pay no attention to anything else. If Jeanne turned up dead, and someone connected to Stern was caught for it, it would throw everything into flux.

If that happened *after* the merger, maybe they could do a better job minimizing it.

Tomorrow had to happen for Stern. The endgame also had to happen for Martin, but he was going to stay with Jeanne tonight, gun out, making sure she got through the night safely. Too many people had been taken from him. Too many things. He wasn't going to let anything happen to *her*.

He left the roof, tasting bile in his mouth again.

CHAPTER
SIXTY

Donne parked his car a block away from the Amaker Motel. He didn't want anyone to mark down his license plate when he left. And if Jeanne was there, he didn't want anyone to see him getting into the car to flee the crime scene.

His heart was jackhammering as he walked the parking lot scanning the cars. There weren't many, but none jumped out at him screaming *Jeanne!* Knocking on each door would certainly attract attention, and with Jeanne in hiding, she wouldn't answer the door unless she knew who it was. There had to be an easier way.

Donne sank back into the roughage opposite the parking lot. He crouched down and watched the doors of the motel rooms, waiting for her to make her exit. They had to eat, didn't they? He checked his watch. Nearly 6:30. Hopefully, she hadn't already left.

Food. That was it.

Donne pulled his cell phone and dialed the front desk. The phone was answered by a man on the third ring.

"I'm here to deliver a pizza for Jeanne Baker, but she didn't leave a room number," he said.

"Nobody told me they ordered a pizza."

"Are they required to?"

"She usually calls down and tells me when food is coming."

A wave ran over Donne.

"Guess she forgot, but this pizza is getting cold."

The man sighed and he heard the clicking of computer keys. "Two-fourteen," the man said.

Donne said thanks and hung up. She was using her own name. Either she'd gotten lazy, or she felt sure she wasn't being followed or tracked. It didn't matter. He had his answer. It was time for payback.

Crossing the parking lot felt like crossing the Sahara. Every step was an eternity, and by the time he reached the spot where the concrete met the asphalt, he was doused in sweat. His fingers itched, and the gun in his pocket felt like it weighed three tons.

The steps were just as difficult, and he had to catch his breath at the landing. His shoulder and chest ached. It felt as if his body were trying to stop him from going forward. Donne gripped the railing and breathed deep, wiping his brow. At the top of the stairwell, he got his bearings and made the left toward room 214. As he did, he pulled the gun from his pocket, hefted it, and checked the safety.

The room was only two doors away from the staircase. Donne stopped in front of it and knocked. A shadow crossed over the peephole. Donne raised the revolver and aimed. There was a muffled voice. He heard locks clicking.

The door swung open and Jeanne Baker faced the barrel of the gun. Donne flinched when he saw her.

"Jesus Christ, Jackson," she said. Her eyes were wide, and her breath came in small gasps.

"Let me in," he said. His shirt was soaked through.

"Okay, okay. Relax."

She moved out of the way. It was a suite, and the first was a living room. A dive like this actually had suites. There were papers and books strewn about on the couch and living room and coffee in the maker. But the sights didn't register with Donne, as fog clouded his vision.

His dead fiancée was standing in front of him.

Again.

This time Bill Martin was nowhere to be found.

"Talk to me, Jackson," she said.

"Why should I?" Donne's voice shook. So did the gun.

"Put the gun down. You're not right."

Donne took a step forward and grabbed her by the arm. He pulled her in tight and jammed the barrel into her chin. Jeanne didn't scream, but chirped when the metal touched skin.

"You lied to me. You've always lied to me. About Bill. About your death." He spat the word. "And then you let *him* shoot me, you just let him."

Jeanne tried to pull away, but Donne held her tight.

"I spent the last six years thinking about you. When Bill told me the truth … it took me until now to get over it. To get right." He breathed deep. "And then you come back. You can't do this to me any longer. You won't."

Donne tensed his finger. Jeanne closed her eyes. The trigger felt the pressure and started to move.

His nightmare was about to end.

"Mom?"

A small voice from the bedroom. Donne loosened his grip.

"Mom, are you okay?"

Jeanne opened her eyes. A tear dripped from her right.

"Stay in the bedroom!" she shouted.

Donne looked over her toward the bedroom door. A small boy stood there. He was in bathing trunks and T-shirt. A tremor ran through Donne's body. His gun hand fell to his side.

"William," Jeanne said. "Stay away." Her eyes went to Donne. "You will not touch him."

Donne blinked. Once. Twice. Air caught in the back of his throat.

"Who is that?" he asked.

Jeanne said, "My son."

William ran to her and wrapped his arms around her waist. Jeanne put a hand on his shoulder and pulled him tight. Donne stumbled backwards.

"How old is he?"

"Don't hurt my mom!"

"He won't," Jeanne said. "Don't worry, baby. He's not going to hurt anyone."

"How old?"

It all swirled into focus. The books strewn on the couch were comic books. There were action figures off to the right, Iron Man and Doctor Doom. The room smelt like coffee and chlorine.

"Six," Jeanne said.

Suddenly aware of the gun in his hand, Donne jammed it back in his pocket. Quick math. Quick math.

"Is he ..." Donne trailed off.

Jeanne gave a short shake of her head. Ice formed in Donne's throat.

"Bill?" Donne asked. His voice was a whisper.

Jeanne looked at the orange carpet. The feeling went from Donne's legs, and he dropped to his knees.

Jeanne whispered something to the boy.

"No," he said. "He's going to hurt you."

She shook her head. "No, he won't. I promise. We have to talk."

"Who is he?"

"An old friend."

"Friends don't hurt other friends."

Donne said, "I'm sorry. I'm sorry. I'm not. I won't."

Ohmygodohymygodohmygod.

"We're playing a game," Jeanne said.

William let go of his mother and stared at Donne. His mouth curved into a frown and his hands balled into fists. He held the pose for a few seconds, then turned and went back into the bedroom. But not before he retrieved his action figures.

"Why didn't you tell me?" Donne asked. "Why did you just leave me like this?"

Jeanne exhaled. "Now you know why I came back."

CHAPTER
SIXTY-ONE

"I've missed everything, Jackson. His first word. His first step. His first haircut. I missed his first day of school. Me. His mother. I missed it all. So I came back."

Donne said, "But you got kidnapped."

Jeanne walked over to the couch and sat down. After looking toward the bedroom door to make sure it was closed, she exhaled. Donne got off his knees and sat on the floor. It felt like his chest was empty, the only remnants of his insides the constant throb of his wound.

"I was tired of hiding, tired of missing William grow up, and I made a mistake."

Donne didn't miss her words. The image of the boy walking in here, seeing his mother with a gun to her throat, ran laps around his brain.

"What would you do to see your own child, Jackson?"

The throb had its own rhythm now. It sambaed against his pectoral muscle. "He's not mine."

"Would you lie, cheat, and steal?"

Donne slammed his fist into his open left hand. "Does Bill know?"

"He's known a long time. Since before—"

Donne tapped his pocket.

"I was happy, Jeanne. Finally."

"How dare you? It was my son." Jeanne shoved her hands in her pockets. "My dad is dying. My mom can't do it on her own."

They let that sit in the air. Donne put his arms straight out behind him and leaned back. His back cracked and his shoulder whined. His eyes felt heavy, and they burned. Sleep called him as the last bits of adrenaline escaped his body.

Donne shook his head. "You should have stayed away."

"And what would have happened to William? He'd roam the streets like Oliver Twist?"

Donne laughed. "Ever the English teacher."

Jeanne didn't return the chuckle.

"That was our problem, Jackson. It wasn't the drinking. Not the coke. That was a part of it, but not the whole thing. But you didn't know me. You never knew me. English? I was working in the education department. And you never even knew that."

Donne pulled his knees in and leaned forward, hugging them. His back cracked some more.

"You cheated on me," he said. "Then you told me you wanted me back. Two weeks later you died. Or ran."

"And you cheated on me, remember?"

Vaguely.

"You weren't a good person back then, Jackson." She rubbed her chin where the barrel of the gun had been. "And it doesn't seem like you've gotten any better."

Jeanne got off the couch and went over to the counter. The mug clattered against the Formica top, and she picked it up. After emptying a sugar packet and adding cream, she poured a cup of coffee. Judging by the smell, she must have just made it. Jeanne didn't offer, but Donne didn't want any.

"What did you know? Why did you hide?"

Jeanne shook her head. "It doesn't matter anymore."

Her words fell flat. There were too many holes, too much damage done for it not to matter. Donne looked around the room for signs of anyone but Jeanne and William. Nothing.

"Where's Bill?" he asked.

Jeanne shrugged, and gulped some coffee. The mug was

steaming, but the heat didn't seem to bother her.

"Come on, Jeanne. What's the point of lying now?"

She turned to face him and leaned against the counter. Took another sip of coffee.

"Have you ever heard of a scorched earth policy?"

Donne didn't say anything.

"I want to start over with William. I don't want to hide anymore. I want to be able to spend time with my parents. I want to be more than what I was. No more lying. No more fear."

Donne patted his pocket.

"So you're going to run again?"

"I don't want to. Have to be near my dad. But Stern …"

William knocked something over in the other room. He called out an apology.

"You're in with him, aren't you?" Jeanne asked. Her voice was steady. She rolled her shoulders and then took another small sip of coffee.

He didn't answer. The woman he'd loved and then mourned for so long was standing in front of him, unharmed. She was drinking coffee, talking, hitting him with sarcastic barbs, and wanting to start her life over. For Donne, the room should have been spinning. Instead, the waters were calm.

"How else could you have survived getting shot like that? It was Henry's building. He had to help you." Jeanne shook her head.

The words weren't coming.

"So, then what? As payback, he wanted you to kill me?"

"No. Yes." Donne said. "It felt like it was all me."

Jeanne nodded. "He pushed you to it. That's what he did in the army."

Donne thought back to his time with Stern. Thought about Luca telling him to lay low. Bigger things were ahead.

He adjusted his jaw and felt the joint pop like a knuckle. Tension eased in his neck for an instant.

Donne thought about Jeanne's words, let them settle in his brain. *Scorched earth* stood out.

"Where is Bill?"

"I don't care," Jeanne said. "I only care about my family."

Donne opened his mouth, then froze.

"You're not the woman I knew," Donne said.

Jeanne tilted her head back and finished off the coffee. She put the mug down and let it rattle on the Formica again. It tilted, but held its edge and settled back into place.

"You've never been the man I thought you were." Jeanne walked toward the bedroom. "I am going to play with my son."

Donne sat on the carpet until she closed the bedroom door. He exhaled, and pushed himself to his feet. His body ached, and he felt hollow. Donne went to the door and unhooked the clasp. He turned the handle.

All of the air left in him went out of him. He reached down to his pocket.

Bill Martin stood on the other side of the threshold.

CHAPTER
SIXTY-TWO

Bill Martin was faster. He was always faster. Always able to think on his feet.

His fist connected with Donne's jaw, snapping his head back and sending him stumbling back into the hotel room. The pistol in Donne's pocket landed on the floor with a *thunk*. Donne rolled to reach for it, but Martin — again — was faster.

"You're dead," Martin said. He stepped over Donne, fists clenched. He was between Donne and the revolver. "I killed you."

"That rumor is gaining steam."

Donne stood up and brought his right arm up to ward off any blows. His left arm hung limp at his side. It was screaming at his brain, however. He must have landed on it funny and destroyed whatever healing had been going on.

Martin reached into his jacket, but Donne had seen that move before. He turned on his heel and ran out on to the hallway leading toward the stairs. Martin shouted something — a phrase — but it came down the hallway garbled, and Donne didn't understand. The acoustics of the motel weren't made for public arguing, apparently. Privacy was a selling point.

He took the stairs two at a time, but could hear footsteps on the concrete behind him. Donne leapt the last three stairs and landed on asphalt. He rolled to his right, into a bush. Now both his shoulder and his chest were screaming at him.

At the very least, if Donne were shot here, there would be witnesses. The motel manager would have to call the police. Martin would be screwed. Donne's former partner barreled down the last flight of stairs, his focus on the parking lot. When he hit the last step, Donne leapt out and tackled him, wrapping his right arm around Martin's waist. They both went down in a heap.

Donne's chin dug into the asphalt and his teeth clattered together. He could taste copper in his mouth. Meanwhile, Martin moaned as he rolled on to his back. Donne pushed himself to his feet and pushed Martin's gun away with his right foot. Then he walked over and kicked Martin in the ribs. Martin grunted and grabbed at them.

Donne said, "Leave me alone."

Through gritted teeth, Martin asked, "What did she tell you?"

"That you were living your life."

"In that case, tomorrow I'm going to get these ribs checked out." Martin rolled toward Donne. Donne kicked him again. Martin curled into the fetal position.

"You're getting off easy," Donne said. With his right wrist, he wiped blood away from his nose. The screaming pain had turned to white noise. There was so much, his body barely noticed it. His nerves had been overworked, and now they were just giving up.

Or maybe he was going into shock again. Either way, he didn't care.

"The hell you know?" Martin asked. "Don't know anything."

He started to uncurl himself, but Donne took a quick step forward. As if he were going to be kicked again, Martin curled himself up. The grass rustled beneath him.

"Jesus."

Martin spat on the ground. Donne couldn't be sure, but the shade looked red. Maybe he'd cracked a rib or two. Donne bit his lip to keep from chuckling. This was a long time coming.

The front desk manager—cell phone in his hand—had made

his way out on to the front walk and was staring at the two of them. He yelled that the two of them needed to knock that shit off or he *would* call the cops. The accent made it seem like there had been a time when he'd bluffed. Donne waved at him as if to say *No worries*. Then he turned his attention back to Martin.

"Stay the hell away from Stern. Just help her." Donne tried to rolled his shoulder and loosen it, but it wouldn't move. He was going to have to drive one-handed.

"Will you be there tomorrow?"

Donne didn't answer. There was nothing to say, no reason to give anything away. Just listening to an old man spin his bullshit and go home. Martin was toast.

"Because I sure as hell don't want to see your face again."

Donne didn't bother anymore. He started to walk through the parking lot. The gravel dug into his heels with each step. He'd counted ten steps when he heard Martin's voice call his name.

Turning around, Donne expected to see Martin aiming at him. Instead, Bill was sitting up, hugging himself. His face was red. He grimaced.

"Jackson," he said. His voice was hoarse and dry. "I just want you to remember one thing …"

Donne kicked at the ground without looking, like a bull preparing to charge.

"Just remember, I won." Martin grinned.

Grunting, Martin got up, and walked toward the stairs. Donne watched him climb them all. Each step Martin took seemed to take an immense amount of effort, like his legs weighed tons. When he reached the top, he looked over the railing to give Donne another glare. The breeze blew his hair askew.

Donne waited.

Martin walked the two doors down to 214, Jeanne's room. He pushed the ajar door all the way open, stepped inside, and closed it.

Donne stood there and waited for her to kick him out. He counted three hundred seconds in his head. Over the hotel roof, the sun had set casting a long shadow across the parking lot. The air grew cooler, and the breeze was stronger.

Jeanne's door remained closed.

Donne gave it another minute, then turned and walked to his car. As he did, he dialed Luca.

"It's done," he said.

"That means, after tomorrow, all loose ends will be tied up."

Donne took a breath. "Like hell."

He hung up.

CHAPTER
SIXTY-THREE

Donne rang Kate's buzzer. He saw her look out through her venetian blinds to check who it was. Just like she always did. For a moment, he thought she wasn't going to answer.

But she did.

She was standing at the open door waiting for him. Donne stopped and waited for her to speak.

When she didn't, he said, "I screwed up. Bad."

Then he fell into her arms. She pulled him into her apartment and shut the door.

HE TOLD her everything. Stern's way with words. How he stalked Jeanne and Bill. Kate listened, red-eyed and silent. No questions were asked. And if she judged him, he couldn't tell.

When he was done, she pulled him in for another hug.

"You could have messed up," she said. "But you didn't."

"For once," he said, holding her as tight as he could.

And then she laid it all on him. Everything she found. Everything about the mob. The merger.

Donne's gut twisted at the words, realizing how close he'd been to helping it along.

"No one has to die," she said. "We can stop this. Tomorrow. We'll go to the police."

Donne nodded.

"Will you stay tonight?" she asked.

"I want to," he said. "But they might find me. I can't let them get to you."

He kissed her deeply and left.

SOMEWHERE AROUND midnight, Donne's cell phone rang. The sleepy haze around him faded for a moment, and first he reached for his alarm clock. Then he snatched up his phone and answered, his eye catching too late a phone number he didn't recognize.

"''lo?"

"Jackson." The voice was weepy but familiar. "Jackson? Bill just left."

It wasn't Kate. It was Jeanne. The sleep induced haze was still clearing, and kept him from asking how she got the number.

"I miss you," he said. The words came slowly and seemed to stick together on his tongue.

"Jesus. Are you with it?"

He could hear William saying he was trying to sleep. The shot of adrenaline in Donne's stomach cleared his vision.

"I'm fine," he said. The words weren't Velcroed to his tongue this time, but there was no guarantee he'd be able to keep speaking clearly.

A muted baseball game flickered on the TV. It was one Donne didn't care about. A National League game, and the pitchers had to bat. Took half the fun out of the game. Before Jeanne spoke again, the Cardinals' pitcher grounded out. Big surprise.

"I'm in trouble, Jackson," Jeanne said.

"You're always in trouble."

"No, not what I meant. I mean Bill left, and I tried to stop him but he wouldn't listen."

A local car dealership commercial was on TV. It looked like the owner was screaming, but with the TV muted Donne couldn't hear it. He couldn't read lips either. Another beer would have made it really funny.

"Why are you calling me, Jeanne?"

"Because I screwed up again."

Donne turned away from the TV. "How?"

"He's going to shoot Henry Stern tomorrow. At the press conference."

Like Pavlov's dog, Donne's body reacted to Jeanne's words. His heart began to pound and his palms got slick.

"No," Donne said. "He doesn't have to."

He tried to sound cool, but he was sure his voice was shaking. *Scorched earth*, Jeanne had said. Bill took it literally. Donne would be without a college degree, without a fiancée, and without a lifeline job from the man who saved his life.

"He wants to save me." She paused. Donne heard movement. "Stern was always going to be in my life. With him dead, I would have a shot at a fresh start."

"I have evidence," Donne said. "You'll get your start. I promise."

Another pause. Donne looked for meaning in the pauses but could find none. It was as sad as looking at the bottom of his pint glass.

"You have to stop him, Jackson." Jeanne spit the words out.

The baseball game came back on TV. A real hitter was up for the Brewers, the first baseman. He swung and missed at the first pitch. Donne unmuted the TV but lowered the volume. The hum of the crowd was soothing.

"This is not how I want William to learn about me and his father. I don't want his father to be a murderer. I can't teach my son that lesson. That can't be one of the first things he learns."

Donne tried to hold the words back, but couldn't. "What do you think your son will feel about you faking your death?"

Strike two. The first basemen muttered something at the umpire.

"Help me, Jackson."

"How is he going to do it? I need details."

Adrenaline and heat now pumped through Donne's veins. The jolt was better than any cup of coffee.

"He's going to shoot Stern. That's all I know."

"You're sure." Donne rubbed his face. "Call him. He doesn't have to do this!"

She shouted, "I've tried. He's not picking up his phone. Help!"

Donne hung up.

CHAPTER
SIXTY-FOUR

The door to the building was unlocked, even at 7 AM. A stroke of luck, maybe, but Martin would take it. He adjusted the baseball equipment bag on his shoulder and entered the Robert F. Jenkins building. The halls smelled of newly laid wax, though the stairwell still had a Lysol scent hanging in the air. The lemon-lime smell gave him a slight headache.

He was falling apart.

Martin's hands shook and had been shaking since that morning. The weight of the baseball bag tugged at his shoulder and kept him from taking the stairs at a quicker pace. At each landing, he stopped to catch his breath. He also listened for custodians, faculty, students, or anyone else who could have been milling around. He heard no one. In a way, he was disappointed. Lee Harvey Oswald got to brag about curtain rods. Martin amused himself by trying to come up with reasons he'd be carrying a baseball bag in a science building.

No believable excuses came to mind, though. For the best.

He pushed the door to the roof open and stepped out into the warmth. The breeze was light and steamy with humidity grabbing the air. The smell of seawater helped ease the Lysol out of Martin's nostrils.

Looking out over the campus, Martin could see the stage.

No one was working on it now. The speakers had been set up properly, and some red, white, and blue bunting had been hung. Two New Jersey state flags stood on the stage, one at each staircase. There was only one American flag. Martin guessed the bunting made up for it.

He unzipped the baseball bag and pulled out his rifle. It was unloaded, which was what he wanted. No accidents. He was only going to load the weapon when he needed it. He laid the rifle on the ground. There was no hurry; he had a few hours. Next he pulled a bottle of water from the bag, opened it, and took a small sip. The forecast today would drain the fluid from your body. He needed to stay hydrated.

At the same time, leaving the roof to use the bathroom would be embarrassing.

Martin looked out across the parking lot, past his lone car. He could see the beach, and a few people starting to set up camp. Two umbrellas were popped open and someone else was standing at the shoreline, letting the water rush over their ankles.

If only, Martin thought.

He dialed Jeanne. The phone rang three times, and Martin's gut tightened. Then she answered.

His muscles relaxed. "I'm here."

"Don't do this." She sounded far away. Speakerphone or Bluetooth, probably.

"Keep your eye on the news."

Kent State, Virginia Tech, University of Texas. They'd all gone down in infamy. Martin was about to cross the same line.

"You can't do this."

Martin closed his eyes and realization sank over him. "Where will you be?"

"If Stern dies, I'm not going to tell you. You won't find me."

"Do you have William with you?"

"Of course."

"I'm doing this for him." Martin closed his eyes and waited out the pause. He knew what the answer would be before she said it.

"No."

His hands shook even harder now, and it was difficult to keep the phone to his ear. A rock formed somewhere in his abdomen.

"Have a good life," he said.

Martin took the phone away from his ear and was about to push the button to end the call. He stopped when he heard Jeanne's voice. One last time.

"Bill," she said. Then a sigh.

"Yes? I'm here."

Martin clutched the phone as tight as he could. *Just give me something*, he thought. Some words of encouragement. A "Be careful." Something to make it all worthwhile. He tapped his pocket with his free hand.

"Think this through," she said. The words were flat and even. "There is another way."

"I have." Martin bit his lip. "There isn't another way."

"Jackson—"

Martin put the phone down and stared back out at the ocean. He couldn't turn back now. In a few hours, Jeanne would have what she wanted. A new life, no fear. Henry Stern would be gone. Jackson Donne would be a memory.

And himself?

Martin watched the man wade deeper into the ocean and dive under a breaking wave. He waited for the guy to reappear, brush the water out of his face, and do it again. He counted off the seconds. Counted to thirty, and still saw no one. A sharp edge of the rock inside him dug into his guts. He grunted. No one emerged from the water.

And it was too soon for the lifeguards to be on duty. Martin sat forward. A few feet left of where he was staring, the man popped out again. Then dove under one more time. Martin sat down on the gravel and watched him do his laps. An hour passed, and more people appeared on the beach, the sand polka-dotted by different umbrella shades.

He looked back toward the campus. People were starting to mill around, closer to the stage. A few people had taken their seats in the audience. They were typing on computers, probably press.

Martin went about the process of checking his rifle. Each part was oiled, clean, and ready to go. He checked the baseball bag to make sure he brought everything, checking each item off a mental checklist.

Everything was there. The plan only relied on one more thing. Jackson Donne had to put all the pieces together. He probably would. He always seemed to. And Jeanne was great on the phone the night before, putting just the right amount of panic and fear into her voice.

In his wildest dreams, this wasn't the path he expected his life to take. The moment he found Jeanne and shot Donne was supposed to be the beginning of a happy ending. Now he was left with nothing. He smiled, though. Jeanne and William would be free to start over.

And Bill Martin would be the catalyst.

CHAPTER
SIXTY-FIVE

Jeanne's call had kicked sleep out the door. He spent the rest of the night tossing and turning, and the morning came with something resembling a hangover.

The pain sat right behind Donne's eyes, squeezing them against their sockets. His stomach rumbled, and phlegm was caught at the back of his throat. The Advil hadn't kicked in yet, though the Gatorade cooled his esophagus. The tie around his neck wasn't helping much.

At the entrance to the parking lot, Donne showed a guard the pass Stern had given him. The rest of the campus was open, but anyone related to the press conference for the merger had been directed to one lot. Cops would patrol the other lots, but not until closer to start time. Martin was here already. He had to be, because he wasn't stupid. He'd beat the system.

The hot summer sun didn't help with his hangover sensation, the rays digging deep into the black fabric of his suit. The smell of the sea, however, was refreshing, and he took in as much of it as he could while he walked. Some press members were trying to make their way through the light security, which consisted of having their laptop bags checked. Donne recognized a few of the sportswriters. He wondered how the merger would affect the columnist who wrote a yearly piece about why UNJ should have a football team. Privatization would make that jump extremely unlikely. The Twitter snark would be extremely high today, especially if the conference went off without a hitch.

Donne would make sure that happened.

He showed his pass at security and made his way over to the stage. The metal creaked a bit against the breeze, and the first step sagged under his step. Luca spotted him and crossed the stage toward him. He wore a black suit as well.

"What the hell are you doing here?" Luca asked.

Donne nodded at the military guys roaming the perimeter of the setup. "The state troopers, they usually do this."

Luca worked his jaw. "You can't be here."

"I know why you're here. And what the senator's plan is."

Luca shrugged. "Too late now."

Donne gave him a smile. He looked out at the crowd filing in. The laptop carriers were the press. The others were faculty from both Ben Franklin and UNJ. They were the only people invited. The students were excluded.

"Students protesting today?" he asked.

"Go home, Jackson." Luca cracked his knuckles.

"Hope none of the photographers were snapping pics just then."

Luca's hands dropped to his side.

"Nervous?" Luca nodded toward Donne's waist.

Donne was suddenly aware he'd been tapping his right pocket repeatedly. He jammed his hands in his pockets, bunching the bottom of his suit jacket against his wrist.

"It's the suit," Donne said. "Have you seen anything suspicious?" He couldn't remember.

"That's not my job. Or yours. Go home."

"Half the parking lots on campus are wide open," Donne said. "The security line is more lax than at a football game. Loose ends?"

"I meant you and your girl, if you don't get the hell out of here."

"Don't you touch her."

"Try and stop me."

Donne looked out over the crowd toward the rest of the

campus. The buildings blocked the view of the beach. No one wandered the quads, and only a few people loitered around the student union. To his right, a few workers were changing the last remaining flags on the streetlights. No longer did they only say UNJ. They read BEN FRANKLIN–NEW JERSEY UNIVERSITY. Donne didn't know what they'd change the mascot to.

"Come on," Luca said. "Get moving. The boss is going to be here soon, and we're gonna get started. You know the private sector, always working."

Donne nodded and headed down the metal steps. He could feel Luca staring at his back.

CHAPTER
SIXTY-SIX

Donne made his way through the press corps, noting that all the seats were filled now. People were just waiting for Henry Stern to show up. Rumors circulated that the governor would be there too, but Donne knew he wouldn't be. This was Stern's baby, and he'd negotiated long and hard to keep the state boss out of it. The governor got to handle the beach rebuilding after Sandy as the payoff.

As he got to the back of the audience, he started to hear the clicking of cameras. He turned to see Stern getting out of a black SUV. Two built guys he didn't recognize flanked him and escorted him to the stage. Not using state troopers — a big show of how good private firms were. If Stern's military buddies were doing security, Martin was going to have a hell of a gauntlet to pass through to escape.

If he was even here.

Donne watched Stern climb to the stage and look out over the audience. The presidents of both universities — soon to be renamed chancellors of their respective campuses — followed. They clapped at the press corps and faculty members. A few people returned the applause, but it seemed as if no one was sure what was appropriate. Stern looked out over the crowd and caught Donne's eye. He gave Donne a thumbs-up. Donne didn't return it. He instead headed out on to campus.

He started at the student union, checking for errant backpacks or suspicious packages. Bombs weren't Martin's style. Donne wasn't even sure if Martin had the patience to make one. Not with the way his hands had been shaking the last few times they crossed paths. But Donne did a sweep anyway, finding nothing but two sophomores sipping coffee and chatting about summer classes and if—after the merger was official—they'd have to take extra classes.

"Ladies and gentlemen, if we all could take our seats. We're going to get started in just a few minutes."

The speakers crackled and boomed as the press liaison spoke. The entire press conference would be heard throughout the campus. Donne expected it was being simulcast on the Ben Franklin campus as well.

He turned toward the quad and continued his sweep.

BILL MARTIN opened his eyes when the press was asked to take their seats. He pushed himself up off the gravel and walked over to the edge of the building. The stage was full now, but Martin couldn't make out who was who. There were just a bunch of guys in suits sitting behind a podium.

The breeze had picked up a bit and was going to make the shot a bit trickier. Not impossible, but not the easiest he'd ever done. Once, when hunting, he'd taken a galloping deer out at three hundred fifty yards in a rainstorm. The deer collapsed midstep, and it took ten minutes for Martin to track down the body. But the venison meat on that kill was one of the sweetest he'd tasted.

He hoped Jeanne appreciated today just as much.

Scanning the crowd, Martin noted everyone's focus on the stage. Even passersby had stopped to listen. The campus appeared empty, except for scattered people near the student coffee shop and throngs of onlookers near the stage.

Except for one guy in a suit strolling toward the quad. Martin went back to his baseball bag and took out his gloves, scope, and a clip of bullets. After putting on the gloves, he took his handkerchief from his pocket and wiped the entire rifle down, focusing on the trigger, trigger guard, and stock. Then he slapped the clip into the gun, and carried it back to the edge of the roof. Before attaching the scope he took a second to look through it. Worked like a charm.

He made out Henry Stern sitting between two old, balding men. They all had BF-UNJ pins on their lapels. The pin was obnoxious, and Martin was shocked they hadn't picked a sleeker logo yet. He swept his vision back to the lone man walking in his direction.

Jackson Donne.

Martin attached the scope to the gun. He trained it on Donne as he walked. The kid didn't even flinch. No fucking clue.

"Ladies and gentlemen, on this historic day, allow me to introduce you to the chancellor of the University of New Jersey campus, Hans Clark."

Martin adjusted his aim back toward the stage. He took account of the breeze and aimed about three inches above Stern's head. Gravity and physics would take care of the rest.

But he couldn't shoot yet. That wasn't the plan. It had to be midspeech in front of everyone. He was going to make sure Jeanne knew what he'd done for her. That she'd see it on the news that night, where ever she was.

At the same time, he hoped William would be asleep. That the boy would never see this footage. Or at least never know who'd taken the shot.

"As HAS already been said, this is an historic day for our institutions. Taking the University of New Jersey and merging it with Ben Franklin College will help turn our schools into a private university on par with Princeton. It will allow our enrollment to be more selective and our faculty to focus on their strengths."

Donne shook his head at the spin. This was all about saving the state money and cutting taxes. He wondered how many meetings the higher-ups at the university had to have to figure out a good way to spin this for academics.

And he wondered if they knew exactly what was going to happen to some of their donation money. Where Luca and

Stern were getting it, and what they were doing with it.

But, if he just kept his mouth shut, Donne would have a full bank account for a long time. As the thought passed through his mind, a spider crawled across the inside of his chest.

As the chancellor prattled on, Donne walked over to the freshman dorm and tried the door. It was locked. He didn't have a passkey to get in. Probably something he should have asked Luca for. If he were going to do a true inspection, he would have to check all the buildings. And he should have been here well before anyone else had arrived.

The headache behind his eyes, finally starting to fade, reminded him why he was late.

Donne looked across the quad at the Robert F. Jenkins building. He scanned the outside first floor and saw nothing out of the ordinary. He checked each window, looking for a misplaced blind or twisted curtain.

Nothing.

His eyes ran up the sidewall toward the ceiling, looking for movement. Something shimmered in front of him.

Donne blinked.

More movement.

Donne broke out in a sprint for the door.

CHAPTER
SIXTY-SEVEN

As Donne bounded up the steps, he could hear the announcement that Henry Stern would speak next. The voice was muffled through the thick walls, but he could still make out the words. There wasn't much time.

He grabbed the handrail with his left arm and tried to pull himself with his momentum, but his shoulder gave way. Donne fell forward and slammed his chin into the metal step. His front teeth dug into his tongue, and Donne tasted blood. After getting up, he wiped his mouth and turned his wrist red. Donne spat blood on to the floor and continued.

The door to the roof wasn't locked, surprisingly. It wasn't even barricaded. When Donne pushed the handle in, the door swung open into the sunlight. He could hear crashing waves and the sound of Stern's speech as clear as glass. The sun made him squint as he canvassed the roof and found a crouching Bill Martin looking over the edge.

And into the scope of a rifle.

"Bill!" Donne shouted the word. Speaking made his tongue burn.

Martin pulled back from the edge of the roof and looked toward Donne.

"You're just in time, kid," he said. Then he turned back to the gun.

"Don't do this, Bill." Donne strode across the roof, stopping a yard from Martin. Donne didn't have many options. If he tried to grab or tackle his former partner, there was a good chance they'd both topple off the roof. Plus, with his shoulder weakened, Donne didn't expect to win any fights.

Not even with an old guy.

Talking was his only way out of this. Maybe, just once, he could get Bill Martin to listen to him. To trust him.

"You pull that trigger, Bill," Donne said, "and you're going to destroy your life."

Martin's shoulders flinched. "Yeah. That's what I'm worried about."

Henry Stern was talking about the glories of both universities. His speech was highlighting the science departments of both schools and the developments they'd made in neuroscience. Once they combined their forces, they could be one of the top private research units in the country.

"You think they won't track this back to you?"

"I have that covered," Martin said. His back went up slowly as he took a long breath. Then back down again.

Donne took a step forward. Bill Martin pulled the trigger. There was a single *pop*. Martin stood up, turned, and tossed the rifle at Donne. Instinct took over and Donne caught it. An instant later, the screams of the crowd carried to them.

"Got him," Martin said, looking over the edge of the roof.

Donne looked at the rifle in his own hands. Then dropped it. He took two steps back.

Martin walked past him over to a baseball equipment bag. For the first time, Donne noticed the gloves on Martin's hands. He dashed over to the edge of the roof to look at the crowd. The members of the press had pushed forward toward the stage and were all shouting. On the platform, Donne could make out Stern's legs as two men in suits hovered over him. One of the chancellors had slumped over in his seat.

There were two other men in suits running toward the building. One of them was Luca. The bodyguard looked up toward him and yelled something. It wasn't help. It wasn't a one-syllable word.

Donne whirled toward Martin, who now held a pistol. It wasn't pointed at Donne yet.

"Why did you do this, Bill?"

"You know why. For her." Martin shrugged. "For me too."

Donne shook his head, while still keeping an eye on the pistol. It looked familiar. "She didn't want this."

Martin laughed. "Of course she did. Now she's truly free."

"They're going to track this back to you, Bill. You don't know these people. They're going to track it back to Jeanne too. You screwed up."

Martin shook his head. "Nah. I tried to stop you."

Donne felt the breeze at his back. The words Martin said didn't register with him. Something wasn't right. Maybe he misspoke.

"First shot. Even with my hands shaking." Martin laughed. "I never was able to get true revenge on you, Jackson. Never really torture you the way I wanted."

"You shot me. You took Jeanne from me."

Now there were sirens in the air. More than one. Over Martin's shoulder toward the beach, Donne could see cop cars and an ambulance careening toward the campus.

"And you still survived. You didn't die. You didn't crumble. You put your life together. Meanwhile, I have nothing. I'm sick. Jeanne's gone. Eileen. And I don't have a job." Martin lifted the gun from his side. "I have nothing left."

"Bill …" Donne put his hands in the air. He heard the door to the building open and slam shut.

"This is yours," Martin said, holding the gun out. "You left it at the hotel room."

Donne's stomach did a swan dive to his ankles. His throat closed.

"I came up here to try to stop you. I'm a cop. That's what I do." Martin turned the gun. "But you were too quick. You shot me."

"Bill, don't." Donne fumbled for words. "Ballistics. Evidence."

"Yeah, because cops have always loved you. I'm sure they're going to work real hard."

"Don't—"

"If you ever see her again," Martin said. The gun was aimed at his own chest. His thumb was through the trigger guard. "Tell her I always loved her."

The gunshot made Donne flinch. Martin fell backward as a red splotch formed at his chest. A cloud of dust arose as his body hit the ground. The gun skittered away.

Donne rushed to his side and knelt. Martin's breaths came in wet gasps. Donne touched his chest and felt the wet warmth run over his hand. Martin's eyes were wide and unfocused. He seemed to be looking at the sky.

Donne said Martin's name. Martin coughed and spat blood from his mouth. One more hard gasp.

Then nothing. His eyes glazed over, and his lungs stopped working.

Donne checked for a pulse, but it was too late. He fell back on his ass and rested his hands on his knees. He looked at the specks of blood on his wrist and wondered how much of it was from his mouth and how much of it was Martin's.

He could hear shouting in the corridor. Luca was close.

Then one word popped into Donne's head.

Run!

CHAPTER
SIXTY-EIGHT

Donne bolted toward the door, only to be met by Luca and two other men. Air came in heaves and gasps, his chest tightening as he watched Luca survey the scene. The two men walked over to Martin. One knelt and put his ear next to the body's nose and mouth. Seconds later, he shook his head.

Luca looked Donne up and down, slowing his gaze at the bloodstains. He stepped in, nose-to-nose.

"What the hell happened?"

Donne opened and closed his mouth, trying to find words. They wouldn't come.

"You did this," Luca said. "You waited for Bill to come here? You told me he was already dead."

Donne looked at his hands and saw the blood that covered them. He wiped them on his shirt. Sounds were echoes, and everything was far away. The waves from the beach were loud, however, like someone messed with the balance in his ears. Too much bass, not enough treble.

Luca's voice faded into static. His lips were moving, but Donne couldn't understand him over the rush of the waves. Pressure was pushing on his temples. He opened and closed his sticky hands.

A hand was in Donne's face. Luca was reaching for him.

Donne's heart went into overdrive.

Donne ran. Luca whirled as Donne passed him, and Donne's hearing came back.

"Hey! Wait!"

Donne didn't stop. He hit the stairs and skittered down them, leaping to reach each landing. His knees jarred with each landing, but he kept pushing downward. The taste of copper returned to his mouth.

He hit the front door and busted out into the sunlight. The sirens were all-encompassing now, along with the screech of brakes and footsteps. People were shouting, others were crying, someone was still screaming. Donne ran through the quad, heading back toward the staging area. He could see people taking pictures and two news stations trying to set up live feeds.

The cops hadn't set up a perimeter yet. They were still assessing the situation. Some rushed the stage. Toward the student union, a group of cops huddled next to an ambulance with whirling lights.

Donne hung a hard right and headed toward the parking lot. The metal detectors were knocked over. Some of the crowd must have fled in a panic. Donne hopped the blockade and sprinted out on to asphalt. He pulled his keys and started to press the unlock button.

He looked over his shoulder midsprint and saw Luca following him. Luca wasn't running hard, but was instead jogging and signaling toward the cops. Air caught in Donne's throat, but he pushed forward. He kept pressing the unlock button.

Donne found his car and used the hood to stop his momentum. Vibration from the impact drove up through his wrists like he'd just hit a fastball on the inside part of a bat. He pulled open the door and got in. Through the windshield, he saw Luca picking up speed. Two cops were sprinting in his direction as well.

After starting the car, he put it in gear and peeled out of the parking lot. His brakes squealed as he turned on to the main road, aiming away from the beach. Behind him, two squad cars tore out of the lot as well. Their sirens were blaring.

Donne needed to make it to the Parkway before they closed the entrance down. If he could hit the highway, he'd have a little more freedom to breathe.

Unless they unleashed a helicopter.

It was only then he realized the folly of his choices. By running, he played right into Bill Martin's hands. He looked guilty, even if he wasn't. Even though he tried to stop Martin. Donne's cell phone vibrated in his pocket. He ignored it.

One of the cop cars turned into the lane of oncoming traffic and accelerated. Before Donne could floor it, the car was next to him. Cops cars really had good pickup nowadays.

"Pull over!" The speaker on the cop car was loud.

Donne floored it and pulled away from the cruiser. It wheeled back into his lane, nearly clipping Donne's fender.

"Come on, come on," Donne said. He was doing eighty-five down a Jersey Shore town side street. The traffic light he headed toward turned red.

Donne gripped the steering wheel tight, but didn't brake. He cut through the intersection, and one of the cops behind him made it too. But the second cruiser slammed into a crossing car. The crunch of metal and smash of glass was almost inaudible over the hum of his engine.

At the next intersection, Donne turned right. He thought he was going to lose traction, as the car almost hit two wheels. The turn must have surprised the cop behind him, who kept going straight through the intersection.

Donne exhaled. He could see the Parkway up ahead. The relief wasn't enough for him to let up on the accelerator, though.

Again, his cell phone buzzed. Had his name made the news already?

The cop who'd been following him must have known a shortcut. Three blocks down the road and about two blocks in front of the Parkway, the cruiser pulled out at the intersection and blocked the road. Instinct made Donne release the accelerator. The engine RPMs wound down, but he still fired ahead at nearly seventy miles per hour.

His car could not withstand a straight-up ramming through the police stop. Hell, he'd probably go through the windshield.

And if anyone was in the passenger seat of the cruiser, they were screwed too.

Didn't matter though.

Jackson Donne put the metal to the floor. He could feel gravity press him back into the seat just slightly. His skin tightened over his knuckles and he held the wheel tighter.

"STOP THE CAR." The speakers of the cruiser roared.

Donne gritted his teeth.

One block.

"STOP THE CAR NOW!"

Two blocks.

Donne screamed.

Three blocks.

Donne swerved left onto the parking lot. A trashcan slammed into his hood and then rolled over the roof. A coffee cup splashed against the glass. The cop car was unharmed. His car had made it around. He drove another block on the sidewalk.

Two civilians had to dive out of the way.

The Parkway entrance was up ahead. He checked the rearview mirror and could see the cop car backing up and straightening out on the road to continue pursuit. Donne imagined they were radioing ahead to state troopers as well. But if Donne played it right, he only had to make it ten miles on the highway.

The *whup whup* of helicopter blades could be heard overhead. Donne peeked through his sunroof and could see the state trooper chopper following him. Of course.

Donne picked Parkway north and kept the pedal on the ground. He was pushing 120 mph, and two cars had to swerve out of the way of his merge. An overpass loomed up ahead, and Donne thought it could work to his advantage. The state cops hadn't caught up yet. Procedure meant the locals had to stop at the entrance to the highway. His only worry was the chopper.

As he neared the overpass, Donne weaved on to the shoulder.

The rumble strip pounded against his ears. He slammed on the brakes and came to a stop just under the pass. Donne counted to twenty as the chopper passed above him. He just needed them to get far enough away that it was hard for them to turn around.

The *whup whup* faded and Donne accelerated. He merged in at the speed limit, mixing in with traffic. Ahead he could see the tail of the chopper as it slowed in the air. The next exit was less than half a mile away. With a helicopter in the air, he'd never make it the ten miles he'd planned. He'd have to be more creative.

He was pulling off the exit before the chopper had made its way back in his direction.

CHAPTER
SIXTY-NINE

Another shore town. He didn't even know the name of this one. Ocean Grove? Ocean Town? Something along those lines.

Donne dumped his car as soon as he got off the Parkway, leaving it in a supermarket lot. He jogged across the lot and made his way toward the street that led to the beach. He undid his tie as he walked and dropped it and his jacket into a dumpster. Across the street was a beach shop. Donne ducked inside and, with the only cash he had, picked up a bathing suit, a beach-themed T-shirt, and sandals. He got changed into the dressing room, leaving the rest of his clothes behind.

Before he left the shop, he checked his cell phone. Kate had called twice. Donne turned the GPS locator off and walked down to the beach. He called her back. The phone rang while he found a spot on the sand.

"Where are you?" she asked.

"Can't tell you," he said. She could probably hear the water crashing.

"You didn't do this. I know you better than that."

The knot in his stomach eased. He'd expected a question, not a statement. He squinted in the sun looking out over the beach. It was moderately crowded, full of people on their day off sitting in plastic chairs. He and Kate rarely came to the beach, and when they did, they never sat in the sand. They went somewhere like Point Pleasant and had beers on the boardwalk. They played Skee-Ball and redeemed tickets for T-shirts with stupid sayings.

They had hoped to support the Sandy rebuild this summer by spending a ton of cash there. He never gave them the chance.

"I didn't," he said.

"They think you did. You have to run."

"You—your dad. You can help me."

"I don't think I can," she said.

She was right.

"Where will you go?"

"Some place with good craft beer, Kate. You know me."

A situation popped up in his mind. One he hadn't even considered. Bill Martin had talked about being sick and not being able to steady his hands. Not an easy condition for a sniper to have. It was possible Stern survived the wound. Maybe it didn't hit any vital organs. Maybe the bullet dug itself into his shoulder.

Bill Martin had missed Donne at close range. What could he hit at three hundred yards?

"Did Henry Stern live, Kate?"

"No. They said he got shot in the head. Oh my god, you *were* there?" She sniffled, a sound Donne had become all too used to recently. "The car chase on the news. Was that even you? Jesus, tell me they're lying to me, please."

"Who have you talked to?"

Please say the cops.

"Someone from Henry Stern's protection committee."

Donne's ribs constricted, trying to crush his lungs. "Guy named Luca?"

Donne didn't mind using names. It was unlikely the cops were tracking his calls already. Even if Luca gave them his number, it was too fast to set that up. They should have still been scrambling with crime scene evidence.

"They think you did it. All of them." Kate paused. "Luca— he's so angry."

"Is he still there?"

Donne dropped his head and looked at the sand. A cigarette butt stuck out of a mound of it. He kicked it over with his foot. Particles of sand stuck to his foot. They itched. He slapped some of it off, but it didn't relieve the sensation.

"I'm sorry," she said.

"He's going to hurt you, Kate," he said. He jumped to his feet and started to run back to the street. "I'm coming."

"No. You have to go. Get out of here."

"He's going to kill you!"

"I'm coming to get you right now."

"You can't. They'll find you."

"Who?"

A long pause. Donne listened to the waves and the mumbled, happy conversations of other beachgoers.

"Don't worry," she said. Her voice caught for a second. "I have my beer goggles on. They're very focused."

Donne stopped running. His muscles eased.

A kid on a waveboard wiped out. Out of the corner of his eye, Donne noticed the lifeguard stiffen. The kid popped back up, laughing. The lifeguard relaxed.

"Good luck, Jackson."

Donne hung the phone up, opened the settings, and turned the GPS back on. He got up and walked down to the edge of the water. Out in front of him was a vast blue nothing. At the edge of the horizon was a fishing boat. Beyond that, nothing else. Swimmers were more toward the south. The kid on the waveboard paddled out to find more.

Donne threw his phone as far as he could. It landed in the water with a small splash.

"Beer goggles," he said to himself.

Twenty minutes later, Donne was in a stolen car cruising north. He planned on driving more than ten miles this time.

There were no cops to be found. He made a stop just before the New York border to take all the money he could out of an ATM. He dropped his card at the bank. It was a drive-up ATM, so he had to ditch the stolen car just over the border.

After boosting a 1980 Cadillac, he didn't stop driving for nearly four hours.

KATE PUT the phone down and turned toward Luca. The barrel of the gun obscured his face.

"I don't like loose ends," he said. "Where is he going?"

She rubbed her hands together. He wrists were cold, but the rest of her was warm. It was an odd place to be cold.

"He didn't say."

Luca leaned in close. The gun touched her temple. Kate fought back tears. Just make him talk a little while more.

"I know he said. I'm going to find him. If you tell me, maybe I'll go get him instead."

Kate swallowed. She strained her ears, but didn't hear anything. If only she'd listened to her father and not plastered her address all over the place. He'd always told her that if she wanted to be a lawyer, her home would have to be unlisted. The metal of the gun dug into her forehead. It felt as cold as her wrists.

"He did not say. I wish I knew."

The emails she sent, the phone call she made when she saw him walking toward the door had to have registered by now. She gritted her teeth together and prayed, begged.

"If you don't tell me—" Luca pressed the gun against her even harder. His voice was as sharp as diamonds.

"I really don't know." Her entire body shivered as she spoke.

Then she heard it. The sirens. More than one. 911 had come through. As soon as she saw the guy, just like Jackson described him, walking up the front step, she grabbed her phone and her computer and sent off an email with the files attached. One to her dad and one to the town police chief. It wasn't enough to convict, but it was a start.

Luca flinched at the sound.

"They're coming for you," she said. "It's over."

His face went red, and the gun moved away from her head. Getting up, he ran to the window, peering through the venetian blinds.

"No," he screamed. "I'm not done!"

"Your girlfriend Marie really helped me out," Kate said. "You should have called her back. I have evidence about everything. The board of trustees. Your link to Tony Verderese. All of Henry Stern's plans. And I emailed them right to the cops."

As tough as she tried to sound, her voice still shook. The sirens were deafening now. Brakes squealed in front of her house.

Luca whirled back toward her. "No! This isn't how it happens. It doesn't end this way."

Doors slammed. Voices volleyed outside. Just a few seconds more.

Kate looked at Luca. His face scrunched, his eyes squinted, his cheeks burning. He lifted the gun.

"I will not go out this way."

And too late, Kate realized, the cops weren't going to get there in time. She closed her eyes.

I love you, Ja —

CHAPTER
SEVENTY

B ethel, Vermont, was the perfect small town.

In fact, it could barely be labeled that. Which meant it was perfect for Jackson Donne. Located forty-five minutes from Killington and nestled against a quarry, it felt remote. Far away. There were a few blocks of houses and just enough bed-and-breakfasts for tourists. When Donne pulled into town at nearly nine in the evening, he was able to rent a motel room in cash. No one asked any questions.

No one even seemed to recognize him.

The next week moved at a relaxed pace. Donne found a job doing fixer-up jobs at all the bed-and-breakfasts. He mowed lawns, fixed broken shelves, and attempted plumbing. And all of the owners felt it was easier to pay cash. Meanwhile, he started to grow a beard. After a week, he had enough money to sublet out a small house on the edge of town. The owner was moving to Colorado for the winter for some "real" skiing. He was willing to rent out the house monthly, for cheap. It was another fixer-upper.

Perhaps this was a haven for ex-cons and fugitives on the run. Cash was acceptable, paperwork was scarce, and everyone minded their own business. At the same time, people smiled and waved at him. They made small talk, but never probed.

Donne didn't care. The house had hot water, heat, a kitchen

and a bedroom. He didn't have the Internet and didn't have a cell phone. That was fine, most people couldn't get reception in town anyway. Two Mondays a month—his day off—he would make the hour drive to Waterbury for groceries and beer. The case of beer he got from the Alchemist—Heady Topper—was a double IPA someone had designated the best beer in the world. Donne tended to agree. Soon the employees there started to recognize him.

One of them must have thought he was cute, even with the scruffy lumberjack beard. Once a month, he'd find an extra four-pack thrown his way.

The beer kept his stomach saggy, but the housework kept the rest of him tight. The work did wonders on his wounded shoulder. He almost had complete movement back. By October, he was splitting wood at all four bed-and-breakfasts. At first he'd wake up sore, but within a week the soreness faded. He enjoyed the rhythm of work.

He wondered if name was mentioned on the news. He never checked. Didn't want to know. Somewhere between New Jersey and Vermont, he decided his name was Joe Tennant. That was good enough, and the beard and the beer gut changed his appearance enough if no one looked too close.

No one did.

He missed Kate. And he wondered about Jeanne. Thoughts of both of them tickled the back of his brain daily. He thought about them as he worked. He thought about them when he ate. The thoughts only faded after his second or third Heady Topper.

Curiosity got the better of him the day before the first snowfall. He had finished shopping and picking up his case of Heady. He considered asking the woman at the cash register out, but that broke his rules. The idea of starting a new relationship brought Kate to the forefront of his mind. Memories of her flooded his thoughts—the way she chewed the corner of her hair, how she threw her head back—eyes closed, mouth open—during sex. His hands shook, and he finally gave in.

Pulling into a local coffee shop, he asked if he could use

their computer. He bought a latte and logged into the Internet. A Google search brought up a few news stories that mentioned Kate. And Luca.

Donne logged off and exhaled. A moment passed. Then the entire coffee shop turned toward him as he screamed. They asked him to leave.

He drove home.

That night, as the snow fell and carpeted his lawn, he drank an entire four-pack of Heady Topper and passed out. The next morning, head throbbing, he went out and shoveled all four bed-and-breakfasts. He left his own front walk for last. The snow was heavy and wet, as if the temperature was just barely cold enough for snow.

The tears in his eyes blurred the whiteness away.

ABOUT THE AUTHOR

Dave White is a Derringer Award-winning mystery author and educator. White, an eighth grade teacher for the Clifton, NJ Public School district, attended Rutgers University and received his MAT from Montclair State University. His 2002 short story "Closure," won the Derringer Award for Best Short Mystery Story the following year. *Publishers Weekly* gave the first two novels in his Jackson Donne series, *When One Man Dies* and *The Evil That Men Do*, starred reviews, calling *When One Man Dies* an "engrossing, evocative debut novel" and writing that his second novel "fulfills the promise of his debut." He received praise from crime fiction luminaries such as bestselling, Edgar Award-winning Laura Lippman and the legendary James Crumley.

Both *When One Man Dies* and *The Evil That Men Do* were nominated for the prestigious Shamus Award, and *When One Man Dies* was nominated for the Strand Critics Award for "Best First Novel". His standalone thriller, *Witness To Death*, was an ebook bestseller upon release and named one of the Best Books of the Year by the *Milwaukee Journal-Sentinel*. All three books have been reissued by Polis Books and are available wherever ebooks are sold. Follow Dave White on Twitter at @dave_white.

ACKNOWLEDGEMENTS

If you enjoyed this book, or any of my books, you need to thank Jason Pinter. Jason, the brilliant mind behind Polis Books brought Donne to print and then saved him off the scrap heap two years ago. Without Polis Books, Donne would have gone away like a lot of other private detectives. I am so happy he's back on the page, and for that I am so thankful for Jason and Polis Books.

My wonderful agent Allan Guthrie is also to thank, for early read-throughs, smart advice, and a shoulder to lean on.

No one can get by without good friends: Sarah Weinman, Duane Swierczynski, Bryon Quertermous, Jay Stringer, Russell McLean, Chuck Wendig, Chris and Katrina Holm, Bill Cameron, Thomas Pluck, Angel Colon, Hector Acosta, Dan and Kate Malmon, and Alex Segura. To everyone else in the mystery community too. You've always been there for a helping hand and Twitter pep talks.

And, of course, the family. I am forever in Carol and Martin White's debt—you know because they're my parents. I also thank Thomas White, Jessica Schupp, Eleanore Richard, Thomas Richard, Fred Aguilera, Kristen Richard Aguilera, and Daniel and Brandon Aguilera. Thank you for the support.

To my readers, I hope you enjoyed this book. And all of the other ones. Thank you.

And finally Erin and Ben White. I love you. Thank you for being there for me.